Haven's Hope

by
Dena Netherton

Write Integrity Press

Haven's Hope
© 2018 Dena Netherton

ISBN-13: 978-1-944120-43-6
ISBN-10: 1-944120-43-2

This book is a work of fiction. The author discovered a good deal of fascinating historical information during her research, and to the best of her knowledge and belief, she represented actual historical facts with integrity. Aside from the historical characters and events, names, characters, places, and incidents are either products of the author's imagination or used fictitiously. Any similarity to actual people and/or events is purely coincidental.

Scriptures are taken from the Holy Bible, New International Version®, NIV®. Copyright © 1973, 1978, 1984, 2011 by Biblica, Inc.™ Used by permission of Zondervan. All rights reserved worldwide. www.zondervan.com.

Published by Write Integrity Press
PO Box 702852
Dallas, TX 75370
Find out more about the author, **Dena Netherton,** at her website:
www.DenaNetherton.com or on her author page at
www.WriteIntegrity.com

Printed in the United States of America.
Library of Congress Control Number: 2017944755

Table of Contents

Dedication

To all who love the mountains
and find in their mysterious depths and heights
a kind of metaphor for God.

Chapter One

An urge—powerful, undeniable, somewhere between the desire to adore, and the need to murder—compelled him.

Dade had followed the silver Sebring for almost twenty minutes, impatient for its pretty driver to choose whatever place she needed to conduct business, pull in, and park.

Finally, she signaled her intention to turn. The mall. Of course. So typical of young women with nothing more important to occupy their time. But once she was back safe in his cabin, she wouldn't be wasting any more time window-shopping for indecent clothing, or frivolous, worldly items.

She turned down a parking lane, driving so slowly he wanted to curse. Finally, she pulled into a spot. His pulse jolted when she stepped out of her car and pressed the lock on her key fob. *Beep, beep.* Slinging the strap of her handbag over her shoulder, she walked with quick, purposeful steps down the row of cars in

Macy's parking lot, glancing right and left. Wary, like a deer in the meadow.

"Ruth." He breathed her name like a prayer. Turning his truck down the next lane, he parked, never taking his eyes off his prize.

Hunting a human was different than stalking a deer or a cougar. They ran when they sensed danger. People, well, they were more concerned about looking stupid. So, they didn't look behind to check out someone walking a bit too close. Or double check a policeman's badge. Or any of a hundred sensible things one could do to be safe.

Which was a factor that was going to work in his favor today. Ruth, all alone.

When she drove away from the big estate in the country outside Portland, she was no longer Haven Ellingsen, daughter of Guy Ellingsen, rich bank executive, respected elder at West Hills Community Church. She was Ruth. The Ruth he had craved since he was a boy.

No dapper, blonde daddy would be playing security guard today. The weather this morning had turned all cold and rainy. In the parking lot, folks kept their heads tucked into their coats to ward off the rain, not hearing, not noticing. Perfect conditions for a quick, silent snatch.

His fingers itched to wrap around the trigger of his rifle, but he waited until Ruth had almost reached the south entrance of Macy's before getting out of his truck. Half an hour earlier, he'd been watching her big country estate from an unsuspicious distance not really expecting her to come outside. But then, one of the three garage bays opened and the girl pulled out in the brand-new silver Sebring.

Ever since the day, three months earlier, that he'd watched her and her daddy eat lunch at the café in Monroe, he'd been tailing her. But this was the first time he'd seen her drive by herself. Always ready with the stuff for a quick grab and getaway, he'd followed her all the way from her home outside Beaverton and into town.

So, Ruth hadn't talked. If she had, the police would have been looking for him. They'd never shown up at his place. Never questioned him or Mama or the children. Why? Why hadn't Ruth told the police he'd kidnapped her and held her prisoner in his cabin?

True, he'd threatened her. Told her if she ever got away that he'd kill anybody who helped her, anyone who hid her. But most girls would have squawked once they felt safe. Not Ruth. She was quiet and sweet and gentle. No, not gentle. That rock. He reached down to rub his injured knee. Three months later it still pained him.

He'd wait near the truck. Yes. Wait all night, or seven days, or seven years for the opportunity to love her or kill her. It would be her decision. If he was really lucky, the car just in front of hers would pull out and he could back his truck in next to the Sebring and be ready to grab her when she returned.

He was a man who desired Ruth more than Samson, his Delilah, or Amnon, his Tamar. And he would have her.

♩ ♪♪♫♪

Haven settled into a chair outside the Starbucks, a few stores down the mall aisle from Macy's, and sipped her tall Americano. She'd found Joy's housewarming gift in Macy's quicker than she'd expected, and she wasn't due at her aunt's new condo for another hour. She had just enough time to check her e-mail and send her father a text before she hopped back into her car to brave downtown Portland traffic.

"Haven!"

Haven jerked and almost spilled her coffee. A man's voice. A skinny twenty-something guy with bleached, spiked hair and facial piercings emerged from between groups of shoppers and loped across the aisle, eyes focused like a laser on her. Fear shot like BB pellets through her limbs. She jumped up and slid behind the table before the man got close. As added protection, she shoved her chair between them and reached into her jacket pocket to finger the small canister of mace. He looked vaguely familiar. But familiarity no longer assured her.

He didn't seem to notice her reaction. "Hey, it's been ages since I've seen you. How are you?" He was beaming like he'd just been introduced to a celebrity.

"I-I'm just fine." What was the man's name? Did she know him from school, from church? To stall for time, she leaned over and dumped her empty Starbuck's cup into the trash receptacle. It'd be embarrassing if she couldn't come up with his name.

He dumped his packages on the table. "Wow, last time we talked was at the cast party at Professor Robert's house after that play we did. End of our junior year."

Oh yes, the actor. She let go of the can of mace and reached to shake his hand. The man's name popped into her head just in time. "Matt Halpern. It's so good t-to see you again." Even though he almost gave her a heart attack. Ever since Dade, she hated the sensation of being startled. It made her want to ball her fists and hit something.

She sat down. "You m-must have graduated from the university by now."

"Yep. Back in May. I can't believe I'm seeing you here, at Starbucks. You're like ... famous now."

Famous? She'd played concerts in multiple states, but it took a kidnapping to make her face nationally recognized. She could do without that kind of fame.

"Mind if I join you?" He pulled back another chair before she gave him permission, and lowered his lanky body onto it. Matt's gaze lingered a bit too long on her forehead. They all stared at her scar. Why would it be different with Matt? Just thinking about the jagged red line etched into her forehead made it throb.

Matt hummed along with the background music. Something about his voice unlatched the floodgate of memories from her college years. They'd been in a theater class together. He'd had black hair then.

It was the spring before her mother's murder, and her illness, and Life Ventures ... and Mama and Dade.

"You look great." His gaze swept over her hair. "I love the way you've grown your hair long. It's so dramatic. It makes you look like that 1940s actress, Veronica Lake." Matt pulled his chair closer to make room for a mom and her stroller to pass into the crowded coffee store. "That newspaper article said you were thinking about going back to college soon. Are you going back to the university?"

She hadn't planned to talk about college plans—secret college plans—even with a guy as nice and friendly as Matt. "Probably n-not. Um, we'll see." The less said, the less he'd have to speculate about. No sense in saying something Matt might unintentionally scramble and then repeat to other friends. So far, only her immediate family and her dear friend, Anna, knew where she planned to complete her music degree. She meant to keep it that way.

"Well," Matt struck a dramatic pose, "I'm off to New York in a couple of weeks."

"Really?"

"Yes. I sent this troupe called Opening Lines an audition tape of my latest gig. They adored it. Said to come right out and they'd have plenty of work for me. Isn't that fantastic?"

"Great news. Your family must be s-so proud of you. I s-seem to remember you saying that one day, y-you'd be an actor in New York. And n-n-now you're actually going there. C-congratulations."

Matt tilted his head slightly and a barely discernable question rose in his eyes. Obviously, he'd noticed the stutter. Nice of him not to ask about it. She was so tired of explaining about the brain injury and how it affected her memory and speech, how she was doing speech therapy and, yep, getting better day by day, and, of course, doctors were confident, given her youth that she'd eventually speak without any stammer, and yada, yada, yada.

Matt kept staring, and she tried to hide the need to squirm under his gaze. Silent seconds ticked away. It was pointless to try to explain how her body responded to such a piercing look. Only another victim of kidnapping could possibly understand the sense of vulnerability, the super startle at sudden noises, or the hyper-awareness when out in public.

She woke her cell phone and glanced at the time. The extra

time she'd earned by her quick shopping skills had been consumed sipping coffee.

Apparently, Matt wasn't going to lose the head tilt until she explained. She didn't want to be rude, but Aunt Joy was expecting her to arrive at her condo no later than three thirty. Straightening her purse and package, she took an audible breath. "Well, I have to get going."

"Have you ever thought about New York?" Matt leaned in closer. "I've already made tons of contacts. With your looks, I could introduce you to—"

"Oh, th-that's okay." She stood up. "I'm really more into my m-music. Theater w-was just kind of a fun side activity." She angled her body toward Macy's. "It-it was great to see you again. I'm really h-happy for you, Matt. Good luck in New York."

"Maybe we could do coffee before I go," he called as she headed back to Macy's. "I've got so much more to tell you."

She nodded, held her phone aloft, and gave him a parting smile. "E-mail me. Gotta go. Late for an appointment." She shouldn't have stopped at Starbucks. Now she'd hit rush hour traffic.

♩ ♪♪♫♪

Anticipation raced across Dade's gut like fire on a drought-stricken prairie. His pulse hammered in his ears. Ruth had just stepped out of Macy's. Rain clouds that had been building for the hour she'd been in the mall decided at that precise moment to release their moisture. Ruth looked up, frowned, reached into her oversized bag and pulled out an umbrella. Perfect. She'd be preoccupied having to juggle her purse, her shopping bag, her umbrella, and her key fob.

He pulled the hood of his raincoat over his head and slumped behind a van parked nose to nose with Ruth's Sebring. He held the taser down against his thigh. When she got closer, his aim would be perfect.

She walked quickly. As she approached, the tap, tap, tap of her heels on the pavement kept time with the rapid beat of his heart. No one else was in the parking lot, thank God. His mouth went dry and his breath jerked in and out.

Five cars away ... four cars away.

He got ready to pounce.

Three cars away.

He'd dash the few feet to the truck. Stuff her inside and jump in right after. Duct tape her hands and feet and her mouth. The key was already in the ignition. He could be on the highway in less than thirty seconds.

Two cars away. She reached into her purse for the key fob. Beep, beep.

Tap, tap. Her little shoes stopped at the driver's side door. He took a breath and held it while he crept around the opposite side of the Sebring.

♩ ♪♪♫♪

"Haven."

A man came at her like a mugger from a dark alley. Strength exploded through her arms and legs. She spun around, dropped her purse and bags, and planted her feet. A battle yell burst from her lips as she thrust out her umbrella.

"Whoa, it's me." Matt back-pedaled and put up his hands, palms out. He swept back his raincoat hood for a second.

Haven's snarl faded. She lowered her weapon and clutched at her chest. "D-don't ever surprise me like that again, Matt. You almost g-got the point of this umbrella through y-y-your chest." Heart still pounding, she bent and picked up her purse and packages.

"Sorry." Matt rolled his eyes.

Matt didn't get it. Oh, how the man needed a good lecture. Her father understood, though. Most fathers with daughters understood.

"I forgot to give you this." Matt stayed back but extended his arm toward her. She took the business card and glanced at it.

"My e-mail is different now." He raised his eyebrows. "Um, a bunch of us are getting together at Bambini's Saturday night, if you're interested."

She looked at the card again before stuffing it inside her purse. "Okay … maybe. I'll have to check my … Well, I'll l-let you know." She climbed into the car. "All right. See you Saturday, maybe."

Matt tapped a goodbye on the flank of her car.

She waved, pressed the lock button, started the car and wipers and waited until Matt was out of the way. Seconds later, she turned onto the main driveway to the mall exit.

♩ ♪♪♫♪

A fist slammed into Matt's jaw. The impact threw him against the passenger door of a minivan. He slumped to the pavement. Pain exploded in his head, stars winked inside his eyes, and his vision funneled.

While on his knees, a man's boot entered Matt's central field of view. But his stunned brain couldn't react fast enough to avoid the boot's vicious forward arc. Like a bomb, the impact of the boot exploded shards of agony inside his gut. He clutched his stomach and his whole body quivered in a panic to breathe.

After he caught his first breath, he hunched over and retched.

"No one gets between me and Ruth. You hear me, boy? No one."

The boots turned and stomped away.

Such a cold voice. An outer-space type of cold. Like ninety-three million miles from the sun and on-the-dark-side-of-the-moon type of cold. No actor he knew could have summoned that amount of hatred and fury.

When Matt pushed away from the pavement and straightened, vertigo overtook him. Nausea poured into his gut. His hands shook as he pulled out his cell phone and pressed 911.

Blood dripped from his unhinged mouth. "I n-need help. A man assaulted me …"

♩ ♪♪♫♪

Haven jerked awake and clutched at her blankets. The blast of a rifle shot reverberated in her mind. For nearly a year, the recurring nightmare had thrust her from unconsciousness into seconds of terrifying limbo, until reality battled Dade's image back into the walls of her bedroom.

"I'm in my father's house," she told the bedroom walls. "I grew up here. This is my old bedroom. My desk and my chair. My guitar and my paintings. My books on the shelf. Dade, you are not here. Dade, you cannot come here."

A breeze stirred the maple tree outside her window. She scrunched deeper into the comfort of her pillow and pulled the blankets to her chin.

The dream always took place in the same house. One single rifle blast. Then her tiptoed journey down the long, dark hallway. At the end of the hall, the scene always morphed into a city sidewalk with Dade, looming over the lifeless body of a woman—her mother—rifle in hand.

She stared—horrified—into the murderer's eyes, eyes as cold as the body lying at their feet. "I told you, anyone who tries to help you, pays the price." She opened her mouth to scream but no sound came out. The criminal dragged her into the shadows, back into the dark cabin in the woods.

Haven kicked off the covers and sat up. Until the images of the dream faded completely, she wasn't going to risk trying to sleep again.

A rumble of thunder announced the arrival of a heavy Oregon rain. She got up and crept over to the window to watch the first raindrops strike the glass, then roll and merge in their downward race toward the windowsill. Usually, the sound of rain comforted her. But not tonight.

She'd tried during the daytime hours, through concentrated practice at the piano and on her guitar, to keep at bay the memory of Dade and the mountain cabin where she had once been imprisoned. But the nights—oh, the nights—they were a different story. The dream returned with relentless frequency.

"I'm not safe even here."

Would she ever get over the traumatic events of the past year? She had reconciled with her father. And God had taken center stage again in her heart. The joy of performing had returned, and with that a strong motivation to continue her music studies and finish her degree.

But the memory of being kidnapped, imprisoned, and terrorized, left her with a brain that had forgotten how to trust. Besides her father, no one seemed safe, particularly men. That distrust sat heavy on her shoulders when she ran errands around town. Her body tingled any time a man stood too close to her in the checkout line at the grocery store. Men couldn't all be like that one evil man. But her heart told her otherwise. Memories clung like dust from a coal mine. Dade's touch had dirtied her, made her feel ashamed.

If only she could tell someone what really happened to her. If only she could be a little girl again and run to the safety of her father's strong, sheltering arms. But if she told him about Dade, he'd try to protect her. And that could put his life in jeopardy.

Hadn't she brought this all on herself—and her father—by allowing her panic attacks to get so bad that she'd required special treatment? If she had not gone to Life Ventures … if she had never met Dade Colton … if she had not been on that forest road when he showed up to "rescue" her.

If, if, if.

♩ ♪♪♫♪

Sunday morning traffic into the West Hills Community Church parking lot seemed much heavier than usual. That meant that more than just the regular church attendees had shown up to hear her story of survival in the wilderness. It was scary enough to share her experiences with people she knew. But to speak to a crowd of strangers who knew nothing about her beyond what they'd read in the newspapers? It made her stomach queasy.

Her father pulled into a parking spot and shut off the motor. He glanced at Haven. "All set for this morning?"

She nodded. Not really.

"Want me to offer up a little prayer?"

"Thanks, Dad." Her hands shook like she'd just drunk ten cups of coffee. She stuffed them into her coat pockets.

They bowed their heads.

The polite toot of a car horn interrupted them. Joy's red VW Bug pulled into the next parking slot. Joy lowered her window. "Morning, Guy."

Dad jumped out and came around to her door. "Hey, I thought you said you weren't going to be able to make it this morning."

Joy opened her door and stepped out, juggling keys, sweater, purse and her laptop. She gave her brother a quick hug. "Oh, I made some phone calls and rearranged my schedule. So here I am. I thought your girlfriend was coming today."

Haven came around the car just in time to see Dad's face turn pink and hear Joy chuckle. "No, Sheila had to fly to San Diego to visit her sister."

"Well, tell her I'm planning a nice dinner for you two when she gets back."

"I will." Dad shifted gears, looking at Haven with the same

buoyant, atta-girl expression she'd become familiar with in the last couple of months.

"Are you okay?" Joy slipped an arm around Haven. Her aunt, the professional counselor, always seemed to know when Haven needed a comforting hug.

"She's just nervous about speaking."

Joy squeezed her. "You've played for thousands. I'd have thought speaking would be way easier."

Haven forced half a smile at Joy's upbeat expression. "What are people going to think when they hear me stutter?" She hated the way people so obviously hid their thoughts whenever she spoke. Was it suspicion? Pity? Condescension was the worst.

"Just remember, these are people who've known you all your life, and they love you. Besides, you never know how your story might touch someone."

♩ ♪♪♫♪

Pastor Jensen preached a shorter-than-usual message to make room for Haven's testimony. She sat in the front pew trying in vain to moisten her throat and mouth. What if her legs wouldn't carry her onto the stage? What if someone snickered at her stutter?

At last, the sermon concluded and Pastor Jensen looked down at her. "We have had the pleasure of watching Haven Ellingsen grow up in this church and develop into a fine musician. We've wept with her and her father, Guy, as they mourned the loss of their precious mother and wife, Helen. We've prayed as Haven struggled with her grief and as she went through a very difficult and dangerous time recently. We praise God that He has brought her back to her family and back to us. And now Haven has come this morning to share a little about her journey. Haven?"

Pastor Jensen gave her an encouraging smile. *Here we go. Lord, I need You.* Nerves knotted her stomach as she stood and gripped her notes. *Good grief,* they were clapping for her. They had no idea they were about to listen to a girl who could barely talk. She mounted the steps with wobbly knees, set her notes on the pulpit, and drew a cleansing breath.

"Most of you remember my m-mom. To you, she was a-a beautiful, kind lady who taught Sunday School, sewed costumes and painted backdrops for the drama ministry, and counseled battered women. She played the piano and headed up the c-community soup kitchen and annual coat drive. But to me, she was my best f-friend. Yes, she was my mother, but she was also my teacher, my mentor, my coach, and my c-counselor."

Some of the people in the audience nodded. "B-but that man with the rifle took all of that away when he shot and killed her."

Her throat spasmed, threatening to cut her testimony short. *Oh, God, please help me.* She swallowed and swallowed again. "After the initial s-shock of the murder, then the funeral and police investigation, I t-tried to get on with my life back at the university. B-but it got harder and harder.

W-when my father could see that I wasn't getting over my traumatic memories, he talked me into registering for a wilderness therapy program for people like me who are struggling with traumatic memories. He was convinced it would help. Even though I was skeptical, I went into the mountains and did what my father wanted. It was scary at first. They h-had us doing all kinds of challenging things like figuring out topographical maps, rappelling down the sides of cliffs, crossing streams on ropes stretched across the water, and worst of all, sleeping on the ground … with bugs."

She smirked. "I hate bugs."

A titter of amusement rippled across the auditorium. Someone in one of the back rows exclaimed, "Amen to that, Sister."

Her throat relaxed, and she laughed with the audience. It would have been great to finish right there, but the audience had come for more than memories of her mom and a couple of funny remarks. Her smile faded. "But, you know, th-that survival course was s-so hard and so mind-consuming that I didn't have much t-time for sitting around, stewing. And when we were almost through with the course I began to see how much I'd accomplished. That felt good.

"I guess part of my anger and fear after my mother's murder had to do with this: If a good person like my mother can be cut down in the prime of her life, then who is safe? What is safe? A person you love? Your health? Even your own memories? None of it is guaranteed. It's a terrifying thing to h-have to come to grips with."

She let that thought hang for a few seconds. "After the Life Ventures course finished, I thought I had come through the worst part of my life. Then they told me my father had been in the car accident, and my world fell apart again."

What more could she say? Obviously, her audience was curious about how she got her head injury and why she spoke with a stammer. This should be the time to tell them about what happened to her. Looking down at her notes, a big blank spot in her notes, with a question mark on the margin, shouted at her. She needed to say something. They were waiting, being so patient and understanding. But her head injury was as much a mystery to her as it was her audience. Like a gaping, dark hole, her brain refused to cough up any memory of the event.

She could tell them about the little, hidden cabin, finding Gregory's Bible, and coming to realize that God was very near even in the midst of bad circumstances. She could share about becoming friends with Anna and how that relationship had blossomed.

But, to tell them about being a prisoner of Dade and Mama? Never. Someday, perhaps, her father would know the truth. But not yet.

Her gaze settled on her father's tender face. "Since coming back home, I-I've been regaining my memory, but it's slow, so please don't be insulted if I walk right b-by you someday and don't remember you. Not all the bits and pieces of my former life are back yet. M-most of the time I can talk like a normal person. But I-I'm sure you noticed that I sometimes stutter or get m-my words turned around, especially when I get nervous or upset.

"The only time I don't stutter is when I sing. So, let me finish with this hymn. She took a deep breath and sang in a strong voice:

Great is Thy faithfulness, O God my Father.
There is no shadow of turning with Thee.
Thou changest not, Thy compassions, they fail not.
As Thou hast been, Thou forever will be.

When she finished singing, Pastor Jensen joined her on the platform. "Let us pray."

Haven bowed her head. *Thank You, Lord. That wasn't nearly*

as bad as I thought it would be.

♩ ♪♪♫♪

He'd taken a seat in the back row of the auditorium so he could slip out quickly in case she spied him. For a brain-damaged woman, she hadn't done too bad a job telling her story. Obviously, she was protecting him by leaving out any mention of him. It was possible she hadn't even told her daddy about him.

Her silence sent a clear message: "Dade, find me. Bring me back."

And as for protecting herself, well, church people can be awfully judgmental. How many of them would believe she'd been in his cabin for three months without any carnal activity?

He had slumped in his seat, pulse throbbing in his temples during the whole of her presentation. Ruth had worn a skirt to show off her legs. Her long hair had turned blonde again. The men stared at her, and his jaw hurt from clenching his teeth.

He hadn't been able to get a better look at her after the service. Well-wishers had mobbed her in the parking lot. Then she and her father drove to a Chinese restaurant for lunch. They were in there a long time. When they came out, he followed them home, then turned around and headed for the interstate. The time wasn't right. Either Ruth was in her daddy's home, protected by a security system, or she was surrounded by people at church or crowds of diners at lunch. He needed to put in some carpentry hours so he had some money. But he'd return in a couple of days to watch her place. Someday she'd venture out alone. And he'd be ready to grab her.

Chapter Two

*Even though I walk through the valley of the shadow of death,
I will fear no evil.*
Psalm 23:4

Having Dad in the car made Haven feel safer on her round-trip to the Washington Cascades to visit the professor and to take a guitar lesson. They crossed the Columbia River on a beautiful early August day. Far below, sunlight glistened on the waves.

It was probably a one-in-a-million chance that she'd ever see Dade again. Even though he was only a few miles away from Anna's when she'd seen him last. He'd have to know by now, if he read the papers or listened to the radio, that she was back with her family. He'd also know that the police were involved in her search and rescue. Hopefully, that'd scare him away.

But the not knowing plagued her. The scar on her left temple started to throb. Maybe she should have told the police everything about Dade. Mama, too. The returning memory of Mama wielding the iron door-stop, and slamming it down on Haven's head, made her cringe. She rubbed her forehead. But who'd believe her? There was no evidence, no witnesses, nothing to indicate she'd been held prisoner at their cabin. Jesse wouldn't talk. Dade would surely have threatened him, and he'd need to keep quiet to protect not only himself but Sarah.

And what if Haven had to go to court? What if she couldn't face Dade? The thought of sitting in court, looking at the man who threatened her life and her loved ones, sickened her. What if she told her side of it and Dade and Mama said everything she claimed was a lie? There'd be no way to prove they did anything bad to her. And with her memory still recovering, anything she said could be disputed. Even the terrifying incident at the cabin when Dade had ambushed her and she'd fought him off with rocks. It would just be her word against his. And all that time in court, Dade would be watching her, getting madder and madder, and he'd be seeing her father sitting there, and probably Joy, too.

She shook her head hard to brush away the track of her thinking. She stole a glance at her father, but he seemed lost in his own thoughts.

They turned onto Highway 2 and exited after a few miles for gas. She stepped out of the car, stretched her legs and breathed in the fragrant coolness of the air, heavily scented with the aroma of Douglas firs and cedars. Northmont College wasn't too far away, and thinking about it gave her butterflies. In a couple of weeks, she'd be moving into a dorm there and taking classes. How would she do? Would she make friends? How many students she met would be aware of her recent experiences? Would that alter their initial perception of her?

"Thirsty?"

She jumped. Her father was carrying a couple of ice-cold bottles of tea and a bag of pretzels.

"What, no corn nuts?"

He looked sheepish. "They're in my coat pocket."

She nudged his jacket open and laughed. A small bag peeked out of his pocket. "You and your corn nuts. I s-swear you must be addicted to those things."

They got back into the car and headed east.

Anna Jaeger, Haven's guitar professor, was waiting at the front door when the car pulled up to her garage. They followed her as she shuffled from the front door to the living room. The professor had already set up a chair, music stand, and footrest. Haven set her guitar case down and opened it. She sat and wiped down the neck and body of the guitar with a cloth while Dad and Anna conversed.

"Professor Jaeger, Haven wants to play some Christmas carols on the guitar for our Christmas Eve service. Oh, and the day before, she'll be at Twin Oaks, where her grandmother lives, to play piano and guitar and sing too. So, there's no way that you can stay up here by yourself for the holidays. I know it's a few months away, but I wanted to make sure you don't make other plans. And just maybe, we could persuade you to bring your guitar for some duets."

"Guy, please call me Anna. 'Professor' seems so stuffy and formal."

Dad grinned. "Sure thing, Anna." He helped her sit in her usual overstuffed leather chair.

"As a matter of fact," Anna said, "Haven and I have already talked about it, and she said I wasn't allowed to refuse her invitation for Christmas."

Haven winked at her friend and started to tune her guitar.

"But it's nice to hear it from you, too, Guy. And, come to think of it, we already have a guitar and piano piece that we've been working on that would be perfect for the Christmas season."

"Then it's s-settled," Haven said. "I'll plan to have the guest room ready for you and-and we'll come get you on December twenty-second. I mean, if th-that's okay." She tilted her head at her father.

Anna sighed happily. "Papa, is that okay with you?"

Dad nodded. "Well, now that that's all taken care of I'll let you two get on with the lesson. Mind if I pour myself some coffee?"

"Help yourself. I made it right before you got here so it should be nice and fresh."

He ambled into the kitchen.

Haven had brought her Christmas carols and she and the professor began to tackle some of the hard spots. Though Christmas was still four months away, she needed as much time as possible to make her performance perfect. She had practiced for hours, trying to reach some of the larger chords. Occasionally, she had to pause while her fingers attempted a strange position.

It was very quiet in the kitchen. Her father must be listening. He always listened. Unlike her mother, he wasn't a musician. But he had a good voice and over time had developed a critic's ear. She winced at her mistakes. He'd notice every one of them, not that he'd ever criticize.

Dad came into the living room with his cup and settled quietly at the other end of the room to watch the last few minutes of the lesson. Good grief, why did he have to pick this minute to come and watch? This was her hardest piece. Her cheeks warmed and her fingers turned clumsy.

"You're going to get it, Haven. Don't get upset," the professor said. "It's a hard chord to play and your hands are small. But I've worked with other students with little hands and they all do eventually get it right. It just takes a while."

"I'm j-just hopeless."

"No, you're not. Why, you're doing music that most of my students wouldn't have done until they'd studied for three or four years. You're doing great."

"She's a perfectionist, Professor," her father said.

"Well, that can be good for a performer, up to a point," Anna said. "Just be careful that you don't expect so much from yourself that you can't live with a couple of mistakes. Even God doesn't expect you to be perfect, just excellent."

Dad clapped his hands. "That's a good one, Professor. I'll have to remember that."

Anna patted her on the shoulder. "That's enough for today. You're making great progress."

"D-do you really think so? Do you th-think I'm going to do okay at Northmont?"

"How are you feeling about going there?"

"Mostly nervous, I guess. I k-keep thinking that all the other students are going to be way ahead of me."

"There she goes again," Dad said. "Anna, she was saying that even when she was a straight-A student, graduating a semester early from high school."

He and the professor exchanged knowing glances.

"Now," Anna said as she closed the guitar score on the music stand, "I'm hungry. How about you two?"

"Well, Dad was s-snacking on corn nuts all the way up here, but I'm hungry."

"Merely an appetizer." He patted his flat stomach. "I'm famished."

The professor held onto her walker. "I have lunch all ready to pull out of the fridge."

"Anna, you got r-rid of the sliding glass w-window." Haven walked over to the back wall and inspected the new French doors. "W-what beautiful doors."

The professor shuffled over and stood behind her. "I was afraid you weren't going to notice. Isn't it nice, and see how the design goes so well with the décor of the room? And now, when I'm in my wheelchair, I can roll it easily right through and onto the deck."

"W-when did you have it done?"

"It's kind of an interesting story. Come on into the kitchen and I'll tell you all about it." Anna led them into the kitchen and pulled sandwiches and a fruit salad out of the refrigerator.

"It was early last month. I was out with Beau, taking him for a short walk down the road and I ran into a neighbor … you know, that nice Italian man, Mr. D'Amico. We got to talking and I noticed that he'd had some work done on his garage. He said that he'd hired this guy to turn half of his garage into an extra bedroom, and he was so excited about it that he ran inside and came back with pictures of the finished room. It looked like such an excellent job and Mr. D'Amico said the guy was quick and polite and didn't even charge as much as he thought it would be. So, I asked him if he had the man's cell phone number. A couple of days later I contacted the carpenter and he said he could come right over."

Anna sat down and poured the iced tea. "You're probably wondering why I'm taking such a long time getting to the point of the story. It's just that the whole thing was strange. When he showed up there was something about him. I can't quite put my finger on it." She shook her head slowly and looked perturbed.

"W-what was so … so … ?"

"Strange? Well, he came right inside, like he already knew the layout of my house. Started taking measurements, asked me just exactly what I wanted. And the whole time his eyes roved around the room like he was looking for something. He came back in a couple of days with all the supplies and got right to work."

Anna took a sip of her tea. "I came in the room occasionally to see how he was doing and to ask if he needed anything. But every time I did he'd ask me questions about how the 'little girl that you helped' was doing.

"Little girl?" Haven rolled her eyes.

"Well, you are petite," her father said.

"Dad," she huffed, "I'm a grown woman." She hated it when some men treated her like an airhead just because she was short and blonde.

"And then he wanted to know if you had decided to go back to school. He'd read somewhere you planned to finish your music studies at the University of Oregon."

Haven shook her head. "I never said that." Had some journalist misquoted her?

"I know," Anna said. "He acted as if he thought I should spill every detail about you. Which I didn't, of course.

"The next time he talked to me he said, 'You must have gotten to be good friends with that girl. Do you ever visit her?'"

Haven pushed her food around the plate. Anna's delicious salad suddenly seemed unappetizing "Why would a-a carpenter be asking you all these questions? It-it seems kind of creepy to me."

"Creepy is the perfect word for it. At that point, I started to get suspicious that he was obsessed with the whole story in the paper. So, I left him alone for the rest of the time he worked here."

"Good for you, Anna." Dad spooned some more salad onto his plate. "What made him think he could pump you for information? Are you sure he wasn't just posing as a carpenter? Maybe he was a news guy."

"No, he was the real deal. He really knew what he was doing with all those tools. He was very tall and muscular, with rough workman's hands. Handsome, too, but he walked with a slight limp."

Haven's stomach dropped like a malfunctioning elevator, plummeting from the ninety-ninth floor. The scar on her forehead throbbed. She glanced at her father, but he seemed to be studying his plate. Pressing fingers to her lips, she fought the nausea that threatened to send her running for the bathroom. Because she needed to hear the rest of Anna's story.

"Then," Anna continued, "after I started avoiding the carpenter, his whole manner changed. He ignored me, but when he looked at me I'd get the feeling he didn't like me. Beau didn't like him, either. He started growling every time the man came over to work. It got so I had to lock Beau up in my bedroom."

"One time he asked if he could use the bathroom, and I said, of course. Then, when I came out of the kitchen, I saw him coming not from the bathroom, but out of the extra bedroom. I pretended not to see, but it sure made me uncomfortable. Well, you know me. Normally, I'd have said something kind of feisty to him about the snooping." Anna shuddered. "But he wasn't the kind of person you get nasty with. There was something intimidating about him, and he had these scary green eyes. When he finished the job, I was extremely relieved to write my final check and watch him drive off."

Haven tried to hide the rising panic. Her skin turned clammy. The thought of that evil man invading her dear friend's home looking for information about her made her light-headed. She excused herself, pushed her chair away from the table and hurried to the bathroom.

Standing at the bathroom sink, she stared at her pale reflection. Her hands trembled as she splashed cold water on her face. "Lord," she whispered, "Anna didn't give Dade any information that h-he didn't already know. She's too smart and cynical to trust any stranger. But he's still after me." She grabbed a towel and pressed it against her forehead. "Why doesn't he give up? I told him I'm not ever going to go back to him. He knows I'm Haven Ellingsen, not that … that Ruth, whatever her name was."

Her parents had always had an unlisted home phone number. And she and her dad were very careful never to share their cell numbers with anyone but closest friends and associates. But what if Dade somehow got some information while he was snooping and figured out where she lived? What if he came after her father or Joy?

It was almost like the man was playing with her, taunting her, knowing she'd visit Anna, knowing she'd see the new French doors. Did he ask Anna all those questions about her because he wanted information or because he wanted Haven to know he was still stalking her? Dade was impossibly clever.

She slid down against the closed door and sat on the cold tiles. Maybe she should go to the police. But would they be able to do anything? The professor had invited Dade into her home to do a job. He didn't force his way inside. And even Anna couldn't prove that he did anything out of the ordinary when he was working here.

A knock on the door vibrated against her back. "Haven?" Her father. "Are you okay in there?"

"I'm fine, Dad. I'll be out in a m-minute." She stood and checked herself in the mirror. Her stomach wouldn't relax, and she heaved a breath to try to dispel the tension.

In another minute, she returned to the kitchen and took her place at the table.

Dad rubbed his chin and watched her with an unreadable expression.

"Are you feeling ill, Haven?" The professor looked concerned.

"Oh, it's nothing. I-I guess I'm just nervous, th-thinking about college and all I've got to do in the next few days to get ready." She took another sip of her iced tea while avoiding her father's eyes. Pretending to study her plate, she said, "So, do you remember the name of that c-carpenter?"

Anna's eyes narrowed. "Hmm, I believe his name was Colson, no, Colter … Hmm. No, it was … wait a minute. I think I still have his card." She thumbed through a small tin containing receipts, miscellaneous lists, and business cards. "Here it is." She handed the card to Haven.

"Colton Carpentry," Haven read out loud. Below that was the carpenter's license number and his contact information. Her fingers tingled at the touch of Dade's card like she'd just been handed a tarantula. She shoved the business card back into Anna's tin.

♩ ♪♪♫♪

On their way home, her father drove in silence. He was probably thinking about work. Or was he thinking about what Anna said today? Did he suspect there was something more to Anna's story?

She turned and stared out the passenger window, furtively brushing away the wetness seeping down her cheeks. This was not going to ruin her life or anyone close to her. Dade was not going to steal her excitement about returning to college. And even if he did find out where she currently lived, she'd be gone in a couple months. And nobody was going to tell him where she'd gone. She'd kept her plans to attend Northmont a secret to all but Joy and her dad and grandmother. And Anna, of course. Not even her friends knew.

Dad cleared his throat. "Sweetheart, what's bothering you? You seemed very upset by Anna's story. Is there something you want to share with me?"

She kept her face to the window to hide her red eyes. "It-it's just something I h-have to sort out myself, Dad. I don't think it's anything y-you can help me with." Her voice caught and she shot a look at her father. His face looked untroubled, but Dad was always good at hiding his feelings if he thought it would upset her.

"I told you months ago that if there's anything you want to tell me, I'm here. I won't judge you or condemn you."

"Dad ..." She turned to face him. It would devastate him to know that she did not feel safe, even in his house. He'd want to know why. Her mouth worked. Should she tell him about Dade?

No, at least, not all the details. Just enough so that he'd be on the alert in case Dade showed up. "Anna's story made me think about my time in the wilderness. Th-there was this strange guy that I ran into while I was living by myself. He wouldn't leave me alone. I finally had to get violent with him."

Her father gasped. "You never told me about this. Are you okay?" His nostrils flared and his hands balled. "Who was this guy? What do you mean, 'violent?'"

He steered the car onto an exit and pulled over.

"I dealt with it, Dad." Well, she hoped. "He was a religious nut. I think he wanted me to be one of his wives or something."

Dad grabbed her hands and stared into her eyes. "Did he hurt you?"

"No, Dad. But it took some convincing to get him to leave me alone." Haven stared at her father's hands, which had gone clammy. "He's gone. I seriously doubt I'll ever see him again."

"Gone? Really gone? You're sure of that? Does he live anywhere near Anna?"

"No. But he saw me going to the professor's house, so he could possibly figure out my true identity."

At his expression of horror, she shook her head. "I'm probably making a big thing out of nothing."

"What's this man's name?" Her father's voice shook.

She had to be careful. She didn't want to involve Dad in an

investigation. "He th-thought he was some sort of Abraham or Moses."

"Good grief, Haven. Is there anything more I should know?"

"I think that's about it. Maybe when my memory gets better I'll be able to tell you more. I'm only mentioning this because I'm going to school in a couple of weeks and I want to make sure people don't talk about where I'm studying. Just in case."

"This makes me re-think your whole Northmont College year coming up."

She frowned. "That's why I hesitated telling you about my experience. Dad, I can't stop living just because someone might have an unhealthy interest in me. Entertainers and politicians and other famous people sometimes have to deal with stalkers. It's the nature of being public."

Her father drew a giant breath, his face stern, and opened his mouth as if he were going to lecture her.

Haven gave his hands a little squeeze. "Dad, I'll be fine. My experience with that nut case was months ago. I haven't seen him since then." And most likely would never see him again. She'd be in college, far away from her father's house, and from Joy, and Nana Bette.

Now that she'd pressed her point about keeping her whereabouts secret, she needed to distract her father from pursuing the matter further. "The main concern I have right now is regaining my speech. I feel like a freak." She reached up to finger the red scar traversing her left temple. "I wonder if I'll ever be n-normal again."

Her father nodded slowly and frowned. "I'm sorry. I've been so happy to have you back safe that I forget how it must be for you." He put his hands on her shoulders. "When I look at you, I don't see a scar. I see a young woman of loveliness and grace. And it isn't just your beauty. It's because you've traveled through a black cave and come out on the other side with a sweetness and strength that makes you even more precious."

When her eyes welled with tears, he said, "You're so much like your mother."

"Oh, Dad." Her voice quavered, which immediately prompted him to pull her to him for a comforting embrace. Her father was a kind man, but that was the kindest thing he'd ever said to her.

Chapter Three

"Hear, O Lord, and answer me, for I am poor and needy."
Psalm 86:1

"I'll have the usual, Fiona." Dade handed his menu to the waitress.

"Burger without cheese, extra pickles, light on the onions," she murmured with a thin, nasal voice as she scribbled on her pad. "Would you like fries or potato salad, sir?"

"Surprise me, little lady." He winked.

Fiona flushed and almost dropped her pad. "Coming right up."

After Fiona left, Dade scanned the bar and dining area of the Remley Pub. Most times the place was humming with activity and conversation. Drinking a beer in the bar always brought him another carpentry job in the area between Ellensburg and Issaquah, which meant that he could stay away from Mama for days at a time.

Lately, Mama had been almost happy to see him go for a few days. She didn't call him "Sir" as much as she used to, and she'd hinted a couple of times about going into town, herself, to buy supplies and goods for Sarah and Rebecca.

He'd have to crush that rebellious spirit in Mama next time he went home. She was getting restless, and restlessness in a woman didn't ever favor a man. No woman of his ever parted ways with him unless he decided it was time for her to go.

Fiona delivered her order at the cook's station and went to a nearby table to wipe it down. He waited until she looked up. Yep, there it was. The shy glance over at him to see if he was watching her. The quick meeting of the eyes.

Too shy to hold his glance, she looked down. Then she raised her eyes again. He forced himself to keep watching her, even though the girl wasn't much more attractive than a tiny gray mouse. Her eyebrows flew up and a slight smile appeared.

He could have any woman, but it was her—plain, no-personality, colorless Fiona— that had his attention. *How does that make you feel, Fiona? Special? Desired?*

He could hunt up a burger anywhere between Remley and Cle Elum. But bagging a woman took more time and skill. He had money stashed away for luring a woman to his side, but that would have been a hollow victory, like reeling in a trout from a stocked pond.

It was his way with women that brought them down. Women want to be wanted.

They pretend that it isn't so. So coy. Ruth pretended, too. All those men at church stared at her, and he could just bet she enjoyed their attention.

The memory ignited fire in his gut. He had a hard time not slamming his palm down on the slick polished table-top.

He needed to calm down. If he didn't, it might ruin his plans. He'd stay focused on the waitress with the Remley Pub tee-shirt. She'll be a useful tool, like all the rest of them.

Women almost always had man-problems. And they were suckers for a little concern and interest. He'd ask, "How's your day going?" When their lip trembled, he'd always say, "Now you just tell me all about it."

Most of them came right out and told him about their selfish boyfriend or abusive husband. "Oh, I'm sorry to hear that." He always added a slight touch on the lady's wrist or the shoulder, with a compassionate slant to his eyebrows. "Anything I can do to help? Here's my number. Call me and I'll come over right away. You just let me know if that man of yours gives you any more grief. From now on, he'll have to go through me to get to you."

He'd seen the bruises on Fiona's arms. The last time he came in for his usual burger, she'd been wearing dark glasses. It didn't hide the shiner above her right eye.

Fiona returned and set a glass of water next to his place setting. "I'll have your burger up in a minute."

He touched her arm before she could walk away. "Fiona, when's your next day off?"

She hesitated and looked confused. "I-uh, I'm off on … Wednesdays and, uh, but …"

She wasn't sending him the right signals. Something was making her hesitate. He had hoped she would act coy, and then ask him what he was thinking about. "That's okay. You don't have to tell me. I understand. You're a real sweet lady."

"It's not that, sir."

"Call me Dade."

"Well," she glanced over her shoulder, "Mickey, my boss, doesn't want me saying yes to invitations. He's ... he's kind of ..."

"Oh, the jealous type." He put a downward spin to his last word.

"He kind of thinks of me as his girlfriend."

"But you don't think of him as your boyfriend, right?"

Fiona nodded, rolling her eyes. "I have to keep on moving or he'll see us and get suspicious."

"I'll save you. Watch this." He waited for Mickey to walk by the kitchen entrance. When the man passed, Dade scowled at Fiona and raised his voice. "When's the burger coming up, girl? It's been at least twenty minutes."

Fiona started, and backed away, her thin fingers twisting the fabric beneath her nametag. "It-it should be ready by now. I'll go check."

Dade winked again.

A slow a-ha spread across her face. "Thanks," she mouthed. She hurried toward the kitchen.

Mickey let her pass but planted himself in the doorway, arms folded across his chest, frowning at Dade.

When Fiona delivered Dade's plate, he raised a Penny Saver Flyer in front of his face so no one could see his lips moving. "Man, that guy sure does watch you."

"Like a hawk," she whispered.

"When are you off?"

"Half an hour."

"I'll be in my truck, around the corner, on Simpson Street."

"I'll be there ... Dade." A smile carved a pink crack across her colorless face.

He bit into the burger, chewed and swallowed.

"Is the burger okay … Dade?"

He gave her a thumbs-up. "Everything's perfect."

♩ ♪♪♫♪

The Cedar Street Mansion reminded Haven of the old mansions she and her mother used to tour in the Portland area. Housing only ten students, it would be so much better than the noisy dorms she'd lived in for most of her time at the University of Oregon. Dad would be pleased.

"You're gonna love Northmont," Ashley, her new next-door neighbor said as she helped carry Haven's things up the wide mahogany staircase. "And the music department is really excellent. I should know; I've been here since I was a freshman. And you couldn't have picked a nicer place to live than the Cedar Street Mansion. It's quiet, and at least half a mile from the other college dorms. I love to jog around here. It's a safe neighborhood, and all the neighbors are nice."

It wasn't the neighbors she was worried about. Using her key, Haven unlocked and swung wide the door to her new apartment. It was indeed a spacious room with a walk-in closet and bath and nice views, just like Mrs. Peterson, the manager had told her. "This is really nice." She strode over to the window.

"Wait till spring." Ashley set the guitar case down on Haven's bed. "Those rhododendrons and roses in the garden are spectacular." She joined Haven at the window. "I like my view a little better, but you can see the garden and the driveway from your window."

Exactly. If anyone unfamiliar drove up to the place, she wanted a good view of the car. Not that she believed Dade would just drive up, ring the doorbell and announce himself.

Haven unzipped her overnighter and pulled out a softball-sized rock, painted red, with white concentric circles. She set it on the table next to her bed.

Ashley lifted the rock and brought it up to her chest like a shot-put. "Now, that's a rock. Any particular meaning for the target on its side?"

Haven gave a half-laugh. "It's kind of a metaphor for my life." A reminder that she had the power to fight Dade and win.

"Hmm, someday, when you're not busy unpacking, I'll have to ask you more about your 'metaphor.'

Good thing Ashley didn't pry. It never felt good having to explain the need for self-protection, even while snug in her new bedroom. Her new friend didn't need the burden of worrying if a madman could gain access to the Cedar Street Mansion.

Where was Dade? Was he still searching for her? Had she succeeded in hiding her tracks? Dade was always—

"Dinner's in half an hour." Ashley strolled toward the open door. "Hey, would you like me to give you a quick tour of the place?"

"Sure." Haven snatched her key and followed Ashley into the hallway.

"I'm in 2B. Katie and Laurie are in the other two rooms down the hall. Six more students downstairs."

Haven accompanied Ashley. The delicious aroma of garlic bread permeated the downstairs. She hadn't eaten since breakfast, and the thought of crunching into a big slice of cheesy toast made her mouth water.

"Down this hall are three more bedrooms," Ashley indicated with a tilt of her head toward her right. Mrs. Peterson's quarters are on the other side of the mansion, next to the dining hall. She's a really nice lady."

Ashley steered Haven into a large room. "This is the parlor. It's not used too much, except when parents come for a visit. But I bet you're going to enjoy the piano. Mrs. Peterson has it tuned regularly. And there are pocket doors so you can close yourself off for privacy.

Haven would have to ask Mrs. Peterson if it would be okay to do some of her practice there. It would save her from having to drive to the music building at night. She stifled a shudder at the thought of stepping out of her car in a dark campus parking lot.

Dade hovered like a ghost in her mind. And from her mind, it was only a leap of a few feet to land the specter of his presence around every corner of every building, in every dark doorway or silent parking lot. Even neurosurgery couldn't remove the frightened response in her brain at the thought of him.

She started when Ashley said, "Let's go into the kitchen."

Stainless steel appliances and countertops gleamed under bright lights. A college student was stirring a big pot of spaghetti sauce. Another young woman pulled a tray of garlic bread out of the oven. And the third woman was dumping salad greens and chopped up vegetables into a stainless-steel bowl.

"Hi, guys. Meet Haven. She just moved in."

They didn't leave their posts, but Haven got hellos and smiles from all of them.

Ashley consulted a schedule printed and hung by the kitchen

door. "You'll have kitchen duty two days a week. That includes cooking and cleanup. Garbage bin is out the back entrance."

A back entrance. Was it secure? Haven walked over and inspected the lock and deadbolt. Metal bars—the kind one would see in a high crime area—had been bolted over the window in the door. Good. So far, the house seemed secure.

"Besides that, we have a schedule for house cleaning, too. Mainly vacuuming and dusting, and sometimes some yard work." Ashley led her out of the kitchen. "Well, unless you have any questions, your tour is over."

Ashley's smile warmed Haven's heart. She shook her head. "Can't think of any questions. Except, I'll be working at Campus Florist a couple afternoons a week. Hopefully, that won't conflict with my kitchen duties here."

"I'm sure we can work around your schedule. We all help each other around here 'cause we're all working and going to classes, too."

"Thanks, Ashley." What a relief. She'd be busy this year, but her schedule seemed to be working out in a manageable way.

She mounted the stairs to her bedroom. So far, so good. Cedar Street Mansion seemed to be a safe place for the next two semesters. Her dad would make sure no one knew where she was studying. Dade knew about her childhood neighborhood, but he wouldn't be able to find out where she had gone.

She'd read about stalkers eventually figuring out where their victims had moved. But that was because the stalking victims had friends or family who slipped up and gave out information.

Haven walked into her bedroom, turned the lock, and sat on the edge of her bed. Aunt Joy would be horrified to know that

Haven was holding onto traumatic memories of being kidnapped and imprisoned without anyone to hear and counsel her. Her therapist aunt would have said that she was only prolonging her emotional struggle by not finding someone she could trust, someone who could listen and remain objective, and provide hope for the future.

Was there anyone else she could tell? A professor? Another student? Who could comprehend the emotional roller coaster of mistrust and guilt set in motion by Dade's abuse and threats? Who could shelter her heart but not become a target for Dade's jealousy and rage?

Only another person who's suffered similar abuse.

Maybe she'd meet someone at the new Bible study she had signed up for. But even in a close-knit group, she'd have to be careful how much she shared. College students weren't always good at keeping secrets.

"Lord, please send me a sweet friend, someone who'll help me, someone I can help, too. I need to be able to start trusting people again."

♩ ♪♪♫♪

September 15th, Journal entry #68

I think I'm going to love this next year. Also, I've already gotten some recruitment letters from four universities and one private college about doing a master's degree. Two years ago, I would have been so excited about this. Now, I have to weigh every decision against my need for security. My head says, "God is in control. He loves me. He's working out a plan that is best for me."

But my heart wants to scream, "Where is Dade? Why can't he leave me alone?"

♩ ♪♪♫♪

Dade exited the highway and turned onto the Oregon county road. He could see the Ellingsen estate long before he turned onto her street. Its terra cotta roof stood out among the three other houses on the street. Ruth's daddy must have paid a pretty penny for that house. Three garages, close to two acres of level land. Nicely landscaped. By the size of the house, he'd estimate it to be at least six or seven thousand square feet. The kind of house a doctor or lawyer or business executive would live in.

He pulled his truck over, two properties down from Ruth's house and idled the motor. When a car passed, he pretended to be talking on his cell phone.

A snort puffed out of his lips. Too bad for Ruth they didn't live in a gated community. He could visit her street any time he wanted, as long as he didn't hang out too long.

The neighboring houses didn't face the street, which was a good thing. Guy Ellingsen usually left the house a little after seven thirty in the morning, leaving Ruth by herself. But there was no way Dade was going to walk onto her property. The security sign posted near the edge of their property warned him off, reminding him that his best opportunities lay in waiting for Ruth to drive into town. Except he hadn't seen her car parked in the driveway for at least two weeks.

Four mailboxes huddled at the end of the cul-de-sac. He drove over to them. Checking the rear-view mirror, he set the brake. It only took him five seconds to walk nonchalantly over to her mailbox, sweep the contents and retreat back into his truck. Putting the truck in gear, he got out of there as fast as he could without speeding.

He drove down the road a mile or two and into a hardware store parking lot where he could go through the Ellingsen's mail.

He'd expected a lot more mail. Didn't rich people get way more than the small pile in his hands? A flyer for ten percent off their next purchase at Michael's. Another for Macy's. Safeway coupons. A letter from some charity he'd never heard of. An envelope from a college in Washington.

Nothing he could use. He dropped the whole lot onto the passenger seat, a deep frown digging grooves around his lips.

He punched the start button on the dashboard. The truck roared to life. Maybe he could hole up in a motel tonight. He could visit Ruth's church in the morning and—

Hold on. A college?

He picked up the envelope from Northmont College. Addressed to 'Ms. Haven Ellingsen'. Return address: Music Department, Northmont College, Issaquah, Washington.

Why would a college from Washington be sending Ruth a letter? The last thing she had stated in her interview on channel five about going to school again was, "I have no immediate plans to return to school. For now, I plan to get re-acquainted with my dad, my friends, and relatives, and work to get my memory back."

Maybe she had recuperated faster than he guessed. But why would Ruth even consider a small, out of state, private college? When she was at Life Ventures, she had told him she studied at the University of Oregon. If she were planning to continue her studies, why wouldn't she return to that school?

He slipped his finger under the envelope flap and ripped it open.

"Dear Ms. Ellingsen,

Congratulations on choosing Northmont College for your music studies. Here at Northmont, we are proud of ..." Blah, blah, blah, blah ... He trailed his finger down the paragraph. More of the usual college introductory stuff. He skimmed the next few lines.

Dade folded the letter and stuffed it into his jacket pocket, his breath hitching. Ruth, not in Oregon. Here it was, mid-September already. She probably hadn't been at her daddy's place for at least a couple of weeks. He didn't know whether to laugh or punch something.

She was in Issaquah. He laughed like a crazy person, shaking his head. About an hour west of Remley. So close he could touch her.

Adrenaline zipped down his arms and legs. One step closer to getting Ruth back.

Three hours later, he stood in the student lounge of Northmont's Music Building. Thank God, it was a Saturday. No classes today, and if Ruth were in the building she'd likely be on the other side, in the practice rooms.

Even if the administrative offices in the music building were open on Saturdays, he couldn't just show up there and inquire about a particular student. But sometimes bulletin boards posted advertisements, including an email or phone number.

He scanned the walls. No bulletin board that he could see. There had to be one somewhere. He'd been in school, years ago. There was always a bulletin board.

A female student ambled down the hallway, studying her cell phone.

"Excuse me, miss," he called, "do you have a bulletin board around here?"

The girl barely looked up from her phone. "Yeah. It's in the hallway, just past the lounge." She pointed the opposite direction and kept walking.

Kids. So rude nowadays. Not concerned about anything except watching YouTube videos or texting friends. On the other hand, since the girl didn't really see him, she wouldn't be able to identify him.

He turned and walked in the direction the girl had indicated. Around the corner, a bulletin board displayed flyers about upcoming performances, advertisements for tutoring, information for various auditions, a music school calendar. Nothing he could use, except ... One index card advertised a quartet that played for weddings, funerals, and parties. "Reasonable rates. Available most weekends."

Hmm. Ruth's name didn't appear anywhere on the bulletin board.

Dade ripped off the index card advertising the quartet. Turning it over, he wrote:

"Female singer wanted. Must also play piano well. Guitar, a plus. Two hundred dollars for a two-hour party. Contact ..." Hmm. Who could be the contact person for the—

Women's voices echoed from down the hall. His hand jerked, and the card slipped from his fingers. Two young women had come down the stairs from the practice rooms and halted at the rear exit. Sunlight poured through the windows by the exit, partially obscuring the girls.

"How about meeting again on Monday, in the lounge, about four?" Ruth's musical voice tickled his ears, sweeping all reason from him. He didn't hear the other girl's response. His focus narrowed, his pulse hammered in his head. His muscles tightened, his breathing jerking in and out like an ambushed deer.

If he grabbed her now, there would be witnesses. He couldn't risk it.

"My car's parked out front. I'll see you Monday," Ruth said to her friend, tilting her head in his direction as she moved toward the lounge doors.

Ruth turned toward him. His neck iced. A sign on a door nearby said, Men's Room. He bolted inside.

Seconds later, her little shoes tap-tapped past the men's room door.

He waited a long time before sticking his head out the door. *Ruth's gone.*

From now on, any more investigations would have to be done by someone else. If Ruth spotted him, she'd either call the police. Or she'd disappear. Either way, she'd win. He couldn't let that happen.

♩ ♪♪♫♪

Fiona peeked out the front window. Her heart thundered when Dade's truck pulled up alongside her house. She slipped on her sweater and grabbed her purse. "Mara, I'm going now."

Her sister came out of the kitchen. "Hold on, I wanna peek at your new guy."

Fiona pursed her lips. Why did Mara always have to judge her latest boyfriend? As if she could pick better men? So far, Mara's dates were all losers.

Mara hurried over for a quick look outside the window. "Not bad. And no tattoos either."

Not bad? The man was jaw-dropping.

Mara released the curtain and backed away from the window, eyes wide. "He's coming up the walk." She stared at Fiona. "And he's got flowers."

Fiona's knees turned to jelly. Dade was actually getting out of his truck, and coming up to the house to get her? No man she'd ever dated had done that. How did she ever score such a great guy?

She answered the door immediately, even though it probably made her look desperate. Why did she care? The man who stood on her front door stoop, holding a bouquet of roses, smiling a toothy grin, was impossibly tall, handsome and desirable. And she had gotten him. Not those other two flirty waitresses, Tiffany and Heather at the Remley Pub. And not Mara, either. She glanced over her shoulder at Mara whose face expressed awe mixed with regret. Good, she was jealous.

"Pretty dress," he said, his green eyes sliding from her hair, which she'd curled, down to her new shoes. She'd borrowed the platform sandals from Mara. It made her at least five feet five.

"Where are we going?"

"Somewhere."

"Mara, would you mind putting these in a vase?"

Mara didn't even look at her. She was staring at Dade.

"Mara?" Fiona put a little edge in her voice.

"Oh, the flowers." Mara shook her head as if coming out of a trance. "Right." She reached for Fiona's bouquet.

"Thank you for the flowers, Dade. That was so thoughtful. I love roses."

"That's only part of the nice things I've got planned for you today." He held out his arm. "Shall we go?"

She could hardly believe this was real. Her heart somersaulted when she placed her hand on Dade's rock-hard arm. She practically sashayed down the steps and across the dirt path leading to the street. He'd opened the door for her, helped her get in. Mickey would've never done that.

Dade started the motor. "I thought we'd go exploring today. Ever been to Issaquah?"

"Not really. I've driven by it a few times on my way to Seattle."

"Well, I think you're going to like it."

More than half an hour went by, and in all that time she still couldn't think of a single thing to make small talk about. Dade didn't seem to mind. He was a quiet guy, but always thinking. Smart guys usually didn't talk too much. It was the stupid guys, the ones with too much beer in their bellies who talked and boasted.

She glanced at his left hand. Funny, she had never thought to check such an obvious thing as a ring finger. She exhaled the breath she'd been holding. *No ring.* But, some guys just took off their wedding ring when they planned to cheat with another woman. Dade's ring finger, however, didn't have a mark on it.

Say something, you goon. "Uh, it's nice weather today."

Dade didn't seem to hear her. What was the man thinking about? Was he thinking about her?

"It's such a nice day," she tried, a bit louder.

Dade blinked, keeping his eyes on the curvy road. "Yes, it is."

"Do you know people there, in Issaquah?"

He glanced at her sharply. "Why would you think that?"

Her stomach clenched. "I-I just thought, well, maybe we were going to meet some friends or something like that."

When he shook his head, his frown wrapped coldness around her ribs. "I-I didn't mean to upset you." Was he already tiring of her?

His face relaxed. "Sorry for snapping at you, Fiona. It's got nothing to do with you. My mind was on some unpleasant things that happened the last time I was in Issaquah."

"I'm sorry. Did something happen with a friend?" She could have kicked herself for being nosy, but she had to know. Was he thinking about another girl?

"I don't want to talk about it, yet. Maybe later. We'll see. Today, I just want to show you a great time." He reached over, engulfed her hand in his giant paw, and gave it a gentle squeeze.

His touch sent pleasure signals throughout her body. He actually cared about her.

When she dared to look up, his eyes held the kind of expression actors in movies wore when they were remembering hard times. Dade had a past. The thought made her want to take his head in her lap, stroke his bearded cheek, and comfort him with her words of enduring loyalty.

Dade nodded as if he had been having an argument in his head and had come to some sort of agreement. "Fiona, I think you and I are starting to feel a connection. Do you feel it, too?"

She stared at him. Had Dade been reading her mind? "I, um, I like you a lot." Could she be honest with him? "I think—"

"Maybe I'm moving too fast. You're a real sweet lady."

"No, Dade. It's not that." Her heart thundered so hard she felt faint. Dade was so honest. Most guys were afraid to share their feelings. Dade said everything he was thinking. It was such a rare quality. "We've only known each other a couple of weeks, and—

"And you're not ready to trust me yet, right?"

"Oh, I trust you. I knew the minute I laid eyes on you I could trust you." Would he reject her, or snicker if she opened her heart to him? She bit her lip for a moment. "You're special, Dade. Really special." She couldn't meet his eyes.

His smile spread warmth through her chest. This couldn't be happening. Nothing this wonderful had ever happened to her. Men always looked at the pretty girls, the ones with curves, the ones who strutted around like they knew everyone wanted them.

"You make me happy, Fiona. I feel like I've been waiting my whole life to meet a girl like you."

"You make me happy, too."

"You don't think I'm moving too fast?"

She shook her head, holding her breath over what he might say next.

"I'm so glad you feel that way because I've got plans for you and I. Big plans."

Big plans? Like marriage? Kids? If she got any happier, she would explode.

"Open up the glove compartment."

"The glove … ?"

"Yep. Pull out the paper in there."

The folded paper in the glove compartment turned out to be a real estate flyer for a house for rent in Issaquah. While she studied the photos, he put his hand on her arm. He winked when she looked up at him.

"Cute, isn't it?" He tapped the paper. "Oh, I know it's kind of cozy. But the house is in a good neighborhood. The landlord would also consider a rent with the option to buy. They always say, "Location, location, location.""

Was he asking her to … ? What did Dade mean? A house for him, or for her, or for both of them? "Wh-what is this?" If she let her heart hope for the best, she'd be disappointed, like always.

Dade raised his eyebrows. "What do you think, honey? Would you like to live there?"

"I-I like it, but Dade, the rent's really high and—"

"Don't worry about a thing. It's all taken care of. You just move in and let me take care of you."

A man wanted to take care of her? Did he expect her to find another job? He hadn't mentioned marriage yet. But if he were setting her up in a house, wouldn't that be the next part of his plan?

She stared at the pictures of the cute little house on Fry Street. Dade must have more money than she had imagined. She couldn't talk, couldn't ask any more questions. All she wanted to do now was stare at the real estate flyer and imagine how life with Dade was going to be.

Even if the place was small, once he bought it, Dade could fix things. He could knock down walls, put in an extra bath, re-do the plumbing. In a couple of years, she'll be pushing a stroller down the sidewalk, and everybody'll be cooing at her baby, saying, "He looks just like your husband."

She didn't come out of her head until Dade pulled his truck up next to a little white house with green trim. He jumped out and came around to her door. Key in hand, he led her up the walk.

The screen door made a racket when she pulled it open.

"Sorry about that. I can fix that with a little oil," Dade said.

She hadn't expected the house to be furnished, too. Dade had thought of everything. How long had he been planning to spring this surprise on her? He must really love her.

"Oh, Dade, I love it. All of it. It's just the right size." She snuggled up to him.

But instead of responding in a romantic way, he pulled away and headed for the kitchen. "You go inspect the place. I'm going to pull some things out of the fridge."

He left her without even a backward glance or a wink. His lack of affection stung. But maybe he was too excited to be affectionate. That had to be it. He won't allow himself to be all lovey until she approved of the house. She started up the stairs. Two bedrooms upstairs, nothing special, but the bath was kind of nice. Maybe Dade could update the fixtures, though.

Back on the main floor, the master bedroom made her insides turn into mush. She came out before he could find her lingering there.

When she walked into the kitchen, Dade placed a tray of canapés and a bottle of champagne and two glasses on the kitchen table.

"Oh, Dade, you thought of everything," she murmured.

"So, do you like it enough to stay?"

He didn't move. Didn't try to hold her. It was like he was holding his breath. This meant so much to him. She meant so much to him. Now was not the time to ask for more details. That could come later. "I'll stay."

His smile lit up his handsome face. Oh, how she wanted to kiss him. Why didn't he move to hold her, claim her lips?

"Issaquah is almost a perfect place to live." He frowned as he poured champagne into their glasses and handed her one.

"Almost perfect? Why isn't it perfect?" Would he say, it won't be perfect until she's settled in the house? She took a sip of the bubbly liquid, her heart thudding, waiting.

"I have a slight ... problem, which I hope you'll be able to help me with."

Dade pulled out a kitchen chair and indicated for her to sit.

She nibbled on a slice of cheese to hide how her body trembled, while he drew something out of his jacket pocket. He laid a three by five photo on the table. "See this girl?"

She wanted to snort. Yes, she could clearly see her. The champagne she'd just sipped burned her stomach. The woman in the photo was blonde and pretty. Why would Dade carry around a picture of another woman? She'd better be his sister or first cousin.

"She's my problem. She took something from me, and I want it back. Then everything will be perfect and I can get on with my big plans."

Leaning over, he shoved the photo closer so Fiona could get a better view. "Memorize that face, Fiona. It's the face of an evil woman, a thief."

Fiona tried to pull the photo over to her side of the table. She hadn't worn her glasses today, and the photo looked a little blurry. But he wouldn't let go. His knuckles turned white where his fingers pressed the photo against the table. Dade's eyes held a look that made her shiver.

"Man, if you hate this girl, there must be a good reason." Fiona hated her already. Had she taken money, property? Humiliated him in some way? Beautiful women were the worst. "She must be a real piece of work."

"You could say that." He downed his glass of champagne in one big swallow. "And I thought, since you'll have some free time on your hands once you move in here, maybe you could do me a favor."

"What do you want me to do?"

"Go to the School of Music and park in the front. It's where the girl—Haven parks. She's a student there. She comes and goes through the lounge entrance. Hang out there and wait for her. Then, when she leaves, follow her, see where she goes."

"That's it?"

"Yes. All I want is information. Don't try to talk to her yet. Don't mess this up. I need you to do this perfectly."

"So, things will be perfect in Issaquah again?" She sneered at the beautiful girl in the photo.

"Exactly."

Chapter Four

Because he loves me, says the Lord, I will rescue him;
I will protect him for he acknowledges my name.
Psalm 91:14

September 18, Journal #71

I am so glad I took that floral decorating class in high school. Campus Florist hired me part-time. I work afternoons three days a week. Dad thinks I shouldn't be spreading myself thin. He's willing to pay for everything. But I said, "No way you're going to do that. I can at least pay for my car insurance, gas, and groceries."

Also, I need to have some money not coming from Dad, just in case Dade ever showed up again and I needed to get away quick. I hope the police never pull me over and look in my car trunk. I don't know what they'd think if they found my get-away-quick bag with emergency supplies and a wad of cash. Who carries that around except someone on the run? I wouldn't want to explain that.

♩ ♪♪♫♪

Haven peered through the window of Campus Florist before stepping outside. Homeless men sometimes hung out on the sidewalks nearby. They were probably harmless. One of them was tall but looked nothing like Dade. Good. No one suspicious out there. Today, she hadn't been lucky. She'd had to park her car way down the street. But at least her shift at the Florist ended at four, long before it got dark.

"Bye, Mrs. Walker," she called to her employer. "See you tomorrow."

Mrs. Walker waved goodbye without taking her eyes off her paperwork.

Haven stepped outside and scanned the area, key fob already in her hand. The walk to her car took her past a sewing and craft store, a coffee and tea shop, and a children's clothing shop. The children's shop was having a fifty percent off all merchandise store-wide sale. Women and little kids crowded the sidewalk where racks of clothing had been rolled out.

"Excuse me, sweetie," she said, trying to get past a cute preschooler who had crawled into the only remaining free space, rolling his toy truck, and making engine noises.

Crowds were good, though. The more people, the better. If Dade were after her, he'd never consider trying to snatch her with so many people around. Once past the crowd, she hurried toward her car, parked a block away.

Empty sidewalks made her way more nervous. Tonight, she needed to go back to school to attend a student recital. Good thing Ashley had offered to drive. Haven wouldn't have gone if she'd had to drive herself because the music school parking lot would be dark by the time the performance ended.

Half a block away from the car she could see the roof of the silver Sebring glinting in the sun, and tension eased from her belly. She clicked the fob.

A woman was coming in her direction, walking slowly, stumbling. Haven clutched her purse closer. Was she on drugs? Or ill? Her clothes looked well-cared for, though she looked pale and awfully thin.

Haven hurried to get to her car before the woman passed, but she looked up. The girl's gaze met her eyes, obviously seeking compassion Asking the girl how she could help was the right thing to do. But involvement in another person's problems wasn't exactly what Haven needed right now. She had her own worries.

"Excuse me, Ma'am, can you help me?" The woman had stretched out her arms like a little child calling for its mama.

Haven's heart melted. She scanned the area around the sidewalk and her car. At least there weren't any men nearby. None of the women at the children's sale were seeing the woman. No, she was barely a woman. More like a girl.

The girl stumbled one more time, lost her balance and fell onto her knees.

"Oh, my goodness," Haven cried out as she stuffed the fob into her pocket and ran over. Crouching, she laid her hand on the stranger's shoulder. "Are you all right? Here, let me help you up."

Most girls weighed more than Haven. Not this one. She might have been ninety pounds, soaking wet. It wasn't difficult to get her up on her feet. "There's a bench over there," Haven whispered. "Let's go sit. Ma'am, what's your name?"

The girl settled onto the bench but kept her face down. Haven sat next to her, keeping her arm around the girl's shoulders in case she slumped again.

"Fiona. My name's Fiona," she murmured. "I had to get away from my boyfriend. I've been walking all day, trying to figure out where to go."

A battered woman? Haven took her hand. "Fiona, are you hungry? Can I get you some food?"

Fiona raised her head. Her eyes were brown. Brown, surrounded by a sea of unbroken white skin. Except for the dark circles that colored the spaces under her eyes. A big bruise—the kind you'd get if you 'ran into a door'—tattooed her left jaw. The poor child. Outrage stirred in Haven's chest. What kind of brute would strike a woman?

"There's a café across the street. I'm going to take you there and get you something to eat."

Fiona shook her head. "I don't want to bother you."

"Nonsense. You're hungry and tired, and I'm off work, so let's go." Haven helped her up.

In another minute they had seated themselves in one of the café booths.

Fiona's voice sounded surprisingly strong when she told the waitress, "I'll have a burger with fries, everything on it, a chocolate shake, and a side of pancakes."

Haven's heart squeezed. The girl must not have eaten in a long time. "I'll have a dinner salad and a slice of Italian bread, and a cup of coffee, black."

Fiona met Haven's eyes briefly before dropping her gaze to her thin hands.

"Fiona, a minute ago, outside, you told me you'd been walking for hours. Are you from Issaquah?"

"I, uh, I'm from … here. … but I don't want to talk about—" She waved her hands as if to dismiss the statement she'd begun but not finished. "My … boyfriend … might be looking for me. He's mad at me. He's mad all the time." She glanced out the window as if the man might be lurking outside, looking for her.

"Maybe we should call the police. I mean, if he's looking for you, wouldn't you want to tell the police about it?"

Fiona's eyes widened and she stared. "Oh, I-I couldn't do that. No, don't call. He, well, he told me … if I ever go to the police, uh, I'd be sorry."

She seemed to notice Haven's eyes studying the bruise on her face. She put her fingers up to hide the mark. "It's not what you think. It was an accident."

"Really?"

"Jake is a good man. Really, he is. He loves me. It's just that he was drinking 'cause he got fired. He's been under a lot of pressure lately. I asked him something and he got upset."

A man loves a girl but hits her? That wasn't love. Dade's image shoved into her mind. "Sit on down there and think on your sinfulness," he'd bawled at her when he caught her snooping in the new cabin he'd been building. He had shaken her till her teeth rattled, and thrown her down onto the floor. She would never forget how he'd gripped her like a rabid animal. No one should have to suffer that kind of abuse.

Under the table, Haven clenched her fists. She swallowed to make her throat relax. "Do you have any money to tide you over? I can—"

"No, no. I have enough for … for … Miss? What's your name?"

It's Haven."

"I just need to get to my bank tomorrow. It's too late today."

"What's your bank? I could drive you to an ATM machine."

Fiona didn't seem to hear her. She stroked the bruise on her jaw and kept her eyes peeled on the street. Haven pulled out her cell phone. All it would take is one phone call to the police. They'd get this whole mess taken care of.

"Isn't it better to press charges?"

Fiona turned and her eyes pleaded. "Please, Haven, I just don't want to be alone. Don't leave me. Don't call the police."

Haven took a deep breath, her finger hovering over the phone. Did Fiona understand what was best for her?

But Haven hadn't called the police about Dade because she had taken his threat seriously. How could she betray Fiona, who might be in a similar situation? The girl was obviously traumatized. Her boyfriend had threatened to make matters worse for her if she told the police. What if she phoned the police, and then Jake hurt Fiona even worse?

That would be awful. She'd never forgive herself.

"I have an idea, Fiona. Why don't you spend the night with me?"

Fiona squinted her eyes. "I don't know …"

"Just for tonight. Jake won't have a clue where you've gone. Tomorrow, if you'd like, you can try calling him. "How would that be?"

Fiona hesitated, her brown eyes studying Haven's face.

For a minute Haven thought she detected anger or something

close to that in Fiona's eyes. But, at last, she smiled for the first time. "Thank you, Haven. I really appreciate it. God bless you for doing this."

The waitress brought their orders, and Fiona grabbed a handful of fries and stuffed them into her mouth.

Haven bowed her head. *Thank you, Lord, for putting me in the right place at the right time for Fiona. Help me to help her.*

♩ ♪♪♫♪

"I was all set to be really mad at you for talking to Haven. But I guess your plan worked. Congratulations, Fiona. You'd make a terrific CIA operative."

Fiona beamed under his approving gaze. "She totally fell for my poor-little-me act." She snickered.

He knew he'd picked the right girl to spy out Ruth. Dade settled next to Fiona on the sofa in the living room of their new house on Fry Street. Needy girls would do almost anything for someone who promises a little love and attention.

"You should have seen her place at that Mansion. All fancy and rich-like. Her closet is full of nice clothes. She's got designer perfume, and a dresser drawer just for her jewelry. Nice stuff, too. I peeked when she went out of the room for a few minutes.

We sat and talked for hours in her room. She even made me sleep in her bed, and she slept on the floor. She prayed for me, kept smiling and smiling, telling me things were going to get better. What a fake. I'll bet she's never faced anything harder than breaking one of her perfect nails."

Dade shook his head. "She's rich all right. Her daddy's paying for that fancy education, and her new car." This was fun. He didn't have to do much to stoke Fiona's hatred of his beautiful Ruth.

"I don't get it, Dade. Why would Haven need to steal from you? I mean, she's definitely rich and spoiled. But why would she need to take anything from you? It sure seems like she's got it all."

Dade frowned. "Don't get me started. It's too complicated. I'll just say, Haven's a woman who will take your love, then throw you into a pit when it suits her." He'd never forget the devastation he'd experienced when Ruth escaped from his cabin.

He slung his arm around Fiona's shoulders. "I'm so glad I've found a woman who's so different from Haven. You'd never do that to me, would you, Fiona?"

Fiona sighed and snuggled into his chest. "Never. You're the best thing that's ever happened to me."

He squeezed her tighter. "You make me happy. And as soon as we take care of business with Haven, we'll be in much better shape." He'd be long gone, with Ruth tied up in his truck, and Fiona? Well, once she realized he wasn't coming back, she could always find another waitress job somewhere.

Fiona raised her brown eyes to his, like a dog begging for a treat. He lowered his lips to hers as a reward.

"So, what's next?" she whispered with her lips near his, inviting another kiss.

"We've got to get her to come over here. Come inside."

Fiona's eyes widened. "What are you gonna do to her?"

"Hey, do you care about Haven?" Dade pulled away.

"No, but I don't want to witness a crime."

He shrugged and drew her close again. "I'm not going to do anything bad. I just want my self-respect back."

"I don't know about getting Haven inside our house. We don't know each other that well yet. She might not be ready to trust me. Besides, I told her my boyfriend, 'Jake' is physically abusive. That might make her afraid to come inside."

"You can tell her Jake moved out, or he's gone for the week, something like that. You already discovered Haven's a sucker for a sob story. If you come across like you're upset and need someone to comfort you, she'll come over. Trust me, I know this girl."

Dade chuckled. "Maybe I could add another bruise close to the other one on your cheek." He balled his fist and Fiona flinched, laughing nervously.

She cupped the bruise. "Yeah, you should have seen her face when she noticed it. It wasn't hard to make her believe in my story. She's pretty naïve."

But not nearly as naïve as his dear little useful idiot, Fiona. A corner of his lip flicked upward. He smoothed his mustache to hide the smirk.

"Get in touch with Haven. Ask her about all her churchy stuff. Show her you want to make your life better. A couple more hours of getting acquainted will convince her you're someone worth knowing."

"Okay, I'll go on over to the Campus Florist tomorrow, right before she gets off work."

He winked. "Good girl."

♩ ♪♪♫♪

September 21st, Journal Entry #74
I helped a young woman named Fiona stay away from her

abusive boyfriend. She's so sweet. I think she needs a friend. I hope I can help her. What kind of guy beats a woman and then claims he loves her? She still trusts him. Is that a good thing? I don't trust anyone, well, except for my dad and Joy and Anna.

♩ ♪♪♫♪

In the Campus Florist, Haven was slipping the last sprig of baby's breath into the floral decoration she'd been working on when a shadow crossed the table. She looked up.

"Fiona! I didn't even hear you come in."

Fiona wore a shy smile. "You were really concentrating on that bouquet when I came inside."

"It's so good to see you. What have you been doing for the last couple of days?" Haven carried the bouquet over to the floral refrigerator and slipped it inside.

"Well, things are a little bit better … with Jake and me. I knew you'd be wondering about me and what happened when I went home."

"Did you want to go somewhere and talk? My shift is almost over."

"I was hoping you'd be free."

"Head on over to Crossway Coffee, next door. I'll be there in five minutes."

Fiona turned without another word and slipped outside.

What a sweet girl. So shy, and gentle. But maybe it was Fiona's softness that made a guy like Jake think he could knock her around and control her.

At least Fiona seemed happy today. Not confused or

disoriented. It was amazing how some food and a good night's rest could turn your mind around.

Maybe over coffee, she could broach the subject of Jake again, and see if Fiona had made any decision yet about getting counseling or legal help.

"Mrs. Walker, I'm on my way out," she called.

"Thanks, Haven," Mrs. Walker called from somewhere in the back of the business.

Fiona had already seated herself when Haven stepped inside the coffee shop. Two twelve-ounce cups sat on the table. When Haven tilted her head, Fiona said, "I ordered for you. You like your Americano black, right?"

"Yes, thanks." She reached into her purse for her wallet.

"And don't even think about trying to pay me back. You've done so much for me, it's the least I can do to say thanks."

She hadn't done much. Giving a girl lodging for the night and a meal wasn't exactly heroic. It was simple hospitality. "You are such a sweetheart."

Fiona looked down at her cup and smiled again. "The other day, after Jake and I had our big fight, I felt like I didn't have a friend in the world."

"Don't you have any family close by?"

"No. They're all east." Fiona waved her arm to accentuate the distance.

"How are things going? Did you two talk?"

Fiona took a sip of her coffee, still keeping her eyes cast downward. "He was jealous. He thought I was noticing some other guy at work. But I told him he didn't have anything to worry about."

"Did … did Jake apologize for striking you?"

"Oh, yes. He was so sorry. He bought me flowers. He said he'd never do it again."

"Do you believe him?"

Fiona's eyes snapped upward. "Of course." Her thin voice turned steely. "Jake's wonderful. He just lost his temper. It's not like him at all to strike a woman."

"I'm sorry, Fiona. I didn't mean to offend you. But I care about you."

Fiona sighed. "I'm sorry, too. I know you're just trying to make sure I'm safe. I shouldn't have snapped at you. We've—Jake and me—we've been fighting a lot lately. I don't know why. He's talked about maybe splitting for a while. I don't know what I'd do if he left. We've been together for a long time. I love Jake."

Her voice quavered, and Haven put her hand on Fiona's. "I'm so sorry." Her own throat tightened, and she forced down her grief over Fiona's situation. This wasn't the time to cry. She needed to stay calm so she could help the girl.

Fiona's gaze softened. "Haven, do you have a boyfriend?"

That seemed like a strange question, coming on the heels of Fiona about to lose her guy. "No, no boyfriend."

"Never? Have you ever been in love?"

"Oh, don't get me wrong. I've had a couple of boyfriends. Nothing serious. Just a few dates, off and on."

Fiona's eyes narrowed. "You mean, no guy's ever been in love with you?"

Haven shrugged. "Maybe. I just haven't stuck around long enough for any of them to say it. I'm not ready for a long-term commitment."

One of Fiona's eyebrows shot upward. "You mean you could wait? What if a guy pursued you and he was the one and only guy who'd ever love you. And if this guy truly loved you, you could turn and walk away? Wouldn't that break his heart?"

"Not if I made it plain from the start that I'm not ready for a serious relationship." She'd seen some of her friends fall for the first guy that came along. Sometimes it worked. Other times …

"I don't get you, Haven." Fiona frowned. "You seem so warm and caring. But then you talk like a cold person when it comes to man-woman relationships."

"It's not cold to tell a man up front that you're only interested in friendship. Any honorable man would respect me enough to believe me when I tell him that."

Fiona sat back, folded her arms across her chest, and shook her head. "You're a strange one."

"There's more to life than just having a boyfriend, Fiona."

"What's better than having a man who loves you? Were you serious when you said no man's ever been in love with you?"

"Well … there was this man … a while ago." Suddenly, she was back at Dade's cabin, hiding her trembling hands behind her back, shuddering when he trailed his big hand down her hair and face. "He thought he was in love with me." A wave of nausea flooded her stomach, remembering him bending over her, planting a lustful kiss on her lips, slipping a gold ring on her finger. "But he wasn't."

Fiona leaned closer, her thin face resembling a fox eyeing a hen house. The tone of her voice went from simply curious, to interrogative. "How do you know he wasn't in love with you?"

Haven frowned. Should she share some of what she'd

experienced? It would feel good to blurt out some truth about Dade, even if she couldn't mention his name. Maybe what she'd gone through might help Fiona recognize what love is, or is not. "I would think that if a man truly loved me, he would love sacrificially. He would put my needs ahead of his selfish desires. It's like that verse in the Bible, 'Love is patient, love is kind. Love considers the other person. Love wants the best for her or him."

She stared past Fiona, remembering how Dade had pressed his hand over her mouth and nose until she almost fainted. "He didn't care about me. He wanted me to be some other woman. And when I didn't want to fulfill his fantasy, he tried to hurt me and terrorize me. That's not love."

Fiona's mouth bunched up like a wrinkled prune. "Jake's not like that." Her words poured out fast and loud. "He thinks of me. He works hard and takes care of me. He told me he trusts me 'cause I'd never betray him. He really loves me. He's—"

Haven put her hands up, palms out. "You don't need to convince me about Jake. I believe you. He sounds like a loving man." Good grief, the girl was so defensive, obviously in love with the unworthy Jake. "Maybe someday I'll find a man who inspires such loyalty in me."

Those words seemed to soothe Fiona, whose lips relaxed into a pretty cupid's bow. Maybe it was time to change the subject. Hopefully, if she kept building her relationship with Fiona, she could help her see that a man battering a woman wasn't normal. And it wasn't likely to stop.

"I'm playing a recital next week at the school of music. I'd love it if you could come. There'll be other musicians playing, too."

"Next week. Hmm." Fiona took out her cell phone and consulted it. "What time?"

"Friday night at seven. My dad and his fiancée are coming up. It would be fun for you to meet them."

"Um, I'll check with Jake. Maybe we could both come." She dumped her empty cup in the trash. "Thanks for inviting me. I'd love to hear you play." Another sweet smile graced her pale face.

"And feel free to bring your friends. We love to share our music with the local community."

Fiona finished logging in Haven's information. "Would you mind giving me your phone number?"

"Sorry." This was always awkward. "I need to keep my number private. Personal reasons."

Fiona's lips drooped. "Oh."

It-it's got nothing to do with you, Fiona." She reached over and touched Fiona's bony hand. "I, um, had some … bad things happen a while ago. Something like what you went through. I still haven't learned to trust people again."

"Really, some guy hurt you, too?"

"Yes. I believed him, but he betrayed my trust. Someday I'll tell you more about it." Haven picked up her purse and jacket. "Time for me to go. You can leave a message at the Cedar Street Mansion. I call them each day to retrieve messages."

"That works. Thanks."

"See you Friday?"

"Oh, we wouldn't miss it."

♩ ♪♪♫♪

"She's a cold one, Dade. Just like you said." The more Fiona remembered Haven's nice place at the Cedar Street Mansion, the more she hated her.

Fiona sliced a cucumber and arranged the pieces on a plate with tomatoes and fresh vegetables.

Dade popped a cucumber slice into his mouth. "What did she tell you?"

"I couldn't believe it. Haven said she would tell any man who just wanted to be friends that she could never care for him."

"Told you. She struts around like Cleopatra, making all the men notice her. Then, when they look, she scorns them with her proud eyes. A girl like that deserves to have her hair dyed plain brown, no makeup, no nice perfume, and have to wear a sack to hide all that pretty shape."

"A burka?" A chuckle burst from Fiona's lips. Conceited girls needed someone to take them down a notch or two.

"That would work."

She was glad he agreed. On the other hand, it wasn't good to hear that her boyfriend notices other women. "Here's the best news. Haven's going to be performing in some sort of musical thing at her school on Friday. And, believe it or not, she invited us to come to it."

Dade shook his head. "How's that going to work? I can't show my face there. What if she recognized me?"

"Oh, I'll make some sort of excuse about you having to work, or something, so you couldn't come. She'll appreciate me coming, though. It will make her truly believe that we're developing a good friendship."

Dade laughed. "You're really getting into this assignment."

His smile made her heart thrill. He put his arm around her and squeezed her close. She would have robbed a bank to keep him smiling at her that way.

"So, here's my plan. She's off work the next day, Saturday. I'm gonna call and leave a message—"

"Leave a message?"

"Oh, I forgot to tell you, she doesn't give out her phone number to anyone, so I have to leave a message at the place she's living."

Dade's smile faded. "Didn't you try to look at her phone when you were at her place?"

Fiona's stomach crawled. Dade's mood could drop from warm to icy in seconds. "I tried. She's got a lock on it. I couldn't get past it.

Anyway, I contact her. She calls me back. I'm crying, almost hysterical. I say, 'Jake's left me. I'm so unhappy. And lonely. Haven, please come over. I don't know what to do. I'm desperate. Help me. I can't be alone.' She comes over to comfort me. Walks right inside."

"And I'm waiting behind the door."

"Like a spider." Fiona couldn't stop the cackle that came from her throat. It was going to be so fun to see the pretty, conceited girl go from all-loving and compassionate to terrified, pleading for Dade to let her go.

And Dade would know just what to do to handle his problem with Haven. He'd scare her, and she'd give back whatever she had taken. And then Dade would only think about Fiona. When he kissed her, he wouldn't be thinking about some other woman.

"You gonna use your taser?"

He nodded, eyes narrowed, staring into the living room at the front door.

She'd only seen people on the news get tasered. This would be fun to see it up close.

His voice sounded strange when he said, "You sure she'll come inside?"

"I'm sure."

Chapter Five

The righteousness of the upright delivers them,
but the unfaithful are trapped by evil desires.
Proverbs 11:6

Haven pulled her car out of the Cedar Street parking lot and sped down the street. Poor Fiona. Just last night she'd been in such good spirits at the recital. But now Fiona was crying so hard it had been hard to understand her. Jake had left her. That much she had gotten from the girl's blubbering. "I don't know what I'll do without him. Please come, Haven. I don't want to be alone."

Haven's stomach churned. No boyfriend had ever left her, nevertheless, she'd experienced how awful it was when you lose someone. You either run to be alone—as she had done when she heard about her father's car accident—or you needed someone's arm around you hearing comforting words. Fiona needed her. How could she stay away, even if she had to enter the house of a girl she barely knew?

Her fleshed crawled, nerves firing warning shots. Ever since she had obeyed Mama and entered Dade's cabin in the woods— and her life changed forever—she had struggled to trust any sort of invitation. Fiona knew nothing of her irrational fear. She'd think Haven was crazy if she said she couldn't come over. No, worse, Fiona would think Haven was the most selfish woman alive to refuse to visit someone in a crisis. It was bad enough being called crazy. But being thought of as selfish was just about the worst thing someone could accuse her of.

Did Fiona have a family member who would be willing to drive over and stay with her for a while?

At the stop sign, she turned left. Her GPS led her three more stops, then another left turn.

Maybe she should offer to stay with Fiona if she couldn't be alone.

Dad wouldn't like it, though. Ever since she'd come back from living in the wilderness, he'd been super protective, asking her where she was going, how long she'd be out, who she was meeting.

But Fiona wasn't dangerous. She was just a girl who'd made some bad decisions. Her boyfriend had left. That was a good thing. Maybe Haven could help Fiona understand that living with a man without being married only led to heartache.

She turned off Oak Avenue, took a few more streets. Turned onto Fry. Fifth house on the right, Fiona had said. A little craftsman style house, white, with green trim. Her hands turned clammy. It was so hard to comfort someone in a crisis. "Lord, help me to say the right things."

There it was. Just like Fiona said. A cute little house. Oh, poor girl. She was in there all by herself.

She pulled over and parked right in front of the house.

A man next door was cutting his lawn. Across the street, two women pushed their strollers down the sidewalk.

She got out and hurried up the walk toward the front door.

Fiona must have been watching for her because the screen door screeched open. Fiona came out onto the porch, letting the door bang shut.

Screech. Bang. The two sounds awakened a horrible memory. Mama, coming out the screen door, letting it bang shut. "Come on in, girl." And she had obeyed the woman. She'd let Mama nudge her up the porch steps. Through the screen door. Into the cabin in the woods.

The horrible memory bludgeoned her, like Mama's iron doorstop. Made her jerk to a halt and try to steady herself. She reached up to stop the blood from pouring down her face. What if another awful person was waiting behind this door? Not Mama. But another wicked and stupid and unbalanced person.

Haven's breath hitched. The sound of the screen door echoed over and over in her head. Mama and Dade, waiting for her to come inside. They had wicked plans for her.

Haven's lips turned numb. Hot and cold erupted and sprinted down her spine. She couldn't catch her breath. "Fion"—

The name caught in her throat. Her tongue stuck to the roof of her mouth. The dark doorway behind her waiting friend yawned like an open grave, its rectangular angles neatly dug to accommodate her coffin.

Giant hands squeezed her throat. White noise crackled, crescendoing into a deafening roar. An immense, inky form enveloped her.

"Haven, come inside." The girl in front of the grave said. "I need you."

"I-I can't ... brea ..."

Fiona didn't look sad. She looked angry. "Haven?" She put her hands on her hips.

"I can't breathe."

Fiona stomped down the steps and seized Haven's hand. "C'mon, girl."

"No. No! I can't go in."

"Why not?" Fiona's grip tightened. "It's all right," she almost snarled. "You'll be fine once you come inside. I need you."

"I can't."

"You said you'd come and help me."

A breeze shifted branches of a maple tree in the yard. Shadows lunged across the front door, with thin wraith-like fingers, seeking, grasping.

"Don't go in." She wasn't sure the voice she heard in her brain was God's voice or her own.

Did her ears catch the sound of something, some tiny movement inside the house? Like scraping against the door? Haven gasped. "You're not alone. Who is that?"

Fiona jerked, blinking rapidly. "It's ... it's just ... Jake. He's back. But I still need you, Haven."

"You-you lied."

The man next door had finished mowing. At the sound of Haven's raised voice, he stopped to gape at them.

"Jake wants to meet you."

"I have to leave. Now." Nausea spread through her gut. Her lips went numb. Saliva filled her mouth and throat. If she didn't get away now she'd heave right in front of Fiona and the man next door.

The looming house seemed to tilt. Her vision funneled to a narrow 'o.' Her body leaned forward and crumpled. Just before the cement came up to meet her, she threw her arms out to shield her face. The rough cement bludgeoned her knees and hands.

Jesus, help me!

Immediately, sunlight blasted back into her eyes. "Get up. Get away," the warning voice called. She broke Fiona's grasp. "Leave me alone. I don't trust you."

Breath jerked her ribs in and out. The fast steps to her car jarred her throbbing head. *Lord, help me to get out of here.*

Fiona followed her all the way to her car door.

"Haven, Haven? Please come back. I'm sorry about not telling you Jake was here. I promise I won't do that again. He just got back."

Haven slammed the door shut and locked it.

Fiona pounded on her window. "Please, Haven, I'm sorry."

Haven pressed the ignition button, slammed the gear-shift into drive, punched the accelerator. Could she still drive? Didn't matter. Get away! Her heart pounded against her chest like a sledgehammer.

In the rearview window, Fiona stood, staring, arms held out as if imploring.

She had to clear her head. "Lord, help me drive. Help me get home."

As soon as she started the car, Goliath released his grip on her. Now, if she could only keep conscious long enough to get home.

♩ ♪♪♫♪

Dade stormed out of the house, truck keys in his hand, and rushed toward his truck. When Fiona tried to say something, he cut her off with a slice of his hand.

"I'm sorry. She—"

"Get on back to the house. I'll take care of this."

He jumped into his truck and roared off in pursuit of Ruth. That stupid Fiona. She couldn't do anything right. How hard was it to welcome someone into your house? Even Mama could do that.

Ruth turned right. She was probably heading home. Good. There was that stretch of country road where he could head her off.

Up ahead, he could just make out a silver vehicle. It had to be hers. He followed her all the way through town and then onto Oak. Ignoring the stop sign, he gunned the engine.

A van turned onto the road, going slow. He cursed. The road curved. He had to chance it. He jerked his truck over into the oncoming lane and sped alongside the van. The van's driver increased his speed, making an obscene gesture.

"You moron!" Dade bellowed out the window.

A blue car zipped toward them, coming from the other direction. Dade laid on the horn and waved his arm out the window. "Get outta my way!" If he slowed down, he'd lose Ruth, for sure.

The blue car wavered at the last minute, horn blaring its outrage. When it pulled to the shoulder, Dade punched the accelerator again. The white van gave up and yielded. Dade yanked his truck back into the eastbound lane.

There she was.

He glanced in the rearview window. Perfect. The white van turned off another street, leaving them alone on the road. Just Ruth and him.

She was driving slow. The back of the Sebring got closer. Closer. He could read the license plate. He moved into the opposite lane, increased his speed. She slowed down. Must've noticed him. She was letting him pass.

He laughed. So polite.

She signaled to pull over. This was so easy.

A sound invaded his head. High pitched. Whiny. He checked the side-view mirror. Flashing lights. A roar burst out of his throat. The Taser and his gun were loose on the floor of the passenger seat. He couldn't stop. Not with this junk. His stomach pitched, and his breath came fast.

He passed the Sebring, raising his arm to shield his face so Ruth wouldn't recognize him.

There was a bridge up ahead. If he got to it quick he could pitch the evidence in the Issaquah Creek. He took a curve and didn't slow. Would that buy him precious seconds?

Two police cars behind him now. The officer must have called for back-up.

His hands shook, his jaw clamped. A dirt road emptied onto Oak. It led to the creek. His tires screamed when he took the turn. The truck could go faster on a dirt road. He'd lose them. For a while. Just enough time to throw away the evidence.

He pressed the accelerator and didn't slow down even at the pothole. The speeding truck almost flipped when he tried to avoid it. He had to slow when the rear of the truck shimmied. His tires spun when he resumed his crazy speed. The flashing lights were gaining. Sirens knifed his ears. A log lay across the road. No way the truck could go over it.

He braked at the end of the road. Grabbed his stuff. Jumped out, took off running. The river was maybe two hundred yards away. He could outrun the police if he kept running and didn't look back.

He could run and run. Those fat guys with their bullet-proof vests could never catch him.

He got off the road, crashed through bushes, vines, ferns. Jumped over logs. He slipped on a moss-covered patch. Almost fell.

Tramping sounds told him they were after him on foot. They wouldn't catch him.

The river was close, now.

Men breathing. Getting closer.

Hands seized his shoulders. He spun before they could take him down. His fist flew outward, finding its mark. That man fell. Another one dove for his legs. He was too quick. He jumped and the man missed his tackle.

He pulled his gun out of his waistband. A black uniform jumped on top of him. Dade pivoted and hunched, got the safety off, aimed. The gun fired. Missed.

He launched another fist, smashing into the officer's eye socket.

Someone pinned his arm. He snarled. Thrashed. Two men threw him onto his face, yanking his arms behind his back. Cuffs snapped into place. Hands frisked, fingers felt along his belt.

"Bruzzoni, you okay?" Moaning sounds coming from the ground nearby from one of the police officers told Dade he'd done some damage to the guy's skull.

Bruzzoni didn't answer.

"Drury, get the EMTs over here."

He couldn't see the other officers, but he heard their steps and their heavy breathing.

The cop he'd socked in the jaw said, "Look at this, Olson. A taser."

"Anything else on his belt?" asked Olson who still had Dade pinned with knees grinding into his backbone. The cop who found his Taser put a knee on the back of his neck, forcing his face into the dirt. Dade cursed under the weight of the man's body. If he could have turned his head, he would've spit at the cops.

Olson snapped on gloves. "Got anything sharp in your pockets? Knife, syringes, needles, anything like that?"

"No, you jerk. Get out of my pockets!" No one ever manhandled Dade Colton and got away with it. "You're killing me. Get off my neck. I'm gonna die."

"We'll ease up when you stop trying to resist," Olson said with infuriating calm. "He only has a wallet in his pocket. Nothing else."

"I demand to know why I'm ..." Dade choked on the dirt in his mouth. "Why I'm being ..."

"Detained?" Another voice said. "How about reckless driving, and doing 84 in a 45 zone? Fleeing the police. Resisting arrest. Shooting at a police officer. Assaulting and injuring a police officer. Pretty serious offenses."

"Lemme see the wallet," Olson again. A few seconds of maddening silence followed while the man must've been inspecting his ID.

"Wait till my lawyer hears about this," Dade growled. "You creeps are gonna pay for this."

Olson ignored his threat. "Mr. Dade Colton," he read the information on the license. "Hair: brown. Height: six foot six. Weight: 240 pounds." He flashed the license in front of Dade's face. "Address, vicinity of Lily. I see you have a PO Box. You live off-grid?"

"Yeah," Dade grunted, barely able to breathe. Once they got him upright, he was going to give Olson a headbutt right in his nose.

"Well, Mr. Dade Colton," Olson continued, "I see that the Glock is registered under your name. Wonder why you have a Taser, too. You must have a lot of enemies."

♩ ♪♪♫♪

October 12th, Journal Entry #81.

I haven't seen or heard from Fiona since that awful day at her place. After a few days, I calmed down. Fiona seemed different at her house, not in a good way, and seeing that shadow at her door brought back so many awful memories. I couldn't get it out of my mind. I'll never forget Mama standing at her screen door with that angry look on her face. Fiona had the same look. After I went home, I hid in my room. I don't know if I'll ever think of Fiona in the same affectionate way. Is that unforgiving? Probably. But the way she talked to me, coupled with my panic attack makes me hope I never see her again.

And to top it off, on my way home after I left her, this crazy driver got behind me. Practically ran me off the road. Classic case of road rage, I guess. The police must have been following the guy because they went zooming by, lights flashing, sirens screaming.

He must have been some sort of criminal. I hope the police got him. He shouldn't be on the road, endangering other drivers.

I called Fiona yesterday to make sure she was okay but she didn't answer. I'm still wondering if I over-reacted at her house.

She shouldn't have told me she was alone when Jake was actually in the house. Why would she plead for me to come over so she wouldn't be alone when her boyfriend was there? It doesn't make sense. She seemed so angry. The way she gripped my arm; totally not the girl I thought I knew.

At work, I was nervously expecting Fiona to walk in and ask to do coffee with me after my shift ended. I'm glad she didn't show up. I don't know how I would have reacted.

This morning I drove over to Fiona's house. The place looks deserted. No car. I peeked through the window. No furniture, either. The flowers on the porch are dying. Maybe she and her boyfriend moved. I'm still praying for her. Maybe I'll call her again—

♩ ♪♪♫♪

Haven's cell phone startled her. She set her journal down and hurried over to her desk to answer it

"Hi, sweetheart."

"Oh, hi, Dad." Her father didn't usually call on Monday. Something was definitely up.

"Are you sitting down?"

His upbeat tone reassured her, and she laughed. "Yes, I'm sitting." She sat on her bed quickly to make her statement the truth.

"Sheila and I are getting married."

Haven's heart almost skipped a beat. *Finally.* Both she and Joy, and Joy's new husband, Jeff, had encouraged Dad to ask Sheila to marry him. "Well, it's about time."

"I wasn't sure Sheila would want to be saddled with an old guy like me."

"Dad, you're both forty-six. Hardly old. When's the big day?"

"Right after the holidays."

"So fast?"

"Why not?" Her father liked to answer a question with a question. "Hawaii is great in December. And we wanted to make sure Sheila had plenty of time after the wedding to fit in catering your recital in April."

"That is so nice of Sheila. Tell her I'm thrilled about you guys getting married, and thank her for offering to cater."

Her father sighed loudly. "Well, now that's off my chest I can breathe normally. How are classes? Do you need anything?"

"Everything's fine." She wasn't going to tell him about Fiona.

"No problems?" Dad had that tone in his voice that always meant he was worried about her.

"If you mean problems with that crazy guy I told you about, then no. He hasn't shown up. I don't know why I even mentioned him." Why had she?

"Good to know. I'm still not telling people where you're studying."

"I think that's a good idea, Dad." Dade might be long gone, but she wasn't going to let down her guard … yet. Just speaking his name made crazy tingles shoot through her arms and legs. Yet, she hadn't seen the man since last April. More than six months. He had forgotten her. Moved on. Her memory was coming back. He had to know she would recover eventually. Dade wouldn't dare come near her if he thought she could recall all that had happened at his cabin. He'd have to wonder if she would continue to take his threats seriously.

She'd read that stalkers sometimes go underground for months at a time, showing up unexpectedly, just when victims thought they were finally safe. One stalker sat in prison for years, and when he got out, went right back to following and harassing the same lady.

But that wasn't like Dade. He has Mama and the kids to look after. He couldn't risk showing up in a town where there were tons of potential witnesses. Besides—

"So, make sure you contact Joy and Sheila right away so you can plan all the plans."

Plans? She had totally spaced Dad's last sentence. "Sorry, Dad, I didn't catch that."

"No worries." He sounded breathless like he was in a hurry. "I'm going to send you an email with Sheila's contact info. Joy's going to call you later this week."

"Dad, I'm really happy for you. Sheila is wonderful. I know you guys are going to be really happy."

Dad didn't say anything for a few seconds. When he did, he sounded all choked up, which made her choke up, too. Sheila was God's blessing for her dad.

"I love you, girl."

"Love you, too."

♩ ♪♪♫♪

December winds and rain blew outside West Hills Church, and Haven shivered in her satin bridesmaid gown even though the sanctuary was plenty warm enough. It wasn't the weather, though, that made her shiver. It was the realization that, with her dad's marriage to Sheila, Haven's life had turned a corner. From now on, the memory of her mother would be relegated to photo albums or fond but seldom-shared anecdotes about Helen at family gatherings. It was another mental adjustment, among the twenty, or forty, or hundred adjustments that came with successfully grieving her mother's death, and moving on with her educational goals, and living in another state.

Sheila had honored Haven by asking her to be her maid of honor and she didn't want to visibly tremble with all the emotions that accompanied her life changes.

Haven pinched herself under her bouquet so no one would see the action. She needed to stay in the moment, to concentrate on how beautiful Sheila looked in her winter-white satin gown, walking like a queen down the aisle on her own father's arm

As Dad and Sheila met, and ascended the stairs leading up to the altar, Haven turned to face them, smoothing the burgundy-colored fabric on her sleeve. The color matched the flowers on the altar and down the aisle.

Her dad looked incredibly handsome. His platinum hair, just beginning to go white a bit at the temples sparkled in the late afternoon sunlight that poured intermittently through the church windows.

"… to have and to hold, from this day forward …" Dad had to stop to steady his voice.

Pastor Jensen smiled at the couple in front of him.

Haven swallowed the lump that rose in her throat, seeing her dad holding another woman's hand, speaking words that had once been spoken to her mom. Mom had been gone for over two years. It was time for Dad to move on, to find love and companionship again. And Sheila was a kind, unselfish, caring woman. Dad couldn't have found a better mate.

Sheila's sweet voice chimed in with her own vows. "For richer, for poorer, in sickness, and in health …"

Haven repositioned her clammy hands on her bouquet of white roses. She was glad Dad had bought a new diamond ring for Sheila. It wouldn't have seemed right to look at Sheila's hand and see the ring that had once adorned Mom's hand.

And with Dad and Sheila married, he would have more to think about than just Haven and her studies and future career in music. Or about the crazy guy who might still be obsessing about her. That was a good thing.

"I now pronounce you husband and wife," Pastor Jensen said. Dad kissed Sheila, the audience applauded, and the recessional music began. And Haven wouldn't have to worry about Dad anymore, either.

At the conclusion of the ceremony, she followed her father and his new wife down the aisle, Mendelssohn's music making tears well in her eyes. Once they reached the lobby, Aunt Joy, wearing a different style of gown but in the same color, whispered, "After we do the photographs, meet me in the south parking lot. We'll drive to the reception together."

An hour and a half later, Haven settled into the back seat of Jeff and Joy's new Toyota and kicked off her high heels.

Jeff started the engine and reversed out of his parking spot.

Joy buckled her seatbelt. "I'm glad we've got a few minutes to visit. We won't have a chance once we get to the reception. Are you going to spend the summer at home?"

"No. I'll probably keep working at my new job at the florist. Unless I decide to go to grad school in the fall. Besides, Dad and Sheila will still be newlyweds in April when I graduate. I think they should have some time alone. Don't you think?"

Joy frowned. "I keep forgetting you're all grown up now. It makes me kind of sad sometimes that you're not still a kid."

"Oh, Joy." Haven leaned forward and squeezed Joy's shoulder. Her eyes moistened and a heaviness dragged at her heart. Once she graduated, would she move back to Oregon? Only if she could be sure Dade had really forgotten her. But how would she figure that out? "I'll be down here a couple of times this summer." She held up her fingers to count, "Let's see, Dad's birthday, Fourth of July, and then I'm playing for—"

"Oh, I know you're coming down for visits," Joy said. "It's just that this is the beginning of the end. Now that you're graduating, you'll probably start playing music gigs all over the country and I'll never see you."

"Hey," Jeff said, glancing in the rear-view mirror with a tone of surprise in his voice. "I've never seen the two of you like this. You're usually so upbeat when you're together."

"I know." Joy sniffed. "It's just that there's a lot of change happening in this family. My baby's not living near me anymore and I haven't quite gotten used to it, yet."

Haven pulled a tissue out of her purse and handed it to Joy. "Now s-stop that. You're going to get me all emotional again. This is not the time or place f-for tears. I'll be back for Spring Break.

And then you're c-coming up for my senior recital."

They pulled into the Hotel parking lot, Joy dabbing at her eyes. "Why not move back to Portland after graduation? Think of all the fun things we could do if you lived close."

"I know, I've thought about it a lot." More than her aunt could imagine.

"And?"

"And it depends on things I won't know, at least for a few months."

"Well, let me know as soon as you decide, Haven."

Would she have a better idea of her future by the end of April when she graduated? Dade had said, "There isn't a town, or relative or lawman or anyone else who could hide you from me because I'd find you." He had said it as he had nearly snuffed the life out of her. He meant every word of his threat. So, where she moved after graduation depended on Dade. Her family's safety depended on Dade.

Dade! Her hand balled into a fist. Oh, how she wanted to slam her fist through the window.

Chapter Six

Our God is a God who saves;
from the Sovereign Lord come escape from death
Psalm 68:20

"I can't wait to see what music Haven's been working on this year," Guy said from the back seat of Jeff's Subaru. The whole way from the Bellevue Inn to the Northmont School of Music, he'd been fighting butterflies in his stomach. If he felt this nervous, what must Haven be feeling like as she waited backstage for her audience to arrive?

His brother-in-law pulled into the parking lot and shut the motor.

"She didn't tell you, either?" Joy asked as she stepped out of the car.

"Not a thing. All she said was that she'd be playing the Mozart sonata I like so much."

"When did Sheila get here?" Jeff asked.

Guy glanced at his watch. "She left the hotel about three hours ago. She's keeping the food and the cake and the decorations a secret, too."

They walked up the steps, past beautifully tended rhododendrons, in full April bloom. Guy held the door open to the lobby, allowing Joy and Jeff to pass inside.

Guy followed signs, which guided him to the left. "There it is," he said with a smile. At home, Haven had always decorated her bedroom door with her artwork. Sure enough, the walls surrounding the auditorium entrance had been decorated with Haven's signature creative ideas: paintings, watercolors, mixed media with blotches of paint, and strips of fabric interwoven under a collage of music scores. Her recital program sat in a neat stack on a music stand by the door.

Joy chuckled. "No one could miss that Haven's been here."

No doubt about it, his little girl—and her sparkling personality and never-ending creativity—had come back after having been buried for a year under a mountain of PTSD. Guy fought to push down the lump that had risen in his throat. Turning his back on Joy and Jeff, he grabbed a handful of programs from the stand. "Let's find our seats."

♩ ♪♪♫♪

Haven stood at the door to the reception hall, her face flushed with the joy that comes from relief that all had gone well.

Sheila had decorated the reception hall with yards of royal blue fabric and sparkling silver ribbon tacked to moveable room dividers, strategically placed to focus attention on the table and the sheet cake. Sheila had even frosted the sheet cake with white and embellished it with blue icing and touches of silver.

The guests mingled, enjoying the hors d'oeuvres and iced tea. A reporter and photographer snapped pictures of Haven with her family and professors. The reporter tried to get her to tell them what she planned on doing now that she was graduating. "Sorry," she said. "I'm still figuring that out, myself."

When the rain began lashing at the building, Haven moved further into the reception hall. Occasional booming of thunder couldn't shake the festive atmosphere inside, though the blasts did send Sheila's hands to shaking as she served cake. One particularly loud rumble also startled her dad. The piece he'd been bringing to Anna almost landed in her lap. Haven had followed a couple of college girlfriends to the door to say goodbye when the lights went out. Startled gasps from the remaining guests rippled across the dark hall, followed by Dad's voice saying, "Sorry folks, just sit tight. I'm sure the lights will be on in a minute."

Haven remained where she was. The last thing she needed right now was to trip over someone or something. In the darkness outside, lights illuminated the walkways crisscrossing the areas surrounding the music building. A tall, narrow shape stood at the foot of the concrete steps to the lobby doors. For a second Haven thought it was a potted tree. But then it moved, took steps toward the window where she stood, through a hedge of low-growing bushes, onto the lawn, onto the flower garden just outside the window where she watched. Closer.

The man—for it was definitely a man—approached the window. Raised his arm. Pressed his hand against the glass, leaned forward. The darkness hid his face.

Was he trying to communicate a need?

Darts of electricity zipped down her legs.

She didn't dare go closer to the window "Hello?" She gestured. "Do you need help?"

The arm shifted. She couldn't tell if the man spoke?

She cupped her hand to her ear. "I can't hear you." No way was she going to open the locked door down the hall and invite him inside.

The figure didn't budge, except for his raised right hand. It closed into a fist except for the index finger. He pointed it right at her.

Haven's throat went dry. Sometimes strange people hung out around the campus. Maybe this was one of those types. Most of the time they asked for money. She usually had a couple of dollars or some change to hand out. But sometimes one of them crowded her, muttered scary, unintelligible words. How does a small woman deal with that?

Lightning flashed. For a split second the man's staring eyes became visible. But only the eyes. They weren't pleading. They weren't angry. And they … just … stared.

Her body went taut. Tingles spread to her hands and feet. Was the man's face menacing, twisted, monstrous? She didn't want to know. It would only give her nightmares.

The man was not normal.

"Move away, girl." Haven took a step backward, then another, never taking her eyes off the man in the window. "Get back to the reception hall."

The cake and punch she'd just consumed turned sour in her stomach.

Inside the reception hall, hushed but excited voices laughed and murmured. Nobody was scared by the blackout.

The lights needed to come on. And soon.

The dryness in her throat wouldn't let her speak. She swallowed. "Dad?"

He didn't answer. "Dad?" she called again, her voice quivering.

"I'm here, Baby."

Haven turned to search out her dad's emerging form in the darkness.

Footsteps drew near, followed by a crash. "Oof! Who put this table here?" In another second Dad was beside her. He touched her, and she grabbed his arm and held on.

The lights flickered, went out again, came back on.

When the lights came on the second time, Haven whirled around to get one last look at the strange man.

Nothing. Whether he was gone or simply obscured by the brightness of the indoor light, was impossible to tell.

"Wow, you're a sight for sore eyes." Dad was grinning at her, squinting in the bright light. "All dolled up and wearing your mother's diamonds. I didn't get a chance to really look at you close up until now. What a beauty."

She smiled up into her father's gentle face, and her heart stopped its war drumming. He spun her around and, taking her into his arms, danced her back into the hall, moving her in the direction of the refreshment table.

"Let's have some cake."

♩ ♪♪♫♪

Haven turned over in bed and glanced at the clock. Even though it was only seven in the morning, the sun was already blazing through her window. It would be the perfect type of day to introduce her parents to Issaquah Valley Church, where she'd been serving for the past two semesters, and to Pastor Miller.

The flush of victory she'd felt last night hadn't left her yet. All was right with the world. The Senior Recital had gone very well. The graduation ceremony next Saturday was the only thing on her calendar. She'd already completed all of her requirements for her degree.

Her only concern now was whether to seriously consider the recruitment invitations she had received from some of the larger state-supported colleges interested in having her join their graduate degree programs. She'd already applied to and been accepted by the big university in Seattle.

She dressed and strolled downstairs for breakfast. Her eyes fell on the mail slots on the wall next to the stairwell. She hadn't bothered to check her mail last night. A number of letters sat in her slot. She sorted through them. First in the pile was another recruitment letter from a college in Seattle. A master's degree was a good step toward getting a doctorate if she ever decided to teach at a four-year college. But did she really want to spend another couple of years stuck in a musty old practice room? She thumbed through the rest of her mail. All advertisements. As she picked up her things and turned to go upstairs. Mrs. Peterson came out of her room.

"Did you get my note, Haven?"

"Note?"

"I put it in your mailbox last night"

Haven thumbed through her mail again. "Oh, here it is. It must have stuck to one of the letters. Thanks, Mrs. Peterson." She read the note quickly, and again more slowly, pondering the message. When she looked up the old woman was still standing there.

"Is my note clear, honey? You look kind of confused."

Haven pursed her lips. "It's just that … well, your note s-says that an old friend came by and he'll come back this morning at eight. But I can't for the life of me figure out who it might be. Did you see him?"

Mrs. Peterson took the note from Haven's hands and looked at it as if she'd never seen it. "Well, Emily spoke with the fellow, but I never saw him. I just wrote what she told me."

"Is Emily h-here now?"

"I'm not sure. You can go and knock on her door."

Haven walked down the hall to Emily's room and knocked. There was no answer and she returned, picturing several possible male students.

The old woman looked apologetic. "I'm sorry I couldn't be more help. Emily just said it was a guy looking for you and that he seemed really anxious to see you."

She glanced at the piece of paper again. "It's all right, Mrs. Peterson. I guess I'll find out who he is pretty soon." She folded the note and slipped it back into her stack of mail. When she got up to her room she locked her door and went and stood at her window, trying to quell a growing uneasiness that gnawed at her chest. Why hadn't the guy, whoever he was, just given his name? She mentally ticked off a list of young men she'd known during her year at Northmont. It could be any one of them. If only Mrs. Peterson had seen him. A description would go a long way in making her feel more secure.

She sat at her desk and tried to distract herself by reading. Time slowed down. She peered out the window several times, checking the driveway for any unfamiliar cars.

At eight, her heart in her throat, she left her room and tiptoed down the carpeted stairs, the rock with a red target on it in her hand. Halfway down, the doorbell chimed, making her jump. She stretched to peer out the peephole, but the only thing she saw was a man's back. Above average height, black hair. Then he turned to face the door and she recognized the prominent cheekbones, straight nose, dark eyes. She put the rock down and threw the door open.

"Jesse!"

Jesse looked down at Haven with a shy smile. She threw her arms around his neck and hugged him hard. Pulling back, she studied him with a combination of wonder and disbelief.

"Come in, come in." She took his arm and pulled him inside. Mrs. Peterson opened her apartment door and glared at Jesse with distrust.

"It's okay, Ma'am. He really is an old friend." Haven beamed. "Do you m-mind if we just sit in the dining room and visit for a while?"

Mrs. Peterson's expression softened. She nodded, stepped back inside her apartment and shut her door quietly.

They went into the dining room and took chairs facing each other. "Wow, you've grown up, Jesse. I almost didn't recognize you at first." Just as she had once guessed he would, he had grown big and broad-shouldered. His close-shaven face could not hide the darkness of his beard, and his dark gypsy eyes, thickly fringed with black lashes, would turn female heads.

Jesse sat quietly for a moment as he studied her. "I'd forgotten about your hair."

"My hair?"

"I always remembered you with a big brown braid and long, baggy dresses." His eyes met hers. "You look … yer … beautiful."

He dropped his gaze and scrubbed his hands over his knees. When he looked up again he wasn't smiling. "Look, it's great to see you. I've been wondering all this time what happened to you and where you went. But that's not why I'm here."

Haven's stomach lurched. Suddenly, she wasn't so happy to see him.

"Fer months I wanted to ask Dade if he'd heard anything about you, but I knew he'd beat me if I so much as brought up yer name."

At the mention of Dade, blood drained from her face. She gripped the sides of the table to steady herself.

"He was different after you left. I mean, he was always … well, you remember how he was. After you got away, Sarah and me and Mama … we all kept away from him. It was like he was boiling under the surface, all the time. He kept reading from the Bible and preaching about 'bringing back his faithless wife.'"

She felt herself transported back to Dade's cabin, fearing the big man's looming presence and his dangerous religious beliefs. She shuddered when the dark memories she'd worked so hard to repress, burst into her mind.

Jesse rubbed his cheek as if to soothe an old wound. "One day he started in on me and how I was the reason you ran away."

She leaned forward. "What did you s-say?"

"I said it wasn't true, but what was true was that you didn't want to stay with him. Then he said it was your choice to come to his cabin. He said you were all mixed up and confused about your old life and wanted him to help straighten you out."

"What? Do you believe that?"

Jesse shook his head and frowned. "I didn't know what to think 'cause I don't know what happened between you two before you came to Dade's place. Why *did* you come?"

The tightness in her neck spread down her chest. It had never occurred to her that Jesse might doubt her. "I don't know, Jesse. My memory is still spotty. I only remember bits and pieces of the last week of Life Ventures and hearing about my dad's accident. I remember wandering in the woods, and Dade finding me. He said, 'You're safe now.' And I believed him. The next thing I remember is being in the cabin with Dade and Mama and you and Sarah, and I couldn't talk well."

"Well, I remember Mama hittin' you and you falling down like you were dead." He shuddered. "It was awful." His eyebrows pinched and he rubbed his hand over his face as if to put it back in order. Then he thrust his head forward. "How come you never went to the police after you got back with your family? Why didn't you tell them about Dade?" A hint of suspicion colored his voice.

"You think they'd believe me?" Haven's voice rose in intensity to match Jesse's. "I'd go to them with this weird story about crazy Dade and how he held me prisoner and they'd just take my word for it? Good grief, Jesse, with my faulty memory, do you think anything I said would stand up in court? They'd say *I* was the unbalanced one. After all, I'd been seeing a psychologist. And I'm the one who was a patient in Life Ventures. Do you think I'd be a trustworthy witness?"

"I could tell them what happened."

"Oh?" Haven's eyes narrowed. "Can you just picture how a defense lawyer would pick apart anything you said? They'd suggest you were jealous of Dade. Believe me, Jesse, I've gone over and over this. We couldn't get him convicted on our testimony. You didn't see him bring me forcibly into his cabin. I came willingly. And as you said, it was Mama who hit me, not Dade."

Jesse jumped up and raked his hands through his hair. "But Dade tried to marry you."

"What does that have to do with kidnapping? I stood there, too afraid to object, and let him slip his ring on my finger. Remember? I let him kiss me. That's what you witnessed. Any jury would wonder why I didn't try to run away earlier. I wasn't locked in a room or tied up.

"And now time has passed. Why didn't I go to the police right away? Why did I hide out in Gregory's cabin for months? Why didn't I immediately head for a town so I could tell them about Dade and Mama? Do you see all the questions they'd ask? Every one of them makes me look crazy and unreliable.

"No, it's better to keep all this quiet. Without absolute certainty that our testimony would put him in prison for a long time, I just can't risk going after him. If only you could have heard him threaten to hurt my family …" She patted his chair. "Please sit down and finish telling me about you and Dade. What did you say when he accused you of helping me?"

Jesse let a big sigh slide from his lips. He slumped onto his chair again. "What could I say? If I told the truth, he'd a probably killed me, and if I made something up he wouldn't a believed me.

So, I didn't say nothing."

He hesitated and stared straight ahead, mouth grimacing as if viewing a horror movie. "Then he started beatin' on me so hard that I ran for it. And I kept running. I wanted to keep going but I kept thinking about Sarah and Rebecca and worrying about them. I wanted to be near in case they needed me."

Jesse's hands closed into fists. "That's when I decided that I'd never call that man my Pa anymore. Now he's just Dade, Dade Colton, the carpenter, Dade Colton, the wife and kid beater," he said bitterly. "So, I got hired on at the grocery store in Hayfork and found a room at the motel."

The beginning of tears stung Haven's eyes. Jesse's suffering under Dade's abuse was just as damaging as hers and had lasted way longer. "Why didn't *you* go to the police, Jesse?"

He shrugged and looked down. "Maybe the same reason you didn't. You live all your life under his thumb and you feel like you can't do nothin' without his say-so. You wonder if maybe yer the one who's wrong."

She nodded. "I was only under his roof f-for three months but I know exactly what you're talking about. I kept quiet because I thought he'd come after me. I guess that was silly."

Jesse stiffened. "Well, uh, well …" He turned and stared out the window at the dense forest behind the Mansion. "After I'd been away for a few months I finally got up the courage to think about going back and getting my sister out of there. But then I saw in the paper that Pa … I mean, Dade'd been arrested for beatin' up a policeman."

"What? When was that? What happened?"

"It was about October, last year. About the time I heard that you got back with your family. The paper said that he'd been pulled over on a stretch of country road for speeding, and when they went to search the truck he went crazy and started slugging. They called for backup and it took six policemen to get him down. And, besides resisting arrest, shooting at and beating up a policeman, they also found all sorts a suspicious things in his truck." Jesse turned to face her. He looked at her with meaning.

"What things?" she asked with a kind of deadness in her voice.

"Things like he was planning on doing something bad, Haven. I mean, there were syringes and knockout drugs, duct tape, a taser, a gun. Like he planned on kidnapping someone and then holing up for a while." His voice turned to a whisper. "Wanna know where he was when they pulled him over?"

She dropped her head, feeling sick. She already knew the answer.

"Issaquah."

"I'm hating having to tell you all this," Jesse said. "You probably thought you'd never hear Dade's name again."

Haven didn't even look up. "So, where's he been all this time?"

"In jail. I guess it's pretty serious when you put a policeman in the hospital."

He'd been in jail all this time. Inexplicably, she wanted to laugh. If she'd only known. That awful man was locked up, and she could have gone about her business at school and work for the past two semesters with a complete feeling of security.

"But that's why I'm here." Jesse reached over and placed his hands on her shoulders. "Haven, he's out. He got released about a week ago."

She caught her breath and jerked her head up, fighting an impulse to run upstairs and pack her bags. "Does he know ... I mean ... is he still looking?" She couldn't finish.

"When I visited him in jail—" He stopped when her mouth gaped. He did a giant shrug. "I guess I was hoping to kinda get an explanation or reason for what he did to us and you." He stopped and looked at her as if expecting her to provide the answer. When she didn't speak, he said, "That was a couple a months ago."

She turned away. Looking at Jesse reminded her of the cabin. And thinking about the cabin made the blood drain from her head. "How did he know where I was? I didn't tell anybody where I was studying. My dad and Aunt Joy and Anna? None of them would have spilled where I was."

Jesse shook his head. "I don't know, Haven. Dade's smart in a real awful way. He lies and he uses people. For all I know he hired a private detective, or got in good with a police officer so he could get information."

"The police?" She returned and sank back into her chair. "If he could con a police officer, then why would I even consider telling them about what he did to me?"

"I'm just guessin'." He shrugged. "Maybe he followed you. Maybe he watched your house."

Jesse rubbed his cheek, his eyes unfocused. "After Dade was arrested the cops must've done some investigating and found out where he lived, 'cause then they found Mama and the girls. They figured out pretty fast that Sarah and Rebecca weren't hers or Dade's. They took the girls and put 'em in foster homes and I don't know what they did to Mama. I never tried to find out.

"Dade and Mama aren't your real parents?" Why had Jesse

never told her that?

He shook his head. "No, my mother's name was Linda Garson. My father was foreign—Hungarian. I don't think they were married. It was a long time ago—about nine years. I was about twelve, but Sarah was so little she probably doesn't even remember. Mama worked as a midwife and she lived in the same trailer park. She used to babysit us. My father wasn't around too much, but when he showed up, he'd give my mother these shots that'd make her feel better for a while. Then she'd get all dressed up and they'd go out for a while. Sometimes they'd be gone for a couple-a days, so Mama would watch us. But I can remember like it was yesterday how Mama used to shake her head and say, 'She's gonna wind up dead one of these days. Then who's gonna take care of 'em?'"

Haven listened to Jesse's story, his words dragging her heart down into a dark pit. "So, how did you end up with Dade?"

"We were living in a small town in Kentucky. My mother got real sick, so the ambulance came and took her away to a hospital in some bigger town. We didn't get to see her in the hospital. Mama went and saw her, and when she came back she said that our mother was dead and that she was gonna be our new mother. She packed us up that same day and we got into her old van and drove a long way. It seemed like we drove for months but it was probably just a few days. Anyway, we ended up in Washington, but we didn't have any money to stay anywhere, so we lived in the van for a while. I guess Mama was afraid the police would come after her for taking us without any paperwork. But that's when Mama met Dade. He told her that he had a nice house where we all could stay and he'd take good care of us.

"Looking back, when we first started living in the cabin, Dade must have told Mama about how he wanted to have a real big family 'cause I remember Mama saying something like, 'I've already had two and I'll bet I can have lots more.' I don't think it was long before they started living together as man and wife. Then, when Mama didn't get pregnant, he must a started to get suspicious about Sarah and me. I remember that they had a big fight, and it finally came out that she'd taken us and that's why we were hiding. Dade was real mad for a long time, and he kinda ignored her for a while. But he musta come to some decision about Mama and us 'cause eventually, he came to treatin' us like we were all family. That's when he started to teach us the Bible and about how God had chosen him to be the father of a new holy kingdom. And we were all gonna be a part of it."

Jesse stopped and eyed her with a nervous look. "So, when Dade figured out that he wasn't gonna git any children from Mama, he tried buying a baby. They brought Rebecca to the cabin one night, and I don't know where they got her from. But that musta not satisfied Dade. I guess that's where you come in. He sees you at that Life Ventures Camp, and you look just like that other Ruth he killed. So, I guess, in his mind, he's gonna start all over with a new Ruth. He's gonna keep you safe from your father, just like he wanted to keep the first Ruth safe from his father. You two are finally gonna be happy and free and you'll have lots of babies, just like the first Ruth wanted. He probably figured that Mama, being a midwife, could deliver all the babies. He spends so much time reading the Bible and inventing new ways of understanding it. He starts thinking he's the new Abraham, from the Bible, and that must make you his Sarah."

"But, why me?" Her brows knit so hard it hurt. *Lord, why did you let this all happen?* "Why doesn't he just find some woman who'd like to be with him?

"I don't know, Haven. He's … what's that word they use?"

Jesse's hands made little arcs above his head as if he were trying to feel for the correct term. He snapped his fingers. "I got it. Obsession. Dade's obsessed with you."

She thrust her hair away from her face. She could hardly take in all that Jesse's story implied. Dade had killed the first Ruth. He'd been sent to a mental hospital. Then he escaped. Even though she had long ago thrown out the letter Jesse had given to her while a prisoner of Dade, she hadn't forgotten the information it had supplied about Dade.

She launched her arms outward in a giant gesture of exasperation. "How in the world did Dade get to be that way? Where'd he come up with his weird beliefs?"

"All I know is what I heard from some old man in Hayfork who used to work with Dade. That Dade's an educated guy. 'Course, that old guy didn't know about him escapin' from a mental institution. That must be why Dade changed his name. Anyway, he worked his way through college and then went to seminary somewhere back east. He wanted to be a pastor. Seems he tried to start up a church and was teaching them his own brand of religion. He got himself kicked out of the seminary 'cause he had some weird ideas about what the Bible says."

"I'll say." The man could justify all sorts of things, like kidnapping, a farce of a marriage with her. Rape. Her skin crawled at the thought of what would have happened if Jesse hadn't helped her get away. Disgusting and totally creepy. "So, after all this happened, what did you do? Did you stay in Hayfork?"

"I got a job working in Tacoma. Got a couple of gigs playing in some small clubs. I started making friends and got a rundown little place to live in with a couple other guys."

Jesse stopped. "You sure you want to hear all this?"

"Of course. There's not a day gone by that I haven't thought about you and wondered what happened to you. Please, go on."

"You know, it's funny. All those times that Dade and Mama were always telling us about how cities are so evil and all. Well, it's true, there was a lot of bad stuff that I saw. But I don't see how all those people in those cities were any worse than Dade. The way he used to knock me and Sarah around. Mama bashing you in the head, almost killing you, and them taking you away from your real family. They were always talking like they were so good and everyone else was so bad." He raised his eyes. There was a hardness in them she'd rarely seen.

"Anyway, Sarah called me and said she wanted me to live close, so we could visit sometimes. So, I moved north. I've been in Seattle for a few months now. I got a job at a restaurant during the day and I keep finding places where I can play my guitar and sing at night. So, I'm doing pretty good right now. I wasn't gonna look you up 'cause I reckoned you'd probably not want to see anyone who reminded you of Dade. But after I talked to Dade and saw how he was still thinkin' about you, I thought it'd be better to warn you." He expelled a big breath. "That's all the history I can give you. I hope it helps kinda sort through why Dade's still determined to keep you as his wife."

"I'm not his wife." A sham ceremony didn't make an unwilling woman a wife.

"Well," Jesse's dark eyes blazed, "he thinks you are. And that's what's driving him. That's the only thing driving him." His big hands were folded on top of the table as if he'd finished telling a long tall tale and there was no more to be said.

"So, what're you going to do?" He turned his cupped hands upward like man begging for alms.

"I don't know yet." She couldn't look at him. His voice sounded so grim.

"Is there anything I can do fer you? Do you need a place to stay?"

Her gaze darted up to his face. That was incredibly generous, but what would it look like, her staying at a man's place? "No … thanks. At least, not yet. I-I have some money I've been saving."

"You let me know, okay?"

"I will." Jesse could have stayed away, not bothered to find her and tell her about Dade. Her heart squeezed. The courageous boy had turned into a courageous man. She reached over and took his hand. "You know, I only got to s-say a quick thank you when you helped me get away. Thank you for risking your own skin for my sake. Thanks for my backpack and the extra supplies, for greasing the hinges, and for your m-magnificent acting when Dade came out of his room. I can't imagine what it would have been like to actually be married to Dade."

Jesse stared at their joined hands. His smile quivered, then steadied. It didn't end as a nice smile, though. It morphed into the kind of smile you'd see on a person's face who's enjoying an evil thought. He relaxed into the back of his seat and folded his arms across his chest. "Oh, he wouldn't a gotten that far. I'd a made sure of that."

He stood and headed toward the front door. Before he turned the doorknob, he said, "Promise me you'll call me and let me know how yer doin'."

Haven faced him squarely. "Years ago, I told you I'd never forget you, and I never will, Jesse." She reached up and kissed him on the cheek, as she had nearly two years ago.

After he left, the house seemed too quiet. Like the quiet that beckons a burglar to peer through the window with his crowbar and his evil intentions. She locked the door and tried the handle. Tried the handle again. And again.

A door was puny protection from a man like Dade. She released the doorknob and ran upstairs, adrenaline making her take two steps at a time. She slammed her door shut and turned that lock, too. Tiptoeing to the window, she drew a sliver of curtain aside. Jesse was gone. Was there anyone else out there? Maybe hiding in the bushes across the street?

Dade hadn't used the scope of his rifle when he'd hunted her last year. He'd used binoculars. Was he using them now? Had he been spying on her those weeks last fall before he had been arrested? He already knew where her father's home was. How in the world had he found out where she was studying?

At least she lived on the second story. She remembered the strange homeless man, standing outside the music building, his hand trying to reach through the window, his eyes staring.

That man. Why was he standing there, staring at her? Her eyes widened like a rabbit caught in a trap. That was him! She pressed her hands to her mouth to stifle the howl that wanted to rip from her throat.

She backed away from the window, arms out, fingers clawing

as if she could fight the demon warrior who always accompanied her terror. He was out. Dade knew where she was. *Help me. Lord.*

She should go to the police. No, the police couldn't do anything. And Dade would find out she squealed on him. He'd come after her, or her dad. It would be so easy. All he had to do was wait with his rifle for Dad to come outside his house. Maybe work on his lawn or something. Pop! Dade would make good on his threat.

Dad and Sheila were expecting her at church later this morning. She couldn't just not show up. By now, they were probably on their way from the hotel. She'd have to put on a good act so they didn't suspect anything.

"You can do this, Haven. Take a deep breath. Check the window." Light traffic passed the Mansion. The morning sun cleared away any shadows that might have held a stalker. Her car was parked a mere thirty or so feet from the front door. She could run to her car and hop in, drive to church, listen to Pastor Miller's sermon, sing praise songs. It would be her last Sunday at Issaquah Valley.

On her way to church, Haven checked her rearview window frequently. No one suspicious followed her. She drove the five minutes to the Issaquah Valley Church. Dad and Sheila were already waiting by the building's entrance. As she hugged Dad, she scanned the crowds of people walking inside.

♩ ♪♪♫♪

"We're really going to miss you, Haven," Pastor Miller said on the steps of the church after the service.

Too bad she couldn't have stayed. She would have loved to keep working with the first through third graders during the summer. Dade made that option impossible. Her lip quivered, forcing her hand to fly upward to hide it. She pictured herself throwing her last rock at Dade at Gregory's cabin a year ago. What if she'd aimed just a hair to the left? Crunched his skull and left him to die an awful, lingering death?

Dad must have caught her odd expression because he quirked one eyebrow at her.

Turning toward the pastor, he reached to shake his hand. "Haven tells me she's been helping lead the Kid's Praise Team."

"Yes," Pastor said. He put his other arm around Haven's shoulder and gave her a squeeze. "She's done some great work with our primary children."

Haven smiled sheepishly. "Sorry I haven't been around so much lately. Been kind of busy finishing school."

"You don't have to apologize. We know how hectic it can get when you're in college. We just appreciated whatever time you could volunteer with the kids."

He started to say something to Dad but interrupted himself. "Say, Haven, have you thought any more about that job I told you about at Fairhaven Community Church? I just talked to their music minister on the phone and they're still looking for a part-time children's music director."

"Well, I haven't quite decided where …"

"Give them a call. It just might be the perfect place for you to hole up while you're deciding what to do next."

What a strange choice of words. She studied the pastor's face. Could he read her mind? Good grief, it was almost as if he knew she was thinking about going into hiding.

Dad looked surprised. "I thought you were planning to go on with more school, Sweetheart."

She squirmed under her father's gaze. "I know I told you that, Dad, but I've been reconsidering if I want to spend another two years studying right now. I'm sort of looking forward to doing some actual work away from academics for a while."

The pastor reached into his pocket, drew out a slip of paper, and handed it to her. "Here's Fairhaven's phone number and address. Pastor Lauer is the man to ask for." He turned to go.

"Thanks, Pastor," she called after him. "I'll think about it." She slipped the paper into her purse.

Sheila took her arm and they started to walk out of the church.

Dad frowned. "Why this sudden drive to get out into the work world? I thought you were all excited to go to the university."

"I was, Dad … a few months ago. But then I had second thoughts. And remember, you said too much time locked away in the music room wasn't good."

"Yes, I remember," he said, "but that was when you were ill." He regarded her silently as if trying to read her true feelings. Then he shrugged. "Oh, it doesn't matter, Haven. Whatever you choose to do right now is okay with us. We're proud of you and all that you've accomplished and we know you'll always choose the right direction."

"And," added Sheila, "we'll support you in any decision you make." She took Haven's other hand and gave it an affectionate squeeze.

They reached the parking lot and Dad helped Sheila into the car.

Haven kept quiet during lunch, hardly hearing her father and Sheila's playful banter. Her churning stomach warned her not to try to eat anything. Now, if only they'd hurry up and finish their dessert so the meal would end and she could return to her room. They drove her back to the church so she could collect her car, and followed her back to the mansion.

Her father accompanied her to the front door. "Are we going to see you anytime soon?"

She squinted in the bright sunlight, wanting to cry. If only she could bury her face in her father's chest and tell him about Dade. If only she could go home with him, safe and protected. But she made herself answer casually, "I already told Anna I'd try to come up for a couple of days. She's expecting me sometime this week. Also, I might look into that job at Fairhaven. Can I come for a visit the week after?"

"We'll look forward to it, Sweetheart." He hugged her.

She waved goodbye to Sheila, kissed her father, and went inside. Through the peephole, she watched them start to pull out of the driveway. Once they were gone, she scurried upstairs.

It did not take her long to pack. Except for her books and music, which were already boxed, she could throw the rest of her clothes, bedding and odds and ends into the back of her car. But she wouldn't leave during the day. Dade might be watching. She'd wait for dark. In the meantime, she wrote out a note and a check to cover the rent and put it in Mrs. Peterson's mail slot downstairs. She left no information for the kindly old widow other than to request she forward her mail to her father's address.

That evening, still shaky and frightened by the possibility that Dade was near, she went down to the kitchen and made herself eat a small meal, finishing it off with a cup of strong coffee. She'd drive all night if need be and sleep in her car, but Dade would not know where she had gone.

When it was quite dark and traffic had ceased on Cedar Street, she quietly carried her belongings downstairs and packed her car. At three in the morning, she pulled out of the circular drive of the Tudor mansion and sped away into the foggy night.

Chapter Seven

"I will lie down and sleep in peace,
for You alone, O Lord, make me dwell in safety."
Psalm 4:8

Haven hadn't even looked at her GPS. She'd decided her best course was to find a motel somewhere nearby and give Anna a call in the morning. And it was certainly better than driving to Dad's and Sheila's home and trying to explain to her dad why she couldn't move back to the Portland area

She didn't plan to give Anna additional information about the creepy carpenter who had worked on her French doors. No sense in laying a burden of anxiety on the professor's frail shoulders. But the professor had connections in the music world to other teachers, schools, and musicians. She might be able to advise Haven about a summer job. Nothing permanent yet. Haven needed time to consider whether she could safely stay in Washington, or figure out if it was necessary to move to another part of the country.

But when she reached the Bothell area, where there were tons of motels, an urgent thought ambushed her. "No. Go north and help the doctor." She jerked the wheel and had to adjust quickly to stay in her lane. Heart thumping, she checked the rear-view mirror, half expecting some angelic being to be sitting in the back seat. At the next exit, she pulled over to the side of the road, shut the motor and sat in the darkness. What doctor? She rubbed the scar on her forehead vigorously. The only doctor she'd ever known was Dr. Meining back in Beaverton.

She clasped her hands and shut her eyes. "Oh, God, I'm so afraid. Sometimes I don't know which thoughts to listen to. Sometimes I think I should just give up running and let Dade find me and do whatever he's going to do. Then everyone I love would be safe from him. Or maybe I could finish him off with another rock … right between the eyes, just like David did to Goliath.

Prodded by that violent thought, she remembered Dade's snarling face as he'd sprawled on the ground, clutching his injured knee. Cursing her. Threatening, "It'll never be over, Ruth."

Why hadn't she finished him off right there and then? Instead, the same Power that had stopped her from committing suicide had intervened again and stopped her from murder. She had aimed her last lethal rock a fraction of an inch from Dade's head. In spite of the injury and misery he'd inflicted on her, in spite of his threats, she had no right to be Dade's executioner.

"O God, forgive me! I know it's crazy and evil to think I'd be justified in killing Dade. But, would you please bring someone into my life I could tell about that awful man? Someone I can trust. Someone who can help me without getting hurt himself?"

Red tail lights of early commuters streaming northward on the interstate seemed to beckon her to join them. Wasn't the music job her pastor had spoken about up north? She reached into her purse and drew out the piece of paper she'd been given at church the day before. "Fairhaven Community Church, Cascade Springs. Talk to Music Pastor Gary Lauer. They're looking for a part-time music assistant."

The potential job up north on I-5 was worth checking out. Her pastor had made an innocent statement about "holing up at Fairhaven," but Cascade Springs might be a good place to hide from Dade temporarily.

She plugged Fairhaven's address into her GPS before steering into the northbound lanes.

An hour later, just shy of Cascade Springs, she pulled into a rest stop. It was too early for most of the shops in town to be open. Shaky and exhausted, she pulled a blanket from the back seat and curled up for a nap.

At ten o'clock, after she had washed her face and changed into fresh clothes in the restroom, she drove into Cascade Springs and presented herself in Fairhaven's office. The receptionist rang the music pastor's extension and within minutes a man appeared, looking barely older than Haven herself.

"Hi, Haven. I'm Gary Lauer, the music pastor." He gave her a hearty handshake. "It's kind of cool that you showed up today. The pastors aren't usually on hand on Mondays, but we're having a special meeting in an hour. Pastor Bernard, our senior pastor, is here this morning, and I'm sure he'd like to talk with you also."

"I'm sorry this was s-such short notice, but I have all my recommendations and references right here." She patted her portfolio.

"Let's go into the conference room. I'll have Lucy give the

pastor a call and see if he can come join us."

A short time later she sat at the long conference table with both pastors. Rarely had she seen a more disparate pair than the two men now facing her. Pastor Gary's round, cheerful face and short stubby body contrasted sharply with the tall, elegant, older man. His face was long, his slender nose hooked, and the deep-set dark eyes that met hers seemed to shine with passion and brilliance. He wore his thick, black hair pulled back into a long ponytail.

The interview went well and Pastor Gary seemed pleased with her musical education, love for children, and experience working with them. "Pastor Miller said you'd be perfect for the job and, after talking with you, I agree."

She shuffled her papers and looked down. Pastor Bernard's dark eyes seemed to pierce her mind and guess at her need to bury herself and her identity in this city where the mountains met the ocean. "I still have a l-lot to learn about working with all the different ages of children. I h-hope you can be patient with me while I'm getting more experienced."

"We're all learners, too, Haven," Bernard said in his soft French-Canadian accent. "I don't know a single soul who is not still in the process of becoming what God intends for him or her to be."

"The kids are going to love you," Gary added. "I know it's only late April, but we'd like you to start soon. We don't have too many music activities going on right now since we just finished our winter/spring kids' concert. We can spend the next few weeks planning some of the music programs for the coming year and you can start meeting some of the children on Sundays."

"That'll be great, Sir." She shook his hand again.

She collected her things. Maybe this was where she was supposed to be.

"Just one more thing." Good grief, this felt awkward. "I really s-should be looking for another part-time job, you know, one that wouldn't conflict with my work here. Do you happen to know about any?"

"Funny you should ask," Lauer answered, "because just yesterday I was talking to a friend, and she's looking for someone to help her at her shop." Pastor Gary raised his eyebrows. "Do you know anything about floral decoration?"

♩ ♪♪♫♪

Haven filled out all the necessary paperwork for her employment at Fairhaven and gave them to Lucy, the church secretary. She gathered her things and was just about to leave when Lucy called to her.

"Haven, Pastor Bernard wanted to make sure to invite you to our Missions Potluck tonight at six. There'll be lots of people there who'll want to meet you."

Seeing her doubtful expression, Lucy added, "We know you just got here, so don't worry about bringing anything. There'll be plenty of food."

Haven nodded, relieved. It would have been difficult to bake a casserole without an oven, much less an apartment. "Thanks, Lucy. I'll be there tonight."

She almost skipped down the church's steps toward her heavily packed Sebring. Just yesterday, her world had seemed as dark as a moonless night in the forest. But today, Pastor Lauer's words had set her on the brink of a whole new wonderful chapter. As she climbed into her car, her growling stomach reminded her that she hadn't eaten since before she'd started this journey. She'd find a cafe to sit and eat and think about her new job.

At the restaurant, she glanced at the address and phone number of Maggie's Flowers one more time. The shop couldn't be more than five minutes away.

After lunch, back in her car, she followed her GPS toward the florist shop. A block past Mercy Hospital, she parked outside the small building with the brightly painted sign: "Maggie's Flowers." The bells on the door jingled as she walked in. A middle-aged woman with curly auburn hair, brown eyes, and a friendly, freckled face greeted her from behind the counter.

"Are you Haven?"

"How did you know?"

"Pastor Gary called and said you'd be coming by. He said you worked at a florist shop in Issaquah while you were going to college."

She nodded. "Campus Florist. For about a year." She pulled out her work references and handed them to Maggie. "I'm only looking for part-time since I'll also have a job at the church."

"That works." Maggie came around the counter. "I'm only wanting someone in the mornings and an occasional afternoon. Is that what you're interested in?"

"That'd be perfect."

Maggie handed her an application. "Why don't you go behind there?" She pointed to a chair peeking out from behind a latticed partition. "There's a table and chair where you can fill this out. Bring it back to the counter and ring the bell when you're finished. I've got some things to do in the back room."

Maggie turned to go down the hallway. "Oh, and feel free to move all those wedding books off the table."

She thanked Maggie and went behind the partition. Just as she finished filling out the form, the shop door opened and closed. Normally, she would have ignored such a minor distraction, but the customer that crossed behind the partition was very tall and the voice that spoke to Maggie, uncommonly deep.

She gasped and shrank down behind a collection of tall flower-filled vases. Her mouth went dry and her pulse throbbed in her scar. Peeking through the diamond-shaped gaps of the partition she studied the stranger's back and profile. Blood poured back into her face and her breathing returned to normal. Maggie's customer, though tall as Dade, looked close to a decade younger. He wore a beard and mustache that might have been neat two weeks ago, but not now. And his thick, unruly blonde hair needed a good trimming. He was dressed professionally in a grey tweed blazer and dark trousers. But even they needed pressing.

"You got it, Doc. I'll have it ready to deliver first thing tomorrow morning," Maggie said.

The man turned and headed toward the door and Haven got her first good look. Not exactly classically handsome, but it made his face more interesting. A long, aristocratic nose and high cheekbones made her wish it had been her, not Maggie, who'd taken his order. His high forehead and intelligent expression blazed in sharp contrast to the general rumpled appearance of his clothing. He had the look of a college professor. All he needed was a pipe between his teeth and maybe a large musty, hardbound book or two tucked under one of his long arms.

After he stepped out, she gathered up her things and returned to the front counter. Maggie was still filling out the man's order.

"Who was that?" She tried to sound casual but her voice must have betrayed her fascination because Maggie looked up from her work and nodded in a knowing way.

"Thor."

Haven chuckled. "You're kidding, right?"

"Oh, I'd never call him that to his face. He's far too dignified." Maggie squinted through the front-facing windows.

Haven followed her gaze. The man's Honda was just leaving the parking lot.

"But you gotta admit he does bear a certain resemblance, don't you think?"

Haven laughed. "Hmm, maybe. But where was his hammer?"

Maggie giggled, too. She set the man's order aside and leaned over the counter. "That's Dr. Petter Eriksen. He's the new ER doc at Mercy Hospital. He comes in here at least once a week and orders flowers to be delivered anonymously to some of his patients that have been admitted, the ones who don't seem to have any family."

"Wow, I've never heard of a doctor doing that."

"Well, that man is something special. I'll bet every young unmarried woman in Cascade Springs wishes he'd look her way … and some older ones, too." Maggie's eyes crinkled into narrow slits and another musical laugh burst from her lips.

With a laugh like that, she and Maggie were definitely going to be good friends.

Maggie read over her application. "Looks like you know all

about this kind of work. Do you think you could come back tomorrow morning, say, about ten? I have some early orders to deliver, but after that, we can get together and start training."

"Thanks, Maggie. I'll be here at ten."

Haven made a quick phone call to Anna to ask her if it would be okay to delay her visit until the weekend. Then she fairly bounced out the front door. *You're too old to act like this ... in public.* And, as if to confirm that, a man in the parking lot chuckled when he saw her bouncing down the florist steps. *Well, I don't care.* Her mind galloped over the millions of things she had to do, including finding a place to live. But those would have to wait until tomorrow. She'd go to the Missions Potluck at Fairhaven that evening and stay in a motel her first night in Cascade Springs.

♩ ♪♪♫♪

That evening, the aroma of coffee and baked casseroles along with animated voices greeted Haven as she entered Fairhaven Church's gymnasium. Pastor Gary spotted her immediately and came over.

"Hi, Haven. Come on over here and get a name tag and then I'll take you around to meet some friends." Gary waited while she printed her name and stuck the tag onto her shirt.

"First person you have to meet is my wife, Wendy. She's looking forward to meeting you."

She followed Gary's thick form over to the dessert table where a tiny, dark-haired woman was busy simultaneously arranging plates on the table and holding on to a squirmy toddler.

"Wendy, this is Haven Ellingsen, our new Children's Music

Director."

Wendy hoisted the toddler higher up onto her slender hip and came around the table. "Good to meet you." She took Haven's hand and her thin face crinkled into a good-humored smile. "We're so glad you'll be working with the children. I was doing it for a while, but it got to be too hectic now that I've got two children and one on the way. And anyway, the program's gotten so big now that we really need someone who's trained in music."

The chubby child in Wendy's arms reached for Haven, who laughed and opened her arms for him. Wendy transferred the little boy to her. "See, even Timmy's happy you're here, and he's a good judge of character."

Haven smiled tenderly as she held the little boy, her heartwarming at his enormous brown eyes. "So, Timmy, do you like to sing?" she asked in a singsong voice, then giggled when he started to bounce his whole body and sing nonsense syllables. She turned back to his mother, delighted. "I can see he's another budding musician."

"Oh, you wouldn't believe how much he sings at home. Give him another couple of years and he'll be in your primary choir."

Haven was just about to reply when Pastor Gary patted her arm. He took Timmy and handed him back to his wife. "Wendy, I see some other people I want Haven to meet."

Haven waved goodbye. "Hope to see you soon, Wendy."

Pastor Bernard took the mic and asked everyone for silence so he could say the blessing. When he finished, all the people began to form lines to get their food.

"There they are," Gary said. "They're just about to get into the second line."

"Who? Where?" Haven asked, but the young pastor was already hurrying ahead. Again, she followed him as he weaved through the throngs of families standing about visiting.

"Erik," Gary called. A distinguished looking middle-aged man with salt-and-pepper hair turned at the sound of his voice and grinned at Gary.

"Hello, young man." The older man approached and clapped him on the back.

Gary shook the man's hand. "How was your trip? Did you get to Bergen?"

"Ya, indeed. We got to see just about everyone. Liv and Sverre send their greeting."

A slim man with brown, curly hair and mischievous hazel eyes popped his head around Erik's shoulder. "Gary, do you know what it's like to run Misty Mountain for two weeks when there's no one around to answer any of your questions? When's the meat delivery? How do you write this invoice? When does the farrier come? And most important, where's the TP? Longest two weeks of my life." He shook his head and sighed dramatically. "Papa, please don't ever leave me alone again in that big lodge while you go gallivanting back to good old Norge." He laid his hand on his father's shoulder and squeezed it affectionately.

Gary returned the young man's grin. "So, Pal, I guess two weeks running the retreat was enough vacation for you. I'll bet you can't wait to get back to work up north again," he said with exaggerated innocence.

Pal rolled his eyes. "Hmm, maybe after another month of rest. But now that Papa's back I can re-start my sabbatical. Maybe even catch up on some sleep."

Pastor Gary seemed to remember why he was talking to Erik and Pal. "Oh, I'm sorry, Haven." He put his hand on her shoulder and nudged her forward. "Erik, Pal, I'd like you to meet Haven Ellingsen. She's our new Children's Music Director. Just hired today."

"Haven, this is Erik Eriksen and his son, Pal."

Haven leaned in and politely offered her hand to Erik and then Pal.

"I wanted you both to meet Haven because, although she didn't say anything about performing, I'm told that she's an accomplished singer, pianist, and guitarist. And," he straightened and assumed a formal air, "I thought you might find her a valuable asset considering all the missionaries, pastors, and families who pass through your venerable doors each year."

Pastor Gary leaned down to her and whispered quickly. "I hope I'm not overstepping my bounds, Haven. Your pastor from college said you're a really good performer and that you've played all over the Seattle area. Erik could really use your kind of talent at the retreat."

"It's true, Miss Ellingsen," Erik said, "we would love to have you play for our guests."

"And if you come, I promise I'll help you with the singing," Pal added with the same mischievous glint in his eyes while pushing out his skinny chest.

"Don't listen to him," Gary smirked at his friend, then leaned in toward her again. "Singing isn't exactly his strength if you know what I mean." He rolled his eyes, then met hers, shaking his head with meaning.

Haven tried to control herself, but Gary's funny, round face and dramatic expressions caught her off guard and she laughed in spite of herself.

Pal kept his lips pressed together as if he were trying to hold in a laugh, too. His eyes twinkled with amusement. Then, just as quickly, he became serious. "No, really, Haven, if we could have your number, maybe we could call and set up a time for you to come and play or sing."

She looked at the young man and his father, recognizing their goodness and the sincerity of their request. How could she say no? Still, she was a little reluctant to give out her cell phone number until she got to know the Eriksen men a little better. "I just got here today s-so I don't have an apartment yet. But I was planning on starting to l-look for a place to rent tomorrow."

"Do you need to be in town?" Erik looked at her with gentle eyes, so like her father's.

"Well, I guess not, but I don't want to have to drive too far. Do you know about a place that's for rent?"

Erik and Pal exchanged looks, then nodded. "We have been looking for the right person to rent our little cabin at the retreat," Eric said. "It's a rustic little place but you might find it safer than living in a noisy apartment in town."

It was getting hard to hear in the gym. Erik leaned down to speak so he could be heard. "Why don't you come to the retreat tomorrow morning and we'll show you the cabin. Then you tell us if it might be right for you. Okay?"

He handed her a plate and they all began to file past the tables, loaded with salads, rolls, fried chicken, baked beans and various casseroles. Another family engaged the Eriksens in conversation and for a while Haven was left to her own thoughts.

She found a table with a group of younger singles and couples and was quickly welcomed into the midst of their discussions.

Later that evening, Pal shared slides and talked about his ministry with native tribes in Alaska. Afterward, he came over and handed her a map he'd hastily scrawled on the back of his notes.

"Please come tomorrow, not just to look at the cabin but to hear a little more about my father's Retreat. Who knows? I have a feeling God may have a special place for you there." He smiled and his eyes held the same sweet expression of the elder Eriksen.

That night Haven sank into her motel bed and drew the covers up over her weary shoulders. But tired as she was, she woke often throughout the night, wondering about the future. Pal's words echoed in her mind. "God may have a special place for you there."

♩ ♪♪♫♪

The retreat was approximately six miles east of town in a heavily forested part of the countryside, bounded on three sides by steep hills. She turned onto a gravel road, bordered by tall firs, maples, alders, and cedars. Farther down the road she crossed under a wooden sign suspended above the road.

"Misty Mountain Retreat Center," she read out loud. "Well, that's an appropriate name." Below, in smaller letters were inscribed the words of Jesus, "Come to me all ye who are weary and heavy laden and I will give you rest."

She drove another hundred yards before the stables and corral came into view. Beyond that were numerous smaller buildings and then, finally, the main lodge. She pulled up to a parking area, shut off the motor and stepped out of the car. The lodge itself appeared to have been built at least a couple of decades earlier. Its foundation and part of the first floor was stone. Above that rose two more floors of imposing log structure. In the front, a wide stone stairway ascended to a deep veranda. Cushioned wicker chairs lined the walls, awaiting tired guests. Large, timber beams formed a support truss under which a beautifully carved front door beckoned, with two massive logs standing like sentinels on either side.

Her gaze swept the grounds. A variety of evergreens dotted the grassy landscape between the main lodge and the other smaller buildings. Deep purple, pink, white, and yellow rhododendrons glorified the grounds. Planters containing impatiens and pansies decorated the base of the lodge and other buildings, and benches had been placed strategically around the grounds for visitors to sit and bask in the beauty of God's creation. Beyond the buildings, the lush forest rose, densely covering the hills. The mingled scent of balsam and horses tickled her nostrils and reminded her of her childhood. She climbed the steps. Her dad would love this place. It had just the right amount of rustic and modern comfort. She rang the bell and waited. An older grey-haired woman opened the door.

Haven greeted the woman and explained her business.

"Come on in, Miss. I'm Mrs. Graham and I run the operations in the main lodge." The woman indicated toward the left. "Why don't you wait in the great room while I find out where that old man has got to?" she said with a certain grumpy affection. Mrs. Graham escorted Haven from the entryway and through a wide doorway to the left where a large, vaulted room, dominated by a massive stone fireplace greeted her eyes. The room was large enough to comfortably accommodate at least fifty people. An overstuffed leather couch, flanked by wingback chairs, decorated with colorful woven pillows, huddled close to the fireplace. Other groupings of cozy chairs sat in corners of the room. Opposite the fireplace, near the wall, stood a grand piano. The walls sported tapestries of Scandinavian design and paintings of mountain scenes. Rustic pewter chandeliers hung from the cross beams.

"Just make yourself comfortable. Sometimes it takes me a while to find Mr. Eriksen." Mrs. Graham muttered something else and left her standing in the middle of the great room, still admiring her surroundings. When no one showed up right away, Haven wandered over to the piano and found it open, as if waiting to be played. Her breeding and good manners prevented her. "A Bosendorfer," she murmured in admiration. "That must have cost a pretty penny."

A book of Edvard Grieg pieces lay open on the stand and she thumbed through its pages. She recognized some of the works.

"I'd love to hear you play some Grieg, Miss Ellingsen." Erik stood just inside the doorway, smiling his gentle smile, dressed in faded denim and carrying work gloves. The man matched his restful surroundings. Or, was it that the man himself lent the place that indefinable aura of peace? "I try to play them," he said, "but I'm afraid I just don't do them justice. Won't you let me hear them the way they were meant to be played?"

Haven came around the piano quickly. She blushed at the thought that Mr. Eriksen may have been watching her the whole time she'd been peeking through his music. "Don't tempt me, Mr. Eriksen," she warned good-naturedly. But she knew her longing to play showed on her face. "I may start playing and never want to stop."

"Please, Haven." He motioned toward the piano. "You don't know how it would please me to hear you play." He smiled and nodded toward the piano once more. "Please." He sat down and waited.

"All right, Mr. Eriksen." She sat on the piano bench and turned the pages. Which piece should she play? Then her fingers began to work their magic on the keys. She forgot everything—her surroundings, her audience, her appointment at the florist—and lost herself in the music. She pictured the windswept mountains and the fjords of Norway, home of her ancestors. When she finished playing she rested her fingers lightly on the keyboard and shut her eyes for a moment, as if to indelibly engrave in her soul's memory the resonance, beauty, and power of the instrument.

Erik took a long breath before speaking softly. "Beautiful. Beautiful. Such a gift you have. I hope you thank God for the talent he has given you."

She looked up. Tears filled the man's eyes. "Thank you, Mr. Eriksen. And I do thank Him. Every day."

Erik stood up. "Well, I guess we should be taking a look at the cabin if you're still interested."

She followed him out the front door, down the stairs and around the side of the lodge. They climbed into a jeep and Erik took off down a narrow dirt road that she hadn't seen when she'd first arrived. Winding around trees and ascending steep inclines, they crossed a wood bridge, under which a spring tumbled and rushed its way down and across the many acres of the retreat. Coming into a clearing, she caught her first glimpse of the cabin. Erik pulled up alongside and turned off the motor.

He mounted the steps to the porch, unlocked the door and she followed him inside. The main room consisted of a living area with an old sofa, end table, an upholstered chair and a wood-burning stove. Bookshelves lined the wall behind the sofa. To the right was a small kitchen with a table and chairs. Through a doorway behind the kitchen, there was an uncomplicated bathroom to the right and a pantry to the left, which completed the east end of the cottage. On the west side behind the wood-burning stove, was a wall and a door and through that, a bedroom.

Erik looked at her dubiously. "I know it's a little rustic and old-fashioned. Perhaps—"

"Oh, it's perfect." She hurried to take it all in, so she could make a quick decision.

"Really?" He raised his bushy eyebrows.

"Yes. It's just the right size and it's so quiet and peaceful. And I won't bother anyone if I need to practice my guitar or singing."

"But can you handle having only a wood-burning stove for heat? And the stove and refrigerator are so small."

Haven stopped and studied the old man. *Lord, if this is where you want me, please help Mr. Eriksen to agree.* "Don't you want to rent this cabin to me?"

Mr. Eriksen hesitated and looked uncomfortable. "It's just that, after seeing you a bit more, you seem to be a very dainty young lady. I'm not sure you'd be comfortable in such a rustic place."

"Mr. Eriksen," she said, "I have lived in places much more rustic than this. Please, let me rent this cabin."

A shadow at the door interrupted their conversation.

"You'd better rent this cabin to the lady, Papa." Pal leaned against the doorframe. "I told her last night that God has a special place for her at the Misty Mountain."

"Well, that settles it." Erik smiled broadly. "All right, young lady, you may rent this cabin."

"Great!" Pal exclaimed as he hurried into the room and shook Haven's hand. "Welcome home, Haven."

"Thanks, Mr. Eriksen … and Mr. Eriksen." She grinned at both of them. "I'll be a good tenant. You'll see."

She checked the time on her phone, "I need to get back to town. I promised I would be at Maggie's Flowers by ten this morning."

They stepped outside, and Pal followed her to the jeep. "When you finish at work, why don't you join us for dinner? After that, I can help you move into the cabin."

She climbed back into the yellow vehicle. "Thanks, Pal. I could really use the help."

♩ ♪♪♫♪

Pal's cousin wasn't usually late for their morning workouts together in the lodge's spacious basement gym. With any luck, Petter would show up before Haven drove away so he could introduce the two. While Haven and Erik talked about her lease and she wrote out her first month's rent check, he punched in Petter's number on his cell phone.

A raspy voice answered, "Hello?"

"Hey, little brother, it's after nine. I thought we were going to work out this morning."

"What in blazes?"

Sounds of a squeaky bed followed by hurried movement left no doubt that Petter had been roused from sleep. "Sorry, Pal. I forgot all about it. Give me ten minutes. Bye."

After calling Petter, Pal kept up a conversation with Haven about anything musical he could think of, all the while checking his watch. He tried to coax her to play another piece on the piano but she declined, saying that she wanted to make sure she got to Maggie's a few minutes before ten. But she promised to be back in time for dinner.

Petter was due any time. Why, of all mornings, did he have to be late? Pal hid his disappointment as Haven got into her car and drove away.

Oh, well. Maybe another time. He headed for the basement gym.

Pal had just started his second set of bench presses when he heard the door to the basement open followed by Petter tromping down the steps. "Well, it's about time." Too bad his cousin hadn't arrived five minutes earlier. It would've been fun to introduce Haven to Petter and see his reaction to the pretty blonde. He lowered the bar to his chest and sighed in mock exasperation. "Man, you'd think I have nothing but time on my hands."

Petter approached and leaned heavily on the bar just as Pal was trying to press one more.

"Uf da," he groaned. "Ease up, Ivar. You'll give me a hernia."

Petter let go and stepped back with a grin. "That's for waking me an hour before my alarm was set to go off." He helped Pal set the bar back onto the holder, gave him a hand up, and sat down on a mat to stretch. "Sorry about being late. Guess I was pretty beat last night."

"I figured it was something like that." Pal blotted his face with a towel. "You usually beat me here by half an hour." He moved to the rowing machine.

After a few minutes, Petter switched to the treadmill.

They were silent for a while. After working up to a jog and doing a couple of miles, Petter left the treadmill and switched to the bench. He gradually added more weights. "Pal, can you spot me on this?"

Pal left his machine and stood over the big man. It had never occurred to him to be envious of Petter's muscular six-foot-six frame or good looks or, for that matter, his success in the medical world. He loved Petter like the little brother he never had. "So, how long did you work yesterday?"

Petter sat up, breathing a little from the exertion. "Kind of long. I pulled a double shift. Dr. Martin called in sick."

"It's not too bad," he said when he saw Pal's face. "You get used to it after a while. When I was an intern I worked longer hours than that."

But it was *too bad*. Pal shook his head while he followed Petter over to the mats to do crunches. At this rate, the doctor would never have time for a real life outside his work. He needed a wife to look after him: a sweet but feisty woman who'd feed him hot, nourishing meals, see to it that he got his hair cut, and worry and fuss over him. And he needed children. And so much more. "You work too much. How are you ever," he grunted between sit-ups, "going to find a wife … and start a family if … you don't get out and meet … some nice … ladies?"

"You know how women are," the doctor said. "How many of them would put up with my schedule? Besides, you said it yourself, women don't much care for geeks like me."

Petter kept up with his crunches as if the conversation were over.

But the subject was not finished. "That's not fair, little brother. I remember that conversation. When I called you a geek, you were still in med school. Now you're living in the real world."

"Ya? Well, I'm still a geek."

"Even a geek deserves a wife and children. You could go on like this for years, taking care of everyone else's health and ignoring your own. Before you know it, you'll be an old man. I'm telling you, Petter, it's time for you to start looking around."

Petter halted and flipped over on his side, eyes narrowed. "What brought all this up? I come here to work out with you and all of a sudden I'm about ready for a nursing home."

"It's-it's ... well ... uh." Petter was the only person who could make him stammer like a schoolboy. He examined Petter's face, trying to gauge his receptivity, "It's just that ... uh, I've met the perfect girl and—"

"Oh, you met a girl." Petter shook his head and frowned. "So that's what this is all about." He jumped up and shoved the thick, shock of gold hair away from his forehead. "Pal, how many times have you tried to fix me up with a blind date? It never works. Never. They're either too religious or homely or both or —"

"This one's different."

"No, Pal. N-O. I'll do my own picking. If I could find a woman who'd respect my passion for my work and respect me for who I am and not try to change me I'd fall at her feet and worship her. But I've never found her." He looked up at the ceiling, took a deep breath and released it. "I doubt that she exists." He bent to give Pal a brotherly knuckle rub on the top of his head. "Thanks for trying, Pal," he said in a quieter voice. "I appreciate your concern." He threw a towel over his shoulder. "I'm going to hit the shower."

After Petter left, Pal stood up and rubbed the back of his neck. "She does exist." He glanced up at the ceiling. "We've just got to find a way to get those two together."

Chapter Eight

*"Think where man's glory most begins and ends
and say my glory was I had such friends."*
W. B. Yeats

That evening, after she had returned from her first day's work at Maggie's, Haven joined the Eriksens and several Misty Mountain guests for dinner in the dining hall of the main lodge.

As they were nearing the end of the meal, Pal, who was seated next to her leaned in and said, "Papa told me how you played this morning. Would you mind playing the same piece for me, too? It's true that I can hardly carry a tune, but I love to hear other people sing or play."

This time she didn't need any prodding, having experienced the pleasure of playing the magnificent piano. She looked over at Erik. "Is that okay with you, Mr. Eriksen?"

Erik's sweet eyes glowed with pleasure. He turned to the two couples who'd been dining with them, "If you want to hear something special, just come and join us in the great room."

Minutes later she was seated again at the grand piano, playing the requested Grieg. Pal sat nearby and listened, eyes closed, nodding his head to the folky rhythm of the music.

When she finished, her audience applauded. Pal opened his eyes, looking like he'd just emerged from a dream. "You play that music like you've lived all your life in Norway. I wish Petter had been here tonight. He would have really enjoyed hearing you … and seeing you.

"Who's Petter?" Haven stood up from the piano bench. "Is he a friend of yours?"

"Oh," he whispered, "he's more than a friend. He's—"

"That was wonderful, Haven," Erik remarked as he approached. "Any time you want to come in here and practice, you're welcome. Besides, the staff would love to hear you, too."

Pal stood up and motioned toward the front door. "Come on, Haven. We should be getting you moved in while it's still light."

She made her goodbyes, thanked Erik for the offer of his piano for practice, and followed Pal out the door. They climbed into her packed Sebring and Pal guided her up the narrow road to the cabin. She unlocked the door to her new home and Pal carried boxes inside.

Walking into the bedroom she pulled one smooth, softball-sized stone from her overnight bag and set it on the nightstand next to the bed.

They carried on a steady conversation as they unpacked her car and she felt herself growing to admire his gentle, witty soul. He surprised her with his strength, wiry as he was, carrying boxes filled with large hardbound books, and easily moving furniture according to her wishes.

He told her how he had felt called to work with native tribes in Alaska, flying in supplies and short-term helpers, teaching, and counseling. As he spoke, she began to form a picture of a man whose passion for serving left no room for a wife or family.

When they had moved the last box and carried in the rest of her things, she said, "Is there anything I can do to thank you for all your help, Pal?"

His leaned up against the front door, but his eyes seemed to gaze at something far away. "Just keep playing for my father, Haven. You have no idea how much your music helps him. You see, my mother was a very fine pianist, too, and he loved to hear her play. But she died about fifteen years ago. He moved us out here to get away from all the memories of her."

Haven felt her heart grieve with her own memories. "It didn't work, did it?"

Pal looked at her curiously. "Nei, and for a while, he was kind of lost. But running this retreat has helped him find purpose again. You may have noticed that my father is a very sweet and gentle man. I think God has used his grief to make him especially compassionate for others who have gone through tragedy or hardship."

She nodded at his words, remembering how she'd felt when she first drove up to Misty Mountain.

"And even though I hardly know you, I felt from the minute we met that somehow you are very much like Papa." After he stepped outside he said over his shoulder, "Oh, there is one more thing you can do to thank me."

She followed him out to the car and waited for him to finish his thought.

"There's someone I want you to meet, only … he's not quite ready yet."

"Not ready?"

"I can't explain it, Haven. You'll just have to trust me on that. But he could use your help, too."

They got in the car and she puzzled over his words as she drove him back to the lodge.

♩ ♪♪♫♪

Mrs. Peterson opened the door and squinted up into the face of the giant delivery man. "Flowers for a …" the man double-checked the name on the tag and pronounced it distinctly, "Miss Haven Ellingsen." He looked up from the flowers and smiled with a lot of teeth.

"Oh, dear, I'm afraid she's already moved, Sir."

The man's smile chilled several degrees. "Well, does she still live in town?" He sounded almost angry.

"I think her family is still in town. They were staying at the Bellevue Inn." She reached for the flowers. "Maybe you'd better let me take them and I'll—"

He jerked the flowers away from her hands, making her jump. "Oh, that's okay, Ma'am," he said, still smiling his tight, too-big smile. "I guess I'll have to return them to the shop." He backed away, turned and hurried down the walkway.

"I think she's moved back to Portland," she called. The man nodded but didn't turn to acknowledge her words as he continued down the driveway.

She stood on the porch and watched him stride down the

street. *Funny, where was his delivery van?* Halfway down the block he got into a green pickup truck and roared away.

♩ ♪♪♫♪

Working with Maggie was even better than her job at the Campus Florist in Issaquah. Unlike her former employer, Maggie let her take orders and help prospective brides plan their floral decorations and bouquets.

After her hours at Maggie's Flowers, she drove to Fairhaven and met with Pastor Gary to work on children's choir plans for the summer and the fall and order music and other materials. On her first day, he'd said, "I would like you to play for the Sunday morning services as much as possible during the rest of spring and on into summer. That will give the parents a chance to see that you really are a musician." And it had worked. Almost from the first day she played, she had already gotten four requests for piano lessons. Gary graciously allowed her to teach those lessons in the choir room in the afternoons.

A week passed. The private little cabin on the outskirts of Misty Mountain Retreat Center was already beginning to feel like home. How soothing to sit on the front porch on a lazy late afternoon, listening to the sound of the river just down the forested hill, or the wind sighing through the cedars and firs. And after a day of delivering flowers, working with Pastor Gary and then teaching two or three piano lessons, it felt good to be in her own quiet place, music softly playing, stirring a pot of soup and baking her own bread.

Nevertheless, when she had the chance to catch one of Jesse's gigs in Seattle, she sacrificed her serenity and made plans to drive there first before spending the rest of the weekend with her dad and Sheila.

Sitting at a table nearest Jesse's small combo, she listened with admiration to the young man's skillful playing and his expressive tenor voice. He looked down at her several times as he played and sang, his face flushed with excitement.

After the set, he came over, hugged her, and seated himself at her table. "I got a new apartment. It's much nicer than the one I left."

"In Seattle?"

He nodded. "It's closer to the University of Washington, which is good since I'm taking a few courses there." A shy half-smile lit his handsome face.

"Jesse, that's wonderful." She held her hand up for a high five, and he smacked it. "I'm so excited for you." She had always thought Jesse was like a racehorse, stomping and snorting to be allowed to stretch out its long legs and fly like the wind. All he had needed was freedom from Dade and Mama.

His smile faded. "I'm sorry I missed yer recital."

"Oh, that's okay. How could you have known about it? Besides, it's probably better that you didn't come."

"Why?"

"Dade showed up."

"What?" Jesse's mouth dropped open. "Did he do anything? Threaten you?"

"Thank the Lord, no. He just stood outside and looked through the window at me. Scared the daylights out of me." Good thing she hadn't actually recognized him until later.

"All those people there and he still shows up." Jesse shook his head. "Haven, you gotta to be careful about going places. I mean, he probably doesn't know where you are now, but he's real smart. You gotta be smarter than him."

"I know, Jesse. I'm trying. I didn't tell anyone except my family and close friends where I moved to. I'm not on any social media sites either. Only a handful of people know my address

"Good." He looked around the bistro as if checking to make sure Dade wasn't in the room. "You're gonna be okay." He beamed at her. "Anyway, I'm so glad you came tonight. I was getting nervous you weren't really gonna keep in contact."

"I said I'd never forget you. Didn't you believe me?" She tilted her head and smiled. "As far as I'm concerned we're friends for life."

"Friends?" Jesse looked a little disappointed. "I'd hoped that one day we could more than just friends."

Her smile faded. She had always thought of Jesse as an ally, a brother, and friend, one who struggled similarly to be free of the memories of Dade and Mama. Startled by the thought that three years earlier Jesse might have helped free her for himself, a cold, sharp sliver of dread pierced her heart. Affection, she welcomed. But a man's love? That was something altogether different and frightening.

Afraid to touch him now, she kept her hands in her lap. "Jesse, what Dade did to me, what he's still doing to me … I-I just can't be close that way. I'm not over it. I don't know if I'll ever feel different. I—"

"It's okay." His gaze slumped to the table. "You don't need to say anything more. I guess I understand. I'd rather be friends with you than nothing. Let's just drop it."

They visited until it was time for Jesse to play another set. Then she stood and shouldered her purse. "I'd like to give you my new cell phone number."

Jesse pulled his cell phone out of his pocket and entered her name in his directory.

She was just about to give him her number but hesitated. "You're not going to be seeing Dade again anytime soon, are you? There's no chance he could get a hold of your cell phone?"

He stood up, too, and grinned. "Don't plan to see him and don't want to."

She laughed and told him her number. Coming around the table, she gave him a hug. "I've got to get going. Dad will worry if I'm not there by midnight."

She released Jesse, but before he could hide it, she caught the pain creasing the area between his dark eyes.

♩ ♪♪♫♪

Haven's weekend with her father and Sheila flew by, though she'd enjoyed every moment with them and Aunt Joy.

The next morning Haven drove her own car to West Hills Community Church for the first service, planning to leave right afterward for the five-hour trip back north. She corralled Pastor Jensen after the service and gave him an affectionate hug.

"So, young lady, I hear your recital at Northmont was a big splash. And your dad tells me you've been working at a church north of Seattle."

Surely, it was okay to tell the pastor she'd known since

childhood. "Yes, in Cascade Springs. Have you heard of Fairhaven Community Church?"

The pastor looked down at his shoes, frowning in concentration. "No … no, can't say as I have."

"Well. It's a fairly big church and they've got some great things going on there. I'm working with the grade school kids, getting them ready to sing at some of the hospitals and assisted living homes in the area."

"That's great," Pastor Jensen said. "I'm so glad you ended up there. Those kids are lucky to have you."

"Thanks. Oh, by the w-way, I'm not telling everybody where I've moved. Just close friends and family. Anybody who wants to know more can just talk to my dad."

"Fine, fine."

She wasn't sure the pastor heard her. He was checking out the long line of people that had collected behind her, all patiently waiting to speak with him. "I'd better go now. Bye, Pastor."

He waved, already turning his attention to an older woman who had stepped forward to greet him.

Haven rejoined her father and Sheila. They followed her back to her Sebring where Haven hugged Sheila.

After she'd climbed behind the wheel, her father leaned on the window sill. "Call me when you get back, okay?"

"Soon as I walk in the door. Promise." She traced an *x* over her heart.

He leaned in farther and gave her a kiss. "I love you, girl," he whispered.

"I love you too, Dad." She started the motor and waved as she drove off

♩ ♪♪♫♪

Dade pulled from the side of the road, eyes glued to the silver Sebring as it turned out of the church parking lot. He drove skillfully, neither following too closely nor staying so far back as to lose the car on a sudden turn.

He followed her onto the interstate, then across the Columbia, past the cities of Vancouver, Longview, and Centralia. As their cars approached Olympia, the traffic picked up and it got difficult to keep the right amount of distance between his car and Ruth's. More than a few times a semi or large RV merged onto the interstate, obstructing his view. He cursed under his breath and gunned his engine to pull around the trucks and keep his eye on Ruth.

Once in Tacoma, traffic increased to the point where rows of cars simply stopped, then crept forward before stopping again.

"What the—What's causing this pile up?" he yelled into the windshield. He had moved into the fast lane to get around a bus and the next time he glimpsed the Sebring it had moved to the far right lane. Too late, he realized Ruth's intent. Signaling and honking aggressively, he tried to move right himself, receiving honks and angry gestures in return from other frustrated motorists. A semi came out of nowhere and pulled forward and blocked his view again. Swearing loudly, he slammed on his brakes and swerved behind the big truck.

After the exit, cars accelerated and he maneuvered his truck to the right lane, craning his neck to see where Ruth had gone. Had she taken the exit or was she simply farther up in the line of cars? He sped up, searching.

No way she could have gotten any farther up. That she-devil must have taken the exit. He checked his rearview mirror once more before committing himself to the next exit, then took the U-turn and merged with the southbound traffic. When he reached the exit where he'd last seen Ruth's car, he scanned the area desperately. He turned east onto the county road. Pulling into the parking lot of a strip mall, he trolled the rows of cars and glanced inside the businesses.

He drove to a quiet spot a ways down the road and idled. Sweat poured down his back. His breath came in sharp, convulsive gasps and the veins in his forehead throbbed.

"God!"

He punched the wheel until his knuckles bled and physical agony stole the power of his fury.

♩ ♪♪♬♪

Haven turned onto the gravel road leading to Misty Mountain. She'd planned on heading directly to her cabin but as she passed the lodge, Pal came down the front steps and waved at her. She pulled over and lowered her window.

"Hi. How was your visit down south?" He leaned down to her level.

"Oh, it was so good to see my dad and Sheila. They really love each other. And I also got to see an old friend on my way through Seattle."

Pal's body language seemed to communicate something more than just interest in her weekend. "Did you need something? You w-waved at me like you had something important to tell me."

"No, not really. Just that it's been a very quiet weekend, and I was wondering if you've had lunch yet?"

She nodded. "I stopped off around Tacoma for a bite. But if you're hungry I'll drive you somewhere for lunch."

"I've got a friend I wanted to see for a few minutes in town. Then we could go get a sandwich or something."

"Hop in." She pressed the unlock button and Pal came around and got in.

"So, where am I going?"

"To the hospital," he said, and then smiled as if he guarded a great and amusing secret.

She pretended not to notice the smile. There was definitely something on the man's agenda besides lunch. *Okay, Mr. Pal Eriksen, I'll play along.* She steered the car back onto the driveway. In fifteen minutes, they had pulled into the parking lot at Mercy Hospital and were walking into the main entrance. He led her down the hall to the cafeteria, walking with a bounce to his step, and he seemed to scan the room expectantly.

"Just who are you meeting?"

He mumbled something in Norwegian, but his tone sounded disappointed.

"What?"

"He's not here," Pal translated distractedly, still looking around. "He said he'd be taking his break right now." He glanced at his watch.

"Who?" She looked around, too, as if she could find the mystery friend.

"Here," he took her arm, "let's go see if we can find him."

"Who, who?" she asked again as they hurried down the hall,

but Pal didn't hear her. She rolled her eyes. "I sound like an owl."

They wound up in the Emergency Department waiting area. Pal went to the desk and spoke with a nurse, then returned looking disappointed again. "My friend's still in the Emergency."

"Oh, no. Is he okay?"

Pal laughed but caught himself. "I'm sorry, I shouldn't be laughing about anyone being in Emergency. No, he's a doctor, not a patient. The nurse said that they just brought in a couple of patients, so that's why he didn't take his break."

He sighed. "I guess it wasn't meant to happen today."

"What happen?"

"Oh, nothing." He took her hand and walked her outside and around to the parking lot. When they got to the car, he had regained his usual cheerful demeanor. "Let's go get some ice cream."

♩ ♪♪♫♪

May arrived with warmer weather and even more things to do at the church. She'd begun her summer music programs with the children at Fairhaven Community and rehearsed each Sunday morning and Wednesday afternoon. It would be a full summer schedule. She had arranged for the various children's groups to sing at church and at several convalescent hospitals and assisted living communities throughout the next ten weeks. Then a break in August to gear up for the fall activities.

Erik asked her to play and sing for his retreat guests on a regular basis and she was compensated, in a small way, for not being able to play in public. Erik was never far off when she came to practice on his piano. Yesterday, she had found him sitting on a bench in the entry hall, just beyond her view, listening to her piano exercises and repertoire. And when he was discovered, he said, "Such a gift you have, Haven. I hope you thank God for it."

Pal had been traveling for the past week, visiting some of the churches that supported his ministry in Alaska, but he returned the first day in May to assist her with the children's choir. He always came with some little toys or candy for the children if they behaved themselves. She had never seen anyone work and play with the children with such skill. He knew how to use his adult authority, yet with such affirming gentleness that the most challenging boy or girl responded immediately. It was obvious that the choir kids adored him. After each rehearsal, Pal always invited her to sit with him and pray for each child.

"How do you do it, Pal?" she asked him after Wednesday night's rehearsal as they drove back to Misty Mountain.

"Do what?"

"Get the children to love you so much?"

"Oh Haven, those kids love you, too. You're doing a great job with them. And you get better every week. I've been watching you. You're a fast learner."

She shook her head. "It's amazing that someone who's so good with kids won't ever have his own."

"I've got hundreds of kids. Here, and way up north." He waved his arm expansively.

"I know." She smiled at him. "Anyway, thanks for helping me. You've really taught me a lot about how to handle a classroom of kids."

He laughed. "It runs in the family."

"What runs in the family?" She tilted her head at him.

"Having a way with kids. You'll see."

"See what?"

Pal looked at her with an amused expression and hummed off key.

♩ ♪♪♫♪

Dade paid the barber and stepped out of the shop, checking his haircut and newly trimmed beard in the window. He moved stiffly along the mall's shops, looking through the windows, sneering at the gaudy dresses pulled tight over the slender female mannequin bodies. He averted his eyes in distaste whenever a young woman passed, wearing makeup and a short skirt. And his gut tightened when he pictured his beautiful wayward Ruth, driving herself all over the state unescorted, dressing in eye-catching clothing, mingling socially, being seen, being admired, talking freely with other men. It made his head ache whenever he thought about her living away from him, away from his protection and spiritual guidance.

He walked into the Big and Tall store and headed for the suit section. Later, in the dressing room, he checked himself from all angles.

"We'll have to do some altering, Sir," the salesman said as he took some measurements.

"How long will it take?"

"You could have the suit by Saturday."

"That's perfect," he said, flashing his smile.

Sunday morning, as he walked toward West Hills Church, female heads turned in admiration in the parking lot and all the way up the steps leading into the sanctuary. He carried his big black Bible conspicuously against his new, gray suit, smiling and nodding his head in greeting as he passed throngs of worshipers on his way to a pew. Once seated, he closed his eyes and bowed his head, so any overly-friendly sorts would leave him alone. But he gave all of his attention to the pastor's sermon. He also sang with gusto on the closing hymn, his big bass attracting the attention of all worshipers within ten rows.

After the service, he waited in the sanctuary entrance patiently, cradling his Bible as Pastor Jensen greeted and chatted with many of his congregation. When the last of these had finished and exited down the steps, he stepped forward and extended his hand.

"Great sermon, Pastor. I particularly liked that part about the adulterous woman when you said, 'if God made the marriage, then it's worth fighting for.' That is so true, Pastor. My wife and I, we have to really fight for our marriage. And I know the Lord is going to keep us together because I just keep praying for His help and guidance."

Pastor Jensen shook his hand again. "I'm sure God will bless you for fighting to keep your marriage together … Mr.?"

"Collins, George Collins."

"So, Mr. Collins, are you looking for a new church?"

"Oh," he said, "I'm just visiting some family down here. Actually, I live up in Issaquah, … you know, where they have that good Christian school?"

"Really. What a coincidence. One of our own young people just graduated from Northmont College. Lovely, young woman. Really talented musician."

Dade swiped his hand over his mustache to hide a twitch. He raised his eyebrows just slightly. "My wife and I knew a girl there who played the piano and guitar. We got to be good friends. In fact, I went to her recital last May. Hugged her, and told her how well she did. Wonder if it could be the same girl."

"Her name's Haven."

"Oh, yes, Haven Ellingsen. Same girl. Man, was she good on that piano. Whatever happened to her?"

"I'm sorry, but I'm not at liberty to share more about Haven."

Dade put his hands up. "I completely understand. No need to apologize. I'm sure the girl is doing great, wherever she chose to go after graduation."

Pastor Jensen shook Dade's hand again. "Great to have you today. I hope you come back."

Another man approached and the pastor turned to greet him.

Dade smoothed his twitching mustache again. So, the pastor knew where Ruth had gone. Most likely, Ruth's daddy had told the pastor and the church staff not to give out any information about Haven Ellingsen. But was it possible someone else knew details about the girl's whereabouts?

Who would know better than the younger crowd Haven probably hung out with when she came to church?

Dade scanned several groups of college-aged kids still talking on the sidewalk. Two girls and a guy looked about Haven's age. He walked over to them. "Excuse me. Do any of you know Haven Ellingsen?"

The young man perked up immediately. "Yeah, I used to date her."

One of the girls elbowed him and rolled her eyes. "Bryan, one dinner isn't exactly dating."

Bryan flushed. "Well, anyway, I know Haven."

Dade forced his face to appear pleasantly neutral. "Reason I ask is, she loaned me some music CDs a few months ago, at Northmont College, and I never got the chance to give them back. Any of you know where I could mail the CDs?"

The other girl pursed her lips. "Um, you could just send them to her home here in Beaverton. The church has the address."

"But she's not living here anymore," Bryan said. "She moved up north, somewhere in Washington.

The first girl rolled her eyes again. "He already knows she was in Washington. That's where he got the CDs from Haven."

The boy shrugged. "The only thing I know is, I was helping in the church office the other day. We're working on the new directory, and I overheard Pastor talking to the secretary. He said something about Haven and a new job in Cascade Springs but not to put her address in the directory.

Dade nodded, frowning slightly. "I guess I'll have to call the church secretary in the morning. I'm sure they'll be able to give me her address. Thanks anyway."

He walked toward his truck, hiding a smirk. Cascade Springs. A town way up close to the Canadian border.

Once inside his truck, he tossed his Bible over to the passenger seat and gave a fierce whoop of triumph. Opening the glove compartment, he pulled out the newspaper articles about Ruth. He ran his fingers over her photo. For the first time in weeks, happiness spread through his gut. "Did you really think you could outsmart me, Little Girl?"

Chapter Nine

"Where both deliberate, the love is slight;
whoever loved that loved not at first sight?"
Christopher Marlowe

Petter jogged briskly around Mercy Hospital for the third time. Four times around was approximately two miles. It would have to do. His lunch break only lasted half an hour. He had just begun his last lap when he saw the petite woman. At first, she was just a blur of a woman's shape with long, light blonde hair, walking quickly in his direction. He slowed to a walk. As she neared, he took in the way her hair cascaded about her shoulders and back, the blue sweater, the plaid skirt that swayed about her curves, the long boots and the bounce to her step. She was carrying a bouquet of flowers, gaily wrapped, and as their paths grew closer to intersecting, she looked up and met his appraising eyes.

He had seen many beautiful women in his twenty-eight years but it was not entirely her physical beauty that made him catch his breath. She had looked down at her bundle of flowers for a moment, never slowing her pace. When she looked back up at him, her face wore an expression of such joy, such sweetness, and good nature, that he forgot to breathe.

She passed him, and he continued walking, unconscious of his movements or that he was walking away from a woman who had just dazzled him. He stopped and remembered to breathe. When he turned around to look again, she was just entering the main entrance of the hospital.

Beautiful girl. He glanced up at a crow which was boldly eyeing him from its perch on an overhanging tree branch. "I suppose you know who she is."

The bird fluffed its feathers as if in a shrug and went airborne.

He jogged back toward Mercy, went through the automatic sliding doors and looked about. He had moved fast. She had to still be on the main floor. Nei, the girl was too fast. He huffed.

He checked the elevators. One was already down on the main level and the other had gone up to the third floor. He waited for the first elevator door to open. No one came out. He hurried in and pushed the button. Seconds later, he stepped out and wandered the third floor, looking fruitlessly for the lovely young woman.

A nurse approached. "Doctor, can I help you?"

He scanned the hallway one more time. "No, I'm fine." He looked at his watch. There was no more time for searching. "Thanks, Nurse."

A few hours later, though, when his shift ended, the girl was still on his mind.

♩ ♪♪♫♪

When Petter's cell phone chirped, he clicked to accept the call from Pal.

"We've got a new renter in the cabin above Misty Mountain. Really nice girl. She's invited me to have dessert tonight."

"Ya?" He narrowed his eyes even though Pal couldn't see his suspicious expression. Pal had that overly nonchalant tone in his voice that warned Petter his cousin was up to something.

"Well, I thought you might like to come, too. She makes terrific cinnamon rolls."

Hmm. Cinnamon rolls were his favorite, although he didn't permit himself to indulge in desserts too often. On the other hand, Pal had something up his sleeve. Anytime he invited Petter to attend a party or a dinner, Pal always introduced him to another of his religious friends, who just happened to be female a hundred percent of the time.

"I told her we'd be there around seven," Pal informed. "We can have dinner at the lodge and then get some exercise walking up the hill.

"You already told her I'm coming, too?" He had to chuckle in spite of himself. "Pal, your confidence is exasperating."

"Oh, and bring your flashlight."

"You really think we'll be there that long?" Petter hoped his cousin caught the impatience in his voice.

Silence met his question. He sighed. "Okay, but remember, you're not going to try to hook me up with this girl, right?

"Boy, are you arrogant, Petter. Do you honestly think every woman is just waiting to get her hooks in you? You have no idea the kind of girl you're about to meet. She's never even hinted to me about being interested in any man, so just relax."

Probably because no man would be interested in her. Blazes.

Knowing Pal, the girl was some sort of nerdy, religious, holier-than-thou, with thick glasses and a grating voice.

Later that evening, as Petter followed his cousin into the clearing surrounding the girl's cabin, the aroma of coffee and cinnamon rolls greeted his nose. "I'll give her half an hour, that's all," he mumbled. "Just enough time to eat, say thank you and then run for it."

"That's what you think." Pal started to whistle a tune off pitch. He clomped up the porch steps noisily, still whistling, and knocked on the front door.

Petter remained below the steps, fighting an impulse to bolt. The door opened and the light from inside silhouetted a slender form. Pal stepped forward and bent to kiss the young woman on the cheek. When he moved aside Petter caught his first glimpse of the petite girl. Drawn irresistibly, he glided up the steps, feeling as if one wrong move might forever dispel the dreamlike image of the woman. Her light blonde hair cascaded about her shoulders and her dark blue eyes gazed up at him with the same sweet warmth of the other moment outside the hospital. When she smiled, his breath caught, just as it had the other day.

"Haven, I'd like you to meet my cousin, Dr. Petter Eriksen. Petter, this is my friend, Haven Ellingsen."

Suddenly, uncharacteristically shy, he awkwardly extended his hand, engulfing her small one.

Haven stepped back and motioned for them to come in. "Please, make yourselves comfortable. I was just about to take the cinnamon rolls out of the oven."

Pal made himself right at home, settling down onto one of the kitchen chairs. But Petter moved into the living area to examine the artistic touches that had transformed the small cabin. Only recently the place had been the weekend retreat of an occasional religious poet or writer needing a quiet place to think and write. He himself had stayed in the cabin for a couple of weeks before he moved into his apartment in town.

Now, new curtains adorned the front window, framed oil paintings added color to the drab log walls. A woven throw covered a worn spot on the old sofa. Dried herbs and flowers hung from the rafters, scenting the room, and her music and books filled the bookshelves. Off to one corner, draped with a scarf sat her guitar. He recognized Rachmaninoff coming from the CD player. But as he sat to join Pal at the kitchen table, it occurred to him that it was not the decorations, the pleasant aromas or the music, but the young woman's presence that filled the room.

Haven pulled the rolls out of the oven and poured thick icing over them. Then she transferred them to a large plate and set them on the table with the pot of coffee.

They enjoyed the rolls and coffee and when she offered cream and sugar, he politely declined. "No thank you, just black, Haven." It felt strangely wonderful to say her name and to look into her eyes at the same time.

"The doctor's not into anything fancy, Haven," Pal said. "He drinks his coffee and tea black, no salt or pepper on his steak, no sugar on his oatmeal, no fancy clothes or car."

"Now that you tell me that, it seems to make sense."

Petter's body tingled when the woman's gaze swept over his hair, examined his face, paused at his wrinkled collar and finally lowered to his scuffed shoes. She smiled.

"What makes sense?" he asked, pretending to be mystified.

He was no movie star type and he hoped Haven wasn't the kind of girl who cared that he didn't give much thought to the state of his clothing or his thick mop of hair.

She faced him and spoke in a quiet, sincere voice. "Dr. Eriksen, you seem to be a very unadorned person: no rings on your fingers, no gold chain around your neck, no fancy watch. Just you and you alone. And that seems to be quite enough."

If he pretended to look like he didn't comprehend, maybe she'd go on.

"No sugar in your coffee, no three-hundred-dollar haircut, and no designer clothing to say you're something other than who you are."

Petter glanced at Pal who was smiling in amusement. "Is that good? I'm not quite sure if I've been complimented or insulted."

Haven stood up to put their plates in the sink. "That's very good, Doctor."

And you're very good, too, Haven. Good to look at and good to listen to.

Haven got up and went into the living area. "Bring your coffee and come and tell me about your work at Mercy Hospital. It is Mercy Hospital, right? I think I saw you the other day, jogging."

They followed her and seated themselves on the sofa. Haven sank into the old upholstered chair across from them, drew her legs up and tucked them under. "Pal's been telling me all about his work in Alaska, but he didn't tell me he had a cousin in the States. I'm curious how you wound up in this area, too."

"There's not too much to tell," Petter said. "I was offered a good scholarship at the University of Washington and decided to take it."

Pal jumped in. "Petter's being way too modest. He graduated first in his class and had his pick of teaching schools. Why he's so smart he—"

"Okay, Pal, I can take it from here." *Blazes!* His cousin was going to make the girl think he was a conceited, arrogant jerk. "I started studying in Oslo, then transferred to Seattle. They must've liked me because I got accepted to the medical school there afterward."

Pal snorted. "Liked you?" He turned to Haven. "They liked him so much he also got invited to do his residency there. And also—"

"The hospital and I were a good fit." Petter turned and raised one eyebrow at Pal, hoping his cousin caught his hint to stop interrupting. "I've been at Mercy for almost a year now."

Haven shook her head. "Aren't specialists supposed to be pushing forty by the time they start their practices? Maybe I'm a bad judge of age, but you don't look more than thirty."

Petter shot Pal another warning glance before he answered. "Let's just say I got a head start in college. So, tell me about yourself. Are you new to Cascade Springs?"

She nodded. "I just graduated from college last month and I was looking for a job where I could work with kids and use my music a little."

"But you work at Maggie's Flowers."

"She only works at Maggie's for extra income." Pal leaned toward him with an enthusiastic thrust of his head. "And don't just take that *using my music a little* for the complete answer, Brother. She's performed all over the Northwest. I think we should get the Cascade Springs Gazette to write a piece on her and—"

Haven's eyebrows flew upward into a panicked expression, and her hands gripped her thighs. "Pal, I-I don't need, uh, please don't—"

Pal immediately shut his mouth.

An awkward silence followed. What in blazes had Pal said to make her react that way?

Pal added in a soft tone, "I just meant that you're being very humble about your music and all."

Haven's face relaxed.

"Haven's a musician, I mean, a real musician. You should hear her play."

"I saw the guitar over there," Petter said. "Is that what you play?" He didn't even try to hide his interest in her.

"Oh, she plays guitar. But you should hear her play the piano," Pal interrupted again. "She played some Grieg the other night and—"

Petter swiveled and put his hand over Pal's mouth. "Would you let her speak?" Petter went over to the guitar, lifted it and carried it over to her. "Play something for me, Haven. I love guitar. I even play a little."

"Little is right," Pal smirked.

"What would you like to hear, Doctor?" Her eyes searched his, making him feel shy again.

"Something I've never heard before."

"Hmm." She looked off for a moment, then set her fingers on the strings and began to play. He sat back, utterly charmed by the music and her skill. Her small hands moved up and down the neck of the guitar like a virtuoso. When she was done he reached over to pluck one of the strings.

"Here," she proffered the instrument, "would you like to play?"

He put his hands up. "Not after hearing you play. What was that piece?"

"That was a 'Sarabande' from the Renaissance period. I was pretty sure you wouldn't have heard it before."

"Where did you learn to play like that?"

"I have a good teacher. More coffee?"

"Haven," Pal stood up. "I think we should be getting home. It's almost nine and Petter's got to be at work really early in the morning."

Petter glared up at his cousin, then sighed when he glanced at his watch. Haven was probably getting tired, too. He wanted to ask her if she'd be working at Maggie's Flowers tomorrow, but that might look like he was prying.

Haven stood up at the same time he did. They bumped into each other and she lost her balance. He reached out quickly to steady her. She laughed, and he couldn't take his eyes off of her.

"Come on, Petter. It's way past your bedtime."

He turned and walked reluctantly toward the front door.

Haven followed them outside and stood on the porch. The light from inside silhouetted her form again. Pal kissed her on the cheek and whispered a thank you.

Pal had a knack for getting to know people quickly. Up until now, it had never bothered Petter that he didn't have the same knack. He stepped off the porch and called, "Thanks for dessert, Haven. I really enjoyed meeting you."

They turned on their flashlights and headed down the dirt road and back to the lodge. When they were out of earshot, Pal turned to him with a smirk. "You seemed pretty mesmerized by Haven. Even though she's one of those religious girls you hate to talk to."

Pal got a jab in the ribs for that.

"Someone like Haven could make me decide not to be a bachelor anymore."

"That's just what I thought." Pal thrust his chin upward the way he always did when he'd won an argument with Petter.

"But I can take it from here, Pal."

Pal shrugged. "I was just getting the ball rolling."

"I appreciate it."

"You're welcome."

♩ ♪♪♫♪

Pal lounged on the leather sofa, sipping his coffee, pretending to read a book. Haven sat at the grand piano in the lodge great room, practicing some of the children's choir music. It had been two nights since his visit to her cabin and still, she had not mentioned one word about his magnificent cousin. He'd seen her the next day and hinted around the subject. But Haven, in a hurry to drive to Maggie's, had only commented about next Wednesday's practice with the junior choir and asked if he would be helping her.

He set his coffee mug down and dropped the book onto the floor loudly enough to get her attention. Haven stopped playing and looked over the music stand at him.

"Well?" He said.

"Well, what?" She raised her eyebrows and smiled.

"What did you think of the doctor? Was he what you were

expecting?"

"Oh, I've seen him lots of times when I've been delivering flowers at the hospital. And I kind of figured that he would be your friend." She laughed when his jaw dropped. "The first day I got here I was in Maggie's Flowers filling out my employment application and he came in to order flowers. Maggie told me he was the new emergency doctor at Mercy Also, you mentioned that your friend likes to run. He was out jogging the other day outside the hospital and I went right by him. I smiled at him because I figured he was the doctor you were trying to have me meet at the cafeteria."

Pal's face turned hot. Had he been that obvious? "I'm sorry, Haven. I wasn't trying to be sneaky. It's just that Petter doesn't know what's good for him."

Haven came around the piano with a puzzled expression and sat in one of the wingback chairs. "What do you mean, 'good for him'?"

Pal looked down, shaking his head. It wasn't going to be easy to explain about Petter, how he could be such a great guy, but difficult and edgy at the same time. "The man has spent his whole life learning and researching about material things. You know … biology, diseases, chemistry … that kind of stuff.

"He was raised by Christian parents, and they didn't just talk; they lived out their faith. Before Petter decided to become a scientist, he had talked about being a minister. He had a real faith."

He swung his legs around to face Haven. "Petter had a wonderful childhood. I know, I was there. We were all close, my parents and his parents and all of the children. We graduated from high school the same year. I was eighteen and he was only fourteen. He started at the university all fired up to become the next great research scientist. But something happened a little later. And he started to question his faith. Now he just says that since it's impossible to know anything beyond the mere physical, he's content to spend his time working on just that.

"But he isn't content." He looked at Haven, wishing he could transport his love and concern for Petter directly into her heart. "He struggles with guilt and blames God for some really bad things. And that's where you come in, my friend." He tapped the back of her hand and met her eyes. "He needs to be surrounded by people who can help him."

Haven tilted her head and frowned. "But what can I do, Pal? I hardly know him. And he's so smart and educated. Even if we got to be friends, why would he listen to someone like me? Who am I?"

"Who am I?" Pal repeated her words. "You want to know what impresses a man? You have so much going for you: your looks, your talent, your sweet personality. And even with all that, you spent the entire evening listening to Petter, not even trying to talk about yourself. It made him even more fascinated with you."

"He was?" She looked at him in amazement.

"Absolutely. And he asked me what you thought of him." Petter had never, ever done that before.

She shook her head. "That's hard to believe."

"So, would you consider seeing him again?"

Haven visibly stiffened. *Had he said too much, too soon?*

"I ... I've been thinking about something ... I've wanted to tell you," she said, drawing out her words as if she needed time to judge them before letting them form on her lips. "I've been thinking about it for a long time. But I believe I've found a friend I can trust." She hunched over, looking small and frightened.

"What's wrong, Haven? Did I upset you?" He had moved too fast, that was clear. But a girl like Haven was worth the risk. For Petter's sake.

"Pal," she whispered. "I need to tell you some things I've never told anyone—not even my father—about my experience in the wilderness. And when I'm through, maybe you can help me sort out my feelings about men. I think I can trust you with this."

She moved from her chair and sat down next to him on the couch. She began in a quiet voice to paint a graphic picture of her betrayal at the hands of a man she thought she could trust, of the horror of being kidnapped by Dade, of her life in the dark cabin, of Mama and the children, the indoctrination and the abuse and Dade's plan for her. She told him that she had decided, days earlier, on giving him only the minimum amount of details. But, after hearing him talk about Petter with such concern, she felt that he could be trusted to hear her story. She described that day at her small hidden cabin in the woods and of Dade's threat to continue to stalk her. She had begun quietly, but as she neared the end of her story, she wept. He put his arms around her and held her securely.

"When I first saw the doctor, so close, at my cabin, I almost panicked. He's so tall and strong looking, like Dade" She looked up at him with wide eyes as if remembering that other man. "When he walked through the cabin door, it brought me back to my being imprisoned by Dade in his cabin. I know, it's irrational."

He started to say something but hesitated. "Did Dade ... hurt you?" He didn't know how to phrase his question. His arm tightened around her shoulder. Haven shuddered, and he knew she understood his question.

"No. Fortunately for me he's got some strange ideas about morality. And one of them is the notion that we couldn't be totally married until he'd built and furnished a place just for us. Jesse helped me get away just in time."

He released the breath he'd been holding. Still, he had to work to hide the outrage that stirred in his soul. "I'm sorry. I had no idea what you were going through."

"It's okay." She patted his arm. "It's something I need to start getting over. Dade is a monster, but the doctor is, well …"

"He's a good man, a very good man, Haven. No, I'll go even farther—he's a great man. Not only is he incredibly smart, but he cares deeply about people and their suffering. It's what makes him such a good doctor. And he has the capacity to love like I've never seen. Maybe that's what drove him away from God."

She wiped her eyes. "Drove him away? How?"

"That's something he can share with you when you get to know him better, little Karita."

Chapter Ten

*"No cord nor cable can so forcibly draw, or hold so fast,
as love can do with a twined thread."*
Robert Burton

May 14, Journal Entry #131

I've never known a man like Petter. He's completely logical and scientific, just the way you'd expect a doctor to be. But then, he's warm and funny and kind. I'm almost afraid to get to know him better. He's the kind of man who could sweep my heart away. Do I want that, knowing I might have to move quickly if Dade finds out where I am?

♩ ♪♪♫♪

Almost a week passed, and Haven had not had a single opportunity to see the doctor again. Pal explained that the doctor had been dividing his time between his hours in the ER and attending a medical seminar in the evenings.

Maggie had suddenly announced that due to her mother's illness, she would be closing down the business and moving to Phoenix, leaving Haven to search the want ads, trying to find another morning part-time job.

Pal had been away visiting and speaking at churches in California, promising her he would be back on her last day at Maggie's.

She had stayed at Maggie's shop during her final afternoon and into the early evening, helping to box up the last remaining items for the rental truck. As they packed, they watched the sky darken and wind lash the trees. Flashes of lightning lit up the horizon. Just as Maggie shut the truck's back and pulled down the latch, the rain and thunder began in earnest. Haven hugged Maggie and helped her climb into the truck's cab. The big engine roared to life.

"You drive carefully. If it gets bad, be sure and pull into a motel for the night."

"I will." Maggie waved and blew a kiss. The rental truck pulled out of the parking lot.

Haven buttoned the top button of her corduroy jacket and hurried for her own car. She climbed in and turned the key in the ignition. Nothing. She groaned and looked down the road. Maggie's truck was long gone. She pulled out her cell phone and groaned when she saw the battery had totally depleted.

The hospital was just down the road but she didn't know anyone there except the doctor, and he was probably still doing his seminar. She hated to run to the hospital and call Erik to ask him to come pick her up. He didn't see too well at night.

Oh well, if she walked fast she could be at the lodge in an hour and a half.

The storm would probably blow over quickly. She popped the trunk lid, ran around back, and snatched her rain poncho from her box of road emergency supplies. She slipped it over her head and locked her car. The wind shoved her from behind as she walked briskly east on Sea View Way. Fog shrouded the way. She'd have to stay way over to the far side of the highway's shoulder, just in case some driver didn't see the reflective tape on the back of her poncho.

♩ ♪♪♫♪

Petter jogged around the hospital for the fifth time and decided to head home. The lightning was a hazard too close to ignore and the rain was making things slippery. Wearing his track pants topped with a sweatshirt and a windbreaker, he perspired slightly despite the cool breeze. He stopped to glance down the street at Maggie's Flowers. Why weren't the lights on in the little shop? Then he saw a young woman walking hurriedly away from store. It took him a few seconds to recognize Haven and when he did, he called out to her.

She didn't hear him and continued her quick pace. He hurried after her. Why would Haven be walking in the dark all by herself? A semi, coming from the opposite direction slowed and signaled its intent to make a left turn. He waited impatiently while the big truck slowly negotiated its turn onto the small road in front of him. After it had passed Haven was nowhere to be seen. He searched the road, looking right and left in the dim light. Then he spied her again, taking the shortcut under the highway. This way would lead her onto a narrow, shoulder-less road, bordered by woods and, in some places, steep embankments. She was headed in the direction of Misty Mountain. Why wasn't she driving her car? He started to jog, rapidly closing the gap between them.

Farther up, a car's lights emerged from the fog and approached. Hopefully, the driver could see both of them walking along the narrow shoulder. He blinked away the rain that smeared his vision.

By now, most drivers would have moved over to give a pedestrian a wide berth. This one stuck to Haven's side of the road moving much too fast for the weather. *Slow down, you idiot driver. I don't want to see you in the ER.* Then, as the car neared, it began to slide toward the left embankment. The driver must have slammed on his brakes in order to gain control. That sent the car into a tailspin on the rain-drenched road. The vehicle hit a long track of water on the road and hydroplaned straight for Haven. Her silhouette, caught in the glare of the oncoming car, froze. He saw her indecision. Her head jerked right and left. There was nowhere to run. *No! Not again.* Adrenaline surged through his torso. He'd never reach her in time. The vehicle was nearly upon her.

He took a giant breath and yelled, "Jump!"

Haven's body moved as if in a series of snapshots. Her form crouched and tensed then exploded off the ground. She shot upward as if from a diving board, soared in a leftward arc, her silhouette disappearing in the glare of the oncoming headlights.

A split second later, the car skidded through the spot where Haven had been, regained control and passed. Haven was nowhere in sight.

Petter sprinted up to the spot where he had last seen her. Blood poured back into his face. At least she was not smashed on the road. "Haven!" he yelled. Listened. He heard nothing but the wind and rain hissing through the cedars. "Haven," he tried again.

Scanning the embankment, he saw something move. Reflective stripes gleamed near the bottom of the embankment. He clambered down, heedless of the danger but taking pains not to dislodge anything that might roll and endanger Haven. As he approached, his heart in his throat, she moved her legs.

"Haven … Miss Ellingsen." When he reached her, he crouched down and called her name again. She gazed straight up at the sky, unblinking and silent.

"Haven." He unzipped his windbreaker, reached into his sweatshirt pocket and drew out a small flashlight. When he shone the light into her eyes, she did not react. Then her eyes focused and she seemed to see him for the first time. She moaned and tried to sit up, but he held her down.

"Don't get up, Haven." He quickly assessed her condition. "Please don't move. Just answer my questions and let me take a look at you." He checked her head and neck for any signs of injury.

"I-I think I'm okay," she said, trying to help him. "I landed on my feet but then I rolled and twisted my knee and rammed my shoulder and side."

But he wasn't going to take her word for it until he was satisfied that her head and spine were uninjured. He gently probed her abdomen. "Why didn't you answer me when I first called you? Did you black out?" He shone his flashlight into her eyes and looked carefully.

"I didn't answer because I was trying to *keep* from blacking out. My knee hurts terribly. And my shoulder … oh, it feels like it's broken."

She took tiny little gasps of air and cried out when he prodded her side.

Could be broken or cracked ribs. A punctured lung. "We've got to get you to the hospital and assess things."

She was shivering, and her hair was drenched. He pulled off his windbreaker and covered her. Then he took out his cell phone and dialed 911.

"Operator, I'm a doctor at Mercy Hospital. I've got a patient – a pedestrian—out here on the corner of Northwest Highway and Hanover Peak Road. Possible internal injuries from a fall. Need an ambulance ASAP."

"Hang in there, Haven. The ambulance will be here in a couple of minutes." He shone the small light in her eyes again but didn't see any ominous changes.

Within seconds, he heard sirens. "I'll be right back. Don't move."

Haven nodded and showed him a brave smile.

She'd sprained her knee and had a hairline fracture in her left clavicle. Thankfully, her ribs were unbroken and her lungs looked fine. He hadn't believed her when she'd said she had not hit her head. How does one fall down a steep incline and not sustain some spine or cranial injuries? But a CT scan and x-rays had shown no other areas of injury. He'd ordered some pain meds, packed her knee with ice, and splinted her left arm.

"I called Uncle Erik to let him know you'll be staying in the lodge for the next few days until you no longer need to take pain meds."

He ran back to his apartment to collect his car and throw a

change of clothes into a duffle. An hour later, as he transported Haven to the lodge, he glanced over at her. His breath caught when he found her staring at him with large, wondering eyes.

What an awful way to spend the evening with the girl he'd decided would be his future wife. How many times had he wanted to drive to her little cabin and knock on her door? But he hadn't been able to think of a plausible excuse for visiting her. She'd see through any lame pick up line, and he'd feel like a fool. He didn't want to blow it, not with this woman. How many chances does a guy get to convince a woman he's the right man for her? So, even though this wasn't the ideal way to spend an evening, maybe this was his only chance.

"Are you still with me?"

"Yes. Getting a bit foggy headed, though."

"That's good. Those meds will help you get a long, comfortable sleep." He took the turn to Misty Mountain and slowed so that the gravel drive didn't jar her.

When he pulled his car up to the lodge, Erik and Pal were both waiting on the porch. He carried her up the steps, mindful of her sling.

"Take her upstairs, first door on your left," Erik instructed.

Pal ran ahead to pull back the covers. Petter carefully placed her on the bed, adjusted the pillows for her head and knee, and covered her with the blankets. He was about to leave to go get some more ice for her leg when Haven looked up at him. "Sorry to be so much trouble, Doctor," she slurred. Then her eyes closed.

Looking at her slender form, a wave of distant memories washed dread into his gut. What if he hadn't been there to rescue her? What if she'd fallen down the embankment and lain there until she went into shock? He shuddered and tried to shake the picture of her crumpled body lying at the bottom of the embankment. The picture was eerily similar to another that he would never forget. "Not this time … not this time," he whispered. He bent over her and gently smoothed back her hair, gazing at her in a way that he wouldn't have if her eyes had been open. He noticed the old scar on her forehead for the first time. Where had she gotten that?

Pal cleared his throat.

Petter jerked up. How long had his cousin been standing at the door? "I'll go get some more ice for her knee. You can go back to bed, Pal. I'll sleep on the couch downstairs so I can check on her during the night." He brushed past Pal.

♩ ♪♪♫♪

She needed to sleep and keep sleeping. Whatever pain meds the doctor had prescribed, they were keeping her from worrying about her swollen knee. Petter was sitting nearby, watching her while he typed medical notes on his laptop. "It's not hard to plan a wedding," he said. "But first you have to get your marriage to Dade annulled."

"What?" She threw the covers back and jumped out of bed. "I'm not married to Dade."

Petter gave her a look like she was a naughty child. "Of course, you are. He told me."

A woodpecker flew down onto her shoulder and started pecking on her swollen knee. It sounded like her knee was made of hard wood. "Stop it. Go away." She swatted at the bird, but it wouldn't fly away. It kept knocking.

"Haven?"

Her eyes opened. More knocking brought her to full wakefulness

"Haven, can I come in?"

"Y-yes. Just a minute." She pulled her covers closer and winced as she tried to sit up. "Come in."

The bedroom door eased open, and Pal stepped in. "I didn't mean to wake you. I can come back."

No, please stay." She sat up some more. "You rescued me from a giant woodpecker."

"Really" He grinned as he looked behind the door and made a motion to peek under the bed. "Having bad dreams?"

"I think my knee is reminding me I need another pain pill."

Pal walked over to her nightstand, poured a glass of water, and handed it to her along with her bottle of medicine. "Your car is all fixed."

"Wow, that was fast. What was wrong with it?"

"Just the battery, Karita. I replaced it and it runs fine now."

"Thank you so much, Pal. I promise I'll pay you back."

"Well, first you need another job. Which brings me to my second announcement. How would you like to work right here in the lodge?"

Her brows shot up, as did her mood. "Work here?" She'd prayed for a part-time job, but this was even better than she'd imagined.

There was another knock at the door and Erik stepped in as if he'd been waiting for the perfect moment. "We could really use your help, Haven. That is, when you get back on your feet."

She tried to sit all the way up but winced at the pain. "But what would I do?"

Erik sat down on the upholstered chair by the bed. "Our second cook just gave her notice a couple of days ago and we really need someone who knows her way around the kitchen. Would you be interested?"

"But I have my work at the church. How would I do both jobs?"

Erik's sweet eyes crinkled. "We could work with your schedule. We need someone to do the prep work and some baking … you know, the breads, the desserts, that kind of thing. Oh, and also, I'd want you to run some errands in town and maybe help me with the books sometimes."

She gave him a small, cautious smile. She wasn't used to being on the receiving end of charity. "Are you sure you're not just taking pity on a poor helpless cripple?"

Erik laughed. "If you accept my job offer, you won't just be sitting around doing nothing."

"And don't let that sweet expression fool you," Pal said with a twinkle in his eyes. "He'll have you earning every penny you make."

"Then I accept, Mr. Eriksen. And thank you very much. I'll work hard for you."

Erik reached over and patted her hand. "I'm sure you will. I'm a good judge of character and I've had my eye on you ever since you moved here."

"You look tired," Pal said. "We'll leave you to rest."

The two men crept out of the room. She settled back into her pillow and glanced down at her elevated leg. She couldn't wait to get back on her feet

♩ ♪♪♫♪

After Petter's shift, he hurried to drive back to Misty Mountain. Relieved to find Haven sitting up, reading, he said, "You look much better. Do you mind if I check you over?" He came over and bent to take a look at her shoulder. "I called your father. I thought he should know what happened to you and how you're doing."

"My father? H-how did you know? How did you get his number?" Her eyebrows slanted with worry.

"I have my sources. He was all set to drive up and see you, but I told him you're resting and that you'd call him tomorrow." *Why did she look so concerned?* "Does it upset you that I called him?"

Haven's eyes clouded. "It's just that I don't want t-to give him anymore to worry about. I gave him a lot of grief in the past, and he doesn't need any more from me."

She pressed her lips into a flat line as if she was afraid her emotions would get the best of her. He'd have to talk to her again when she was back on her feet, and less emotionally vulnerable. There had to be more to this than just memories of teenage angst. "You sure don't seem like the type of young lady who'd have been difficult."

"But I was, Doctor. Very difficult."

He met her eyes and was surprised by the intensity of pain in their blue depths. "Well," he said gently, trying to soothe her, "it's obvious by the way your father talked, that he adores you."

Haven dropped her gaze and fixed them on his forearms as he lifted the covers to examine her swollen knee. "I'm s-sorry for getting emotional, Dr. Eriksen. I … I … just love my father very much."

He waited for her to continue, but that was all the explanation she would give. "So, what were you doing walking at night in a storm all by yourself? It's a good thing it was me following you and not some big bad guy."

Her brows contracted. "My car broke down and so did my phone. I didn't know who I could call so I decided to walk back home."

"That's over six miles. And in this weather." He clucked his tongue. "Why didn't you come over to the hospital?"

"Look, it's hard to explain. I thought you were still taking that seminar, and I didn't know anyone else at the hospital. And anyway, six miles isn't that far."

"Hmm. Maybe not in the day and in good weather."

"Okay, I'm a dummy."

"I doubt that."

He folded his arms and studied her face. "What I can't figure out is you said you landed on your feet. How did you do that? By the way you jumped to get away from that car last night, it looked like you should have landed on your head."

The troubled expression melted from Haven's face and she smiled. "I did a somersault.

What in blazes? "A somersault?" He tilted his head.

"It would have been perfect, except I had to jump so fast that I gave it too much power and I couldn't stick it."

"You sound like a gymnast." The woman was full of surprises.

She nodded, brushing her hair away from her face. "I took six years of gymnastics but I never thought it'd come in handy just taking a walk in the rain."

He chuckled. "So that explains it. A gymnast. Well, I guess you're stronger than you look." *And so beautiful.* He shook his head slowly. "Amazing. I've never seen anything like that. From where I was standing it looked like you had jumped off a trampoline."

He repositioned her pillows and helped her up to a semi-recline. Then he pulled the covers back over her. "You're full of surprises, Karita."

"You're the second person to call me that. What is a Karita?"

"Karita is a Norwegian girl's name. It means 'dear.' My mother had a doll named Karita. Part of a collection." He looked down at his feet with a secret smile before adding, "A little Scandinavian doll with big blue eyes and a very pretty face." His gaze returned to hers. You look just like a Karita. Maybe someday you'll see my mother's doll collection."

He sat down on the upholstered chair and hurried on before she could think about what he had just said. "So, I hear you're going to be working here part-time. That's great. You'll love my uncle. He's just about one of the nicest guys in the whole world."

"Pal said he is a real taskmaster."

He grinned. "Nei. He's just kidding you. Everyone who works for Uncle Erik loves him."

"That's a relief. I mean, I'm ready to work hard for Mr. Eriksen, but I wouldn't want to disappoint him."

"You won't."

"No?"

He reached over and touched her arm. "Uncle Erik never makes a bad hire. And Pal, well, he reads people. So, I'd say you're definitely in the right place."

She nodded and looked thoughtful. Silence followed. Then she pushed herself up a little more and drew the covers with her. "I've been thinking about something, Doctor. How come you were following me last night?"

"Simple." He gave her his most disarming smile. "I was out running and I saw you walking away from Maggie's. And I thought, now why is that girl walking away from Maggie's without her car, and in this weather? So, I followed you. I even called out to you, but you must not have heard me." He sat back and eyed her curiously. "Apparently, you're not afraid to be alone in the dark."

Haven turned her head toward the window. "I got used to the dark a long time ago."

Chapter Eleven

*"Always be prepared to give an answer to everyone
who asks you to give the reason for the hope that you have."*
1 Peter 3:15

Haven lifted the skillet from the shelf above the cabin's kitchen stove.

Thankfully, Doctor Eriksen's assessment of the job at Misty Mountain was more correct than Pal's had been. Once Haven had gone through Mrs. Graham's week-long training, she felt thoroughly acquainted with big kitchen, and institutional cooking and cleaning. Her shoulder was still sore but she could move her arm now and even lift light pots and serving dishes. Erik had taken her into town several times to show her the shops he used and the supplies he usually needed as well as how to fill out the purchase orders.

May was halfway over but even so, she still needed to stoke her cabin's wood burning stove each morning with the split logs Petter had stacked just outside her front door. He had looked in on her several times since helping her move back to her cabin.

Her heart beat faster when she looked out her front window and saw the handsome doctor walking towards her cabin. Trying not to appear eager, she waited until he knocked, then counted off five seconds before opening her door. He was dressed comfortably in a long-sleeved shirt, jeans and hiking boots.

"Are you feeling up to a short walk?" He leaned his elbow against the doorjamb and his gaze roamed the interior of the cabin before coming to rest on her again.

She looked up at his thoughtful and intelligent face. How could she have ever feared that he was anything like Dade? He had been so kind and caring during her convalescence at the lodge. "Which trail were you thinking about? Most of the ones I've been on are pretty steep."

"There's one that crosses the stream and ends up close to the gas station on the state highway. I thought we could stop off there and get a soda."

"Sounds great!" Haven sat down on the sofa to put on her boots while Petter waited at the door.

They left the clearing, stayed on the gravel road, and crossed the wood bridge. They continued down the road toward the lodge until a path exited off to the right. The trail narrowed, and Petter led the way. He slowed as they climbed a ridge.

"How's your knee feeling?"

She took the incline slowly. "Not bad. Give me another week, and I think I'll be good as new."

As they crested the ridge, the trail widened, then descended into a small grassy valley dotted with rhododendrons, tangles of blackberry bushes and evergreens. She wandered toward the edge of the clearing and broke off a packet of pine needles from a nearby tree. When she took a deep breath, she thrilled to the fragrance of moist earth and pine and cedar. She bent her head back to study the hazy beams of sunlight filtering through the tops of the boughs. Above her, a woodpecker scratched and knocked. Bits of bark and debris flew in all directions under the bird's onslaught. She laughed at the red-headed bird and turned toward Petter to point it out.

His arms were folded across his broad chest as he studied her. "It's a funny thing about you."

So like a doctor. His voice had taken on an analytical tone as if he were trying to come up with a medical diagnosis for a mysterious condition.

"You seem so at home here in these woods. But I'm thinking that you'd probably look just as comfortable in a tiara and a ball gown and little glass slippers."

She laughed and tossed her hair back over her shoulder. "Funny you should say that. I often feel as if I'm straddling two worlds: this one and the one I left behind."

He came closer. "What did you leave behind?"

"Oh, the world of musicians and stage halls and crowds and backstage butterflies in your stomach. It seems like a distant memory now."

"Why did you leave that world?" He took another step toward her.

She had crushed some of the pine needles between her fingers and brought them up to her face to savor their fragrance. It gave her time to think. "I needed to make a change, to get away from …" She was almost ready to tell him, but his eyes studied her with a kind of tender expression she couldn't name. What if she told him and it broke the spell? What if he thought less of her?

"Sometimes," she tried again, "you just need to go another direction for a while, just to experience something else. Like meeting you. I've never hung out with any medical people. My whole world was my faith and my music."

Oh, if only he would come even closer. Press her to tell him about her past. Be outraged at her story, as Pal had been. Offer to help her. Petter's kindness, his intellect, and his interest attracted her. A doctor, of all people, had to understand about tragedy. About illness. He'd have to have witnessed the effects of abuse and emotional trauma.

But what if he only pitied her, as he would one of his patients? The thought stung her pride. No, she wouldn't share her story.

She flung the tiny spray of pine needles over her shoulder and stuck her hands inside her pockets. "I thought it would be awful leaving performing. But it hasn't been bad at all. In fact, it's been wonderful. I'm helping your uncle and teaching children and I've met people I'd never have known otherwise."

The doctor was close enough now to touch her. He reached out, and for one deliciously unnerving second, she thought he was going to pull her to him and kiss her. But he put his fingers on her scar, instead. She closed her eyes when he traced the outline of the white thread that began on her forehead and disappeared into her hair.

"How did you get this scar?"

She opened her eyes. A sinking sensation dragged at her breathing. He saw her only as a doctor his patient. She expelled the breath she'd been holding. "I got hit with something big and heavy."

Petter dropped his hand. "Let me help you down the hill." He sounded disappointed, too. He turned toward the path but held out his arm. "Hold on to me, it's steep from here to the river."

Once they crossed the footbridge it was only another quarter of a mile before they reached the gas station. Petter bought some sodas and they sat on a bench in the shade of the building's eaves sipping their drinks.

She looked down at the doctor's hands, remembering the night of her accident. He had nice hands. Big, but well-formed. Not big sausage-like fingers, or thin, spindly fingers. They were just right: strong but skilled. And gentle. The same hands that attended her in the Emergency Department, then cradled her as he carried her into the lodge.

He was gazing off down the road, watching the traffic pass by. He startled her when he spoke, still looking away. "You said your old world was your faith and your music. Is your faith just part of that old world or have you brought that with you?" He turned to face her. The tone of his voice had chilled when he mentioned her faith.

"The way you say 'faith,' you make it sound like it's just another suitcase or article of clothing."

"Isn't it?" He raised his eyebrows and she could have sworn that his upper lip raised slightly into a sneer.

"I could as soon cut out my heart or my liver than live without my faith."

"What? You're going to equate the value of your life with a mere superstition?"

"Absolutely," she said. "It's far more than superstition." She turned to face him. "God is not Someone you can see. But you don't have to see the wind to know it exists. You see the evidence of its presence. You see the leaves flutter and hear its sound and you know that it is the wind."

"Oh, I don't have trouble believing in God." He shrugged. "I just don't have the same high regard for Him."

And there it was, just as Pal had told her. Petter was angry at God. Why, she'd have to find out later. She pondered for a moment, trying to frame another thought. "You're a medical man, a scientist," she said softly and with respect. "You've studied the human body through and through. Now, I don't know much, having only taken biology and chemistry and physiology in high school, but I do remember that the human cell is incredibly intricate, all of its parts cooperating so that it functions successfully. That is evidence of a God who cares."

Petter took another sip of his soda. "I've yet to see evidence of God's concern. When I was younger I used to believe as you do. But He let my little sister die in a horrible car accident. I prayed and pleaded to this 'caring' God to save her. She was the sweetest, most lovely creature I've ever known. But she died. And then I took a look around and I saw a lot of other tragedies happening. If God cares, why does He allow it?"

He turned toward her. "You're young and you've been spared some of life's more gruesome aspects. I hope you never have to see the things I've seen." He crunched his empty soda can and tossed it into a bin on the other side of the porch. "I guess my evidence is different from yours."

A silence simmered for a few seconds before he spoke again. "Come on, let's get you back to your place."

She avoided his gaze and struggled to restrain her tongue. Someday, she would share her own "gruesome aspects." Now was not the time.

They left the parking lot and began their walk back up the county road.

♩ ♪♪♫♪

Dade drove east on the state highway, tired and frustrated from another day of careful inquiries and fruitless searches in businesses around Cascade Springs. So far, none of the churches he'd called employed a Haven Ellingsen. But there were tons of churches in the area he hadn't yet checked on. And anyway, it was possible she had changed her name. He'd spent the day checking with local arts associations and theater groups. He had one more lead to check before he gave up for the day. Just as he was approaching a gas station he saw a tall man and a blonde girl walking on the side of the road. He slammed on his brakes. Another vehicle just missed rear-ending his truck. The driver honked and shouted angrily at him. Dade gunned his engine and pulled crazily into the gas station parking lot, tires squealing as he hurried to turn around. When he drove back onto the road, facing the direction he had just come, the man and the girl were no longer in sight. He pulled over, shut the motor, and jumped out of his truck.

It may not have been her. Ruth wasn't the only pretty blonde girl in the world, or even in Cascade Springs. He glanced up the road. Maybe the man and the girl hadn't even walked this far. Maybe they were heading for that farmhouse across the road. He'd just sit outside and watch the house for a while. And if that didn't turn up anything he'd go back into town and get some supper.

He had to work the next few days. Couldn't live on air. But he'd be back after he collected his next paycheck. He needed to pay a visit to Fiona. He sighed. Sometimes, it was almost stressful having to keep Fiona happy, fed, and ignorant of his life. You never knew when a girl so eager to please as Fiona would come in handy. But once he had Ruth back, he could dispense with Fiona.

♩ ♪♪♫♪

Haven didn't see the doctor for three days and she was beginning to think their conversation at the gas station had discouraged him from continuing a friendship with her. It shouldn't have upset her. She wasn't ready for any kind of romantic relationship with a man.

She had just finished a morning's prep work in the lodge kitchen, wiped down the counters with disinfectant and rinsed her hands, when Pal sauntered in. He poured himself his usual mug of strong coffee, plopped down onto one of the kitchen chairs, and finger-combed his curly, brown hair off of his face.

"I thought I heard you moving around upstairs."

"Upstairs?" She grabbed a paper towel to dry her hands and smiled at him curiously.

"I was working out down in the basement."

"Oh." She wanted to ask, but if she mentioned Petter he'd know she was interested in him, and she wasn't sure she was ready to admit it, even to Pal.

Pal appeared to read her thoughts. "And no, I haven't seen the

Doc. Haven't talked to him lately either."

He waved her over to the other chair. "What's wrong, Karita? Did you two have a fight or something?"

She sat down and shook her head. "I don't think so. But we were talking, and I said some things about God. I hope I didn't scare him away."

She disappeared into her head for a minute while she tried to recall all that she'd said to Petter. No, she hadn't said anything she regretted. "I told him how important my faith was to me, and then he said God let his sister die."

"Did he tell you the whole story?"

"No, he just said that I was young and hadn't seen a lot of suffering."

Pal sighed and looked a little exasperated. He muttered something in Norwegian and the only word she recognized was 'Petter.'

"Haven, have you ever told him about your past, about your mother and your panic attacks and what happened to you out there in the forest with that crazy stalker?"

She avoided his eyes and folded her hands on her lap. "I wanted to, but I just couldn't. That whole thing with Dade. It's so embarrassing. . . I mean, about him trying to make me another wife and all."

"But you told *me*. Don't you think Petter could be trusted, too?" He took her hands in his. "You have absolutely nothing to be ashamed of. You witnessed your mother's murder and you became ill for a while. Don't you think the doctor has seen patients with anxiety disorders before? And as for that Dade guy, don't you think Petter's seen women come into the ER nearly every day who've been beaten up or abused by their boyfriends or husbands? Do you think you'd shock him by telling him a little about yourself?"

"He'll just feel sorry for me."

Pal leaned in a little closer. "Petter really cares for you. He told me. Does that surprise you?"

She looked up and searched his eyes. How could Petter care for her, so soon, after knowing her only a couple weeks? Her heart beat faster. She had misread him, thinking his concern for her was only the concern of a doctor for his patient.

"And I don't think letting him get to know you more is going to scare him away. In fact, he needs to know that you trust him. He's a big boy, Haven. He can handle the truth. And for that matter, so can your father." His voice turned stern. "It's time to start letting your father and the police help you. You can't fight this bad dude without help. There are laws out there to help protect you against a stalker."

"Laws?" She shot him a hard look. "What can the law do? Issue a restraining order? What good is that?"

"Haven, you can start building a case against Dade. He's got a prison record. So, if he ever shows up, you have something on the books to back your story."

He squeezed her hands before releasing them, then stood and picked up his coffee mug. "Next time you see Petter, you tell him about what you've been through. Show him respect by letting him help you. Okay?"

"Okay," she said in a small voice.

♩ ♪♪♩♪

Pal drove down to the hospital that very afternoon and cornered Petter just before he took his lunch break. They sat on the steps next to the back, parking lot, munching their sandwiches. For a second, he wondered if he should let Haven tell her own story. But her story needed to be told sooner rather than later, and he wasn't sure she'd give Petter all the details. No, it was better for him to tell her story. He knew how to talk to Petter.

Petter must have discerned the debate going on in Pal's mind because he watched him warily.

Finally, Pal put down his sandwich. "What's with you and that sweet girl, Petter? Are you avoiding her?"

"Me avoiding her?" Petter's voice went up in surprise. "I got the impression she was a little upset with me the last time we talked. I was just getting up the nerve to go see her again and apologize for anything I said that hurt her."

"Look, Little Brother, she's afraid she scared you away with her talk about God."

"Nei. She said some really intelligent things about what she believes. I just told her I don't happen to agree with her, that's all."

"Are you sure that's all you said?"

"I think so. I don't remember." Petter gazed off as if remembering his conversation with Haven. "Well, I did say that I'd seen a whole lot more tragedy than she has," he said calmly.

"That was kind of arrogant, don't you think?"

Petter shrugged. "I don't think so. Not in my line of work."

"Well, even if you do see awful things every day, that doesn't mean she's never experienced her own bad things." He frowned at Petter. "Has it ever occurred to you to ask her about herself sometime?"

"I have," Petter said with some irritation. "So far, she's been very tight-lipped about her past. I get the feeling she has some dark secrets."

"Then let me fill you in. Two years ago, Haven witnessed her own mother's murder."

"Oh." Petter closed his eyes and dropped his head. "And I said she hadn't seen suffering."

"Right, you did say that. But that's not the end of it."

"Go on," Petter said through clenched teeth.

"Last year she attended one of those wilderness therapy camps to help her cope with PTSD. There was this crazy guy there. I'm not going to tell you everything. Haven can give you more details. But the man kidnapped her, and she wound up being held prisoner for three months by the guy. A boy who lived there helped her escape. But the dude kept hunting her."

Petter almost shouted, "She was kidnapped?"

He almost enjoyed seeing Petter lose his characteristic reserve. It was about time Petter realized he wasn't the only one with tragedy in his past. "And not even her father knows about that stalker out there. And since I'm almost through with my sabbatical I'm handing the baton to you, Petter. You said you really care for her. So, it's up to you to help support her in any way you can think of, and to figure out how to keep this bad guy from finding her."

When he had finished his story, it satisfied him to see Petter's stricken expression.

The doctor crumpled his sandwich wrapper and threw it into his lunch bag. Then he stood up. "I'll go see her tonight."

Chapter Twelve

"Now thank we all our God with heart and hands and voices.
Who wondrous things has done, in whom His world rejoices."
Martin Rinkart

Dade sat in his truck in the Fairhaven Church parking lot and waited for the service to end. He slumped as far down as his long legs would permit, pulling his collar up and his hat farther down. It had been sheer luck that he had spotted Ruth at the Safeway store yesterday. How they had missed each other, both paying for groceries at the same time, had to be God's help. They almost exited the store together, too. But when he recognized her, he grabbed a newspaper and held it up close to his face, pretending to read. His heart pounded when she passed right by him, arms loaded with bags. Good thing they weren't parked close to each other in the lot. Hurrying for his truck, he'd followed her to all the way to the Fairhaven Church where she quickly entered the building. He would have stayed, but a few minutes later, a patrol car pulled into the parking lot and idled. He drove away, circled and returned.

Somehow, in the five minutes he'd been gone, Ruth had come out. Her car was gone. He'd had words for God, then, and they weren't the thankful words he had offered at the Safeway.

Noon. When would the service be over? Two men stood by the church front doors, watching. Churches did that nowadays. Stationed guys at the entrances to make sure no crazed shooter tried to get inside.

His legs were beginning to cramp in his slumped position behind the wheel. Earlier, he'd slipped into the building after the service started, and had taken a seat far in the back of the big sanctuary. Ruth was sitting near the front, holding a notebook and taking notes as the long-haired pastor preached. A skinny man with curly brown hair leaned in to whisper something to her and she smiled in response.

Dade balled his hands into fists and willed himself to breathe normally. He calmed himself with the thought that today there would be no heavy traffic. Today, he would find out where the girl lived. He'd crept out of the sanctuary just as the congregation prepared to sing the closing worship song.

The church double doors opened and people began to stream down the steps and get into their cars. Heart pounding, he watched the doors, waiting for the blonde girl to come out. At last, his patience was rewarded. Ruth emerged, walking next to the curly-haired man and another, older man.

He started his motor and watched the small group climb into a yellow jeep. He kept a little distance between his truck and the jeep, following them through town and onto the state highway, going east. As the other car signaled to turn onto the gravel road leading to Misty Mountain Retreat Center, he slowed, putting more distance between the two vehicles. Waiting until he was sure it was safe, he pulled onto the gravel road. He paused at the overhanging sign, read the scripture quotation, and sneered at the words of Jesus. Coming to the barn and corral area, he scanned the area, then spied the jeep parked just outside the main log building. Ruth and the two men were just going up the stairs. Satisfied, he put the truck in reverse.

♩ ♪♪♫♪

After church, Haven joined Misty Mountain's entire staff gathered in the big dining hall for a special meal to say goodbye to Pal. He would spend the rest of the summer with his Alaskan families. Just before the meal was served Erik, eyes brimming with tears, asked for everyone to surround Pal and lay their hands on him.

"Dear Father, we ask for safety for Pal as he returns to Alaska. We ask that you bless his work. Supply his every physical and spiritual need. Guide him in all your ways."

Haven had placed her hand on Pal's shoulder. Now she gazed down at his bowed head, feeling as if her heart would break. He had become as dear to her as a close brother and it hurt to think that she would not see him again for a whole year.

Right after the prayer ended and the staff lined up to fill their plates at the buffet, Petter walked into the hall.

Pleasure trilled throughout her chest, and when he smiled at her, she held onto the back of her chair to steady her knees. "Have you been here this whole time?"

"Just arrived," he said. "Got two birds to kill."

She couldn't help chuckling. "What?"

"Well, first, I couldn't miss saying goodbye to Pal."

"And the other bird is?"

"Seeing you." He pantomimed pulling back a bow, aiming an arrow and releasing it in her direction.

She laughed again. Bantering with Petter felt downright marvelous. Nevertheless, she put her hands on her hips and pursed her lips. "I'm glad to know you think of me as a bird."

"A bird I want to keep safe."

"Oh." Her tone slid downward. "Pal told you."

"Are you disappointed?"

"No, I'm relieved. Sort of."

"Just sort of?"

When he touched her arm, she wanted to melt into his arms. "I didn't want you mixed up in my problems."

"How could I not be mixed up, Haven? You're a part of Pal's world, and Erik's and this whole place." He stepped closer. "And you're a part of me. I wish you realized—"

"Hey little brother," Pal said, coming up and clapping Petter on the back. "I thought you'd forgotten all about my party."

Petter turned to face his cousin. "I want some photos, Pal. Here, put your arm around Haven. Say cheese."

She threw her hands up to block her face. "You're not going to put this on social media, right?"

"No worries. These photos are just for my eyes."

"Okay," she said, willing the tension in her neck and shoulders to ease and her breath to move normally. Petter was not going to put her safety in jeopardy.

Just before he took their picture, Petter shot her an I'll-get-back-to-you-later glance, pointing to his cell phone.

"Take a picture of me and Papa next," Pal said.

"I'll be back in a minute, Haven." Petter followed Pal over to a table where Erik sat.

She didn't follow them. Didn't want to break the breath-stealing mood Petter had put her in. He had said she was part of his world. If only he could have finished his other thought. What did she not realize?

Pal had said Petter cared for her. That could be simple affection or friendship. But the look on Petter's face right before Pal interrupted him, spoke of more than friendship. There had been a pleading in his eyes. And that was the reason she couldn't move, didn't want to break the spell his deep voice and passionate eyes had cast.

Petter returned with two glasses of punch and handed her one. "I can't stay, Haven. I'm helping a friend do some demolition at his house." He downed his punch and gave her a quick shoulder hug. "I'll try to get down here tomorrow after work." He strode to the door, giving her one last searching look before disappearing around the corner.

If only she realized. Realized what? Was he going to say he loved her? And if he said it, wouldn't it be her duty to warn him that loving her could be deadly?

After the meal, she walked out with the others to see Pal off. His possessions were packed in the back of the yellow jeep. Just the sight made her want to weep. Wasn't that just like him? One big duffel. That was it. He packed light for life, knowing all his tomorrows belonged to God. Pal and his father came down the lodge steps. When Pal saw her, he ran over and hugged her.

Tears welled in her eyes and she wiped them away hastily. "I promised myself I wasn't going to do this, and here I am crying like a big baby."

He looked down at her tenderly. "I'll be back in a year. . . Lawd willin' and the crik don't rise," he said with laughter in his eyes.

She laughed in spite of her tears. "I'm going to miss you so much."

"I'll be back before you know it, Karita. And anyway, you'll have plenty of things to keep you busy and out of trouble." His eyes sparkled. "Remember, that doctor needs your help."

Her eyes widened, remembering the urgent voice in her head six months earlier, calling her up north. Was it Pal's prayers that had led her to this place?

He gave her a kiss on the cheek and whispered, "Just keep being his friend."

Seconds later, he had climbed into the jeep and she watched, the sting of grief piercing her heart, as it rounded the parking area and disappeared down the tree-lined driveway toward the highway.

♩ ♪♪♫♪

Jesse practiced his story until he almost believed it himself. Now he just had to find a way to arrange a meeting with Dade. He'd had a hard time locating the carpenter, thinking it would be a simple matter of calling directory assistance. But that had turned up nothing. After two weeks of fruitless searching, he gave up and hired a private investigator. The professional quickly tracked down

Dade's address and the hardware store where he worked.

He took an evening off and drove down to Tacoma. If Dade thought he could get some information out of Jesse, he'd for sure invite him inside. He parked across the street from Dade's apartment building and waited for the man to come home from work. A little after six o'clock Dade's old green Ford truck pulled into the parking lot. A familiar figure stepped out and strode quickly toward the apartment entrance.

Jesse took a deep breath and tried to summon the courage to face Dade. As he walked toward the apartment hallway he reminded himself that he was a grown man now, in the prime of his strength, and Dade was nearly forty years old. Encouraged somewhat by that thought, he rang the doorbell. Seconds later, Dade's massive form filled the doorway. The intense green eyes glared down at him.

Even though Jesse was now six feet tall, Dade still stood half a head taller. He had changed little in the year since Jesse had fled his rage and his hard fists. He was still as imposing physically and still as psychologically intimidating. Jesse looked past Dade's shoulder and recognized the drawings of Haven tacked to the wall. It gave him strength to go on with his plan.

"What do you want, boy?"

"Just to talk."

"I'm not a talker." The door slammed shut.

"Wait!" Jesse knocked hard on the door. "I got something to say. It's about … Ruth."

The door opened again, and Dade stepped back. "Get inside."

Dade's backpack leaned up against a stack of cardboard boxes. They were labeled, but the print was too small to read from across the room.

Jesse came inside, his belly so jittery it made his voice shake. "I've been thinkin' about what I did back at the cabin."

Dade folded his brawny arms across his chest. "What exactly did you do?"

"I-I helped Ruth git away." He glanced up at the drawings of Ruth again. There was way more than he'd noticed when Dade first opened the door. Maybe twenty or twenty-five sheets of paper tacked to the wall. Dade was a terrible artist. "She begged me to help. Said she'd reward me. She kissed me."

A flicker of fury crossed Dade's face, but he smoothed it away with a rub of his hand across his bearded chin. "Ruth promised you something a man wants." He turned his back, strode into the kitchen, and pulled a can of beer out of the fridge. He took a long drink, then returned to the spot where Jesse stood, rooted like a tree.

"Ruth is ... she's beautiful. She smiled at me." He put on his dumbest expression. It was the most effective thing to do to convince Dade he wasn't plotting anything. Dade's evil brain never could acknowledge anyone else's intelligence.

"Yes, like Sarah's Abraham. Kings wanted her." Dade narrowed his eyes. "You wanted Ruth for yourself."

Jesse closed his hands into fist, digging his nails into his palms so hard it brought tears. "Yes, I was selfish, Pa. I'm ... I'm s-sorry." He made his chin tremble, and his shoulders shake. "But I know now she's not for me."

"And when did you come to this realization?" Dade's voice came out like a hiss.

"After I ran away, I got a job. After a while, I thought about you … and Mama. How hard you tried to train me to be righteous. Ruth never tried to contact me. You were right about her. She's a faithless wife."

"Yes, my wife."

Dade closed his eyes, smiling like one who is experiencing a moment of bliss. As if he were remembering Ruth on the night he'd conducted his sham of a marriage ceremony. Disgusting. The man had no thought or care for Ruth's terror and revulsion that night.

"I've repented, Pa. I wanna help you get her back. Don't you need my help?"

"Why would you do that for me? I thought you hated me."

"Why … what?" Jesse forced reverence to color his voice. "No! You got it wrong, Pa. I was afraid you'd beat me." He made drool puddle at the corners of his quivering mouth. "That's why I ran."

Dade walked over to the wall where the drawings of Ruth stared down at them. He trailed his fingers across one of the sketched faces. "And now she's living on her own. Maybe other men are noticing her. And you're mad at her. She led you astray, same as she did to me. You're jealous, boy."

"Yeah, yeah, I'm jealous. Ruth is bad. She's a liar. I want you to find her and teach her a lesson. Are you … do you still … want Ruth?"

Dade's head made a little jerking motion. "What if I did still want her?"

"I could help you find her."

The phone on the kitchen wall jangled. Dade went to answer it.

Waiting for Dade to conclude his phone call, Jesse glanced down at a pile of mail on a shelf by the door. The two letters on top grabbed his attention. He leaned over to read the return address. It was from Clear View. Way over the pass on I-90. The other was from—

Dade hung up and Jesse whipped around and focused on the big man.

"You were saying?"

"Uh, about Ruth. If you wanted me to help find her and bring her back. Or … do you already know where she is?"

Dade moved nearer, smiling. Not his toothy grin, but the I've-got-you-figured-out smug smile he always wore right before he took Jesse out for another belt-whipping. "I'll tell you what, boy," he said, completely ignoring Jesse's last question, "if you're sincere about repenting, then why don't you come join us." He took a step toward Jesse.

"Us?" Jesse said stupidly, refusing to back up.

Dade nodded. "I've got some friends in the area. Men and women. They like to listen to my Bible teaching. If you're really sincere about your repentance, you should join them. It might take a while before I can trust you again. You'll have to prove yourself to me. First thing you need to do is bring your own woman. We'll need women at the new place."

"The new place? Where is that?"

Dade didn't say anything, just kept coldly staring. He took another step closer, his eyes hard. "And one other thing."

"What do you want me to do, Pa?"

"Look at me."

The fist came so fast Jesse didn't even have time to flinch. It caught him partway between his jaw and his mouth. His vision went black for a second. When it cleared, blood had spurted.

"Now, get out."

Dade opened the door and shoved Jesse out. He was only vaguely aware of the door slamming, and then his feet slogging down the hall and outside to the parking lot. Climbing into his car, he waited until his head cleared before he dared try to drive home.

♩ ♪♪♫♪

Haven's father, and Sheila, Jeff and Joy drove up, as promised, to spend the weekend with Haven at Misty Mountain. Fortunately, only a few small groups had booked a weekend at the Center, so Erik was free to give the Ellingsen party his almost-undivided attention. Haven and Erik gave them a tour of the facilities, driving them up and down the wooded hills, pointing out some of the cabins, the two meeting rooms, the dining hall and the chapel.

Haven was disappointed that Petter had to work on that day, but he was off the next day and spent most of the afternoon and evening with her family. They ate barbecued chicken and potato salad and cherry pie, and her father thrashed the entire group, including Petter, in a game of Monopoly.

After they had collected all the game pieces and put everything back in the box, her father sat back and smiled wickedly.

"Dad, you don't have to look so incredibly pleased with yourself."

"Why shouldn't I?" He flicked imaginary dust off his chest.

"I'm a tycoon, and you're all losers."

"Losers?" The entire family called out simultaneously

Petter laughed. "It's true, folks, Guy did beat us fair and square."

"I don't know." Haven stood up and put her hands on her hips in mock vexation, "As a banker, Dad's got an unfair advantage. I think next time we play, we should give him some kind of handicap."

"Just ignore him the rest of the evening." Joy chimed in, glaring playfully at her brother. "That'll bring him in line. He can't stand that." She winked at Sheila.

"Haven, let's you and I sing some folk songs," Joy said, nudging Haven over to the piano. "Anyone else want to join us?"

"Go ahead and entertain us," Erik said. "Sheila and Jeff want to know more about Pal's mission work." They went and sat by the fire.

Haven glanced out the window. Dad and Petter had disappeared out the front door. Where had they gone? A dart of anxiety jabbed at her stomach. Obviously, they meant to talk about her. What else could they be discussing? Whenever someone she loved and trusted went out to have a private talk, away from her, it usually turned into something unpleasant.

On the last few bars of *Star of the County Down,* Petter and her dad returned. Petter sat down near the piano to watch, which made her falter and miss a few notes on the music score.

"Get with it, Haven," Joy said in a teasing voice.

"It's Petter's fault," Haven said, glancing at the source of her discomfort. "He's purposely distracting me."

Joy moved over, making room. "Petter, come sing with us.

Haven says you have a good voice."

Apparently, there was a little bit of ham in Petter because he jumped up and joined right in with his big, mellow bass, singing, *"From Bantry Bay up to Derry Quey, and from Galway to Dublin town, no maid I've seen like the sweet Colleen that I met in the County Down."*

Dad loved this song, but tonight he didn't join them. He sat down next to Sheila on the leather sofa. She saw him lean in and whisper something to his wife, then look over at her with concern. Uh, oh. Something was definitely up. What had Petter told him?

Seconds later, Dad stood up and stretched. "Well, it's getting late. We should probably be getting to bed."

Sheila glanced at her watch. "Good grief, it's almost eleven. I don't think I've stayed up this late since my single days."

"Us, too." Jeff chimed in, taking his cue.

"Night," Joy said as she moved to join Jeff.

The foursome excused themselves, and Petter followed them to the doorway to say goodnight. In seconds the great room was emptied of everyone but Haven and the doctor. Lately, she'd caught the man staring at her with such warmth in his eyes that just the thought of being alone with him made her face flush. Still seated at the piano bench, she looked up and caught Petter standing at the door, studying her.

"Are you tired, too?" He approached the piano.

She stood up immediately and retreated around the opposite side of the piano. Petter mustn't get too close, not until she'd sorted through her thoughts and emotions. It was bad enough that Pal had told him about her secret past and about Dade. Now that her heart was tumbling irresistibly toward Petter, she'd have to worry about his safety as well as her father's. Keeping her distance from him was the only way to protect him from Dade's murderous jealousy. But each day, it was getting harder and harder to keep her heart reined in.

He headed her off, looming over her. "No, you're not getting away from me." He took her hand before she could withdraw again. "Come and sit with me for a while."

She gasped. For one brief, terrifying second, Petter and the great room faded and her mind transported back to Dade's cabin. She cringed as the man's big, calloused hands gripped hers. A recording of his angry, deep voice played in her head. "Sit down there!"

"Have a seat," Petter said in his deep, gentle voice. He led her to the sofa, pulled the wingback chair opposite her and sat down.

Her lips grew numb. Darts of hot and cold raced up and down her spine while her pulse pounded in her ear. Her breath came in sharp gasps. The big fear. It would be humiliating if Petter witnessed one of her panic attacks. *This man is not Dade. This man is not Dade,* she repeated over and over in her mind, like a mantra, pleading for the rhythm of her heart to return to normal.

He began to sing softly in Norwegian. A simple, lilting tune that sounded vaguely familiar, like a lullaby she might have heard when she was a child. His voice was little more than a murmur. Gradually the rhythm of the song penetrated enough to give her agitated brain something to grasp and hold onto.

Petter must have sensed that her panic was losing ground because he stopped singing and reached over to take her hand. He warmed it between both of his. "Better now?"

She nodded. "Thank you for singing. It always calms me." She gazed at him in wonder. "But you knew that, didn't you?"

"What could be more calming to a musician than music?" He continued to hold her hand.

"Okay, I'm better now." The touch of his hand was doing funny things inside her. She gently extracted it. "What did you want to discuss with me?"

He sat back in his chair. "Sometimes you can tell a lot more about a person when you meet the family. I really like your father. Your whole family, actually. There's a lot of love between you all, and it's great to see it."

She waited impatiently for Petter to go on, feeling her belly start to tighten. Where were his words leading?

"Your father is a good man and I can tell there's nothing he wouldn't do to protect you. Haven, it isn't right that you've kept quiet about what you're going through with—"

"But I've been trying to protect him."

Petter put up his hand. "Let me finish. We men are strange creatures. We have this need to protect the ones we love. And when we can't do that, it makes us a little crazy. We feel like you don't respect us when you don't come clean about your problems."

She let her shoulders slump forward. "You told him about Dade."

"He needed to know about that crazy guy who's after you. Your father is an intelligent and resourceful man. He can keep information from going out in the Portland area that might be picked up by this Dade character." Petter paused, his eyebrows creased with concern. "What bothers me is that weeks have already gone by since you moved here. And during that time Dade might have already gotten some clues about where you moved."

He sighed. "I've seen women come into the ER who've been so physically or psychologically traumatized by their abusers they're afraid to press charges. We always try to convince them that they're better off telling the police—"

Haven jerked to her feet. "H-he said he'd kill anyone t-trying to hide me." She rushed over to the fireplace and looked down at the smoldering embers, seeing Dade's face. Anyone in her place would have done exactly what she had been doing to protect her family. "That day at the cabin, he s-said it'd never be over."

She returned and stood directly in front of Petter, her throat so tight only a hoarse whisper came out. "It makes me s-sick to think someone else could get h-hurt or killed because of Dade's obsession. There were times in the past when I thought I should just go back to him so everyone else would be safe."

Petter stood up and pressed her trembling body to him. "Shhh ... Don't talk like that. You're thinking like a victim like he's already won."

He lifted her chin and bent over to search her eyes. "It's just like that silly game of Monopoly where the winner has the most money and property," he said. "Well, in this case, *you're* the tycoon. You've got everyone on your side: the law, the police, friends, father ... me."

He smiled, and the tender crinkles at the corners of his eyes looked just like Pal's. "You also have your faith."

That was the best thing, and the worst thing Petter could have said. Was he being sincere, or merely applying a crowbar to pry open the lock on her heart? She tilted her head and tried to read his face. But she couldn't see a trace of deceit there.

Petter nodded. "Dade's the loser."

♩ ♪♪♫♪

The next afternoon, Guy's stomach churned at the news he received in response to his phone call to the State Police. Because Dade Colton already had a prison record, the police had taken Guy's charges of kidnapping, imprisonment, and stalking seriously. With a warrant in hand, they responded that same night by sending several squad cars to the Woodland Apartment complex in Tacoma and surrounded each exit. They kicked down Dade's apartment door and found no trace of the man. No clothing, no furniture, no garbage can filled with discarded mail or receipts that would have given some clue about his plans or living habits.

A call to Dade's probation officer the following morning led the police to his place of employment. No, Mr. Colton hadn't show up to work for the last two days. No, he hadn't called in sick or given his notice.

Guy's fists balled when he got the news that his daughter's kidnapper had disappeared. The thought of some lunatic chasing Haven through the woods, threatening her, was almost more than he could deal with. Had other things too terrible to speculate about happened to her, also?

He'd driven her down to the police that morning to make out a report and file a charge against Dade Colton. There was no statute of limitations on kidnapping. The only question was how the courts would interpret the severity of Haven's case.

The police would get him. Colton would have to surface eventually to buy food or gas. His truck would be spotted, his license plate photographed.

Why hadn't Haven told him about that madman? It was a

question that would haunt him for the rest of his life.

As he pulled his car in front of the big stone steps of the lodge, he decided to keep his mouth shut. No sense in scolding Haven about not telling him what she had endured during her time in the wilderness. She'd suffered more than he could even imagine and was no doubt fully convinced that her silence would protect herself and her family. He'd read about victims of abuse and how they wouldn't report it. He couldn't wrap his mind around the realization that Haven had become one of those victims. And she'd been living in his house, carrying around a terrible secret while he drove to work each morning blissfully unaware. Why hadn't he picked up any clues to her suffering?

Haven said goodbye to Sheila and Jeff and Joy at the foot of the steps. Guy got out and helped Jeff load the bags into the trunk. When they finished, he led Haven away from the rest of the family and hugged her hard. When he pulled back to scrutinize her face, she gave her usual "I'm fine, Dad" look. "Are you sure no one has your address?"

"No one, Dad. When I left Issaquah I only gave your address for any of my forwarded mail. Even I didn't know exactly where I was going when I left. And now all my mail and bills just come to my P.O. box. Nothing comes to the retreat. I don't see how I could be traced."

"What about the church or the florist shop? Did you ever talk to anyone on the phone that seemed suspicious?"

"No, not that I can remember. And before Pal left, he went and talked to Pastor Lauer. Gary told him that all phone calls or inquiries having anything to do with me or my work at church would have to go through him first."

"So, everyone at church knows to be on the alert for that nut?" His gut clenched just referring to Dade.

Haven nodded.

"When I get home, I'm going to see what I can find out about this guy. In the meantime, will you please stay around other people at all times? Don't even drive into town by yourself. Promise me."

He took her hand and his stomach churned at the thought of leaving her. "Call me. Every day. If I don't hear from you, I'll worry."

"Okay, Dad. I love you."

He hugged her again. "I love you too, Sweetheart."

He drove away, watching his daughter so intently in the rearview mirror that he nearly ran off the road.

Chapter Thirteen

"Love is free; it is not practiced as a way of achieving other ends."
Pope Benedict XVI

Now that he knew where Ruth lived he could bide his time for a few more days. He could work a few more carpentry jobs and get some more money. It was clear, by watching her comings and goings that she wasn't planning on moving anytime soon. Well, as long as she didn't get spooked.

Even though he hadn't fully stocked his hideout yet, he still planned to come up and watch Ruth one more time. And if some golden opportunity presented itself, if she left her cabin unlocked, if he caught her wandering around her cabin, no one else around, he'd seize her. But now, he could focus most of his time on final preparations.

He had come to know the backcountry well, an hour's drive east on I-90, beyond the Pass, the hundreds of square miles beyond public access and examined only occasionally by state fish and wildlife agencies. Once turned off the interstate, a man and his vehicle could disappear quickly in the rugged, densely-wooded areas. He'd been carrying supplies in for the past two months. A couple more trips into the wilderness and the bunker hideout would be completely ready.

Ruth, his wife, back with him, never to escape again. Back at his former apartment in Tacoma, he'd tried several times to sketch Ruth's face. He tacked several of his attempts on his otherwise bare walls. But, unlike Jesse, his artistic capabilities could not capture the perfection of her features, the flawless skin and her sweet expression.

When he moved out—even though he was in a hurry—he had ripped his sketches off the walls and stuffed them in his glove compartment.

Ruth was a religious woman but misguided in her faith. That's what happened when women went to school and learned more than they could handle. He shook his head and frowned. If only he had had more time to properly instruct her in the truth. If only he had had the chance to live with her as a husband. But there had been too many distractions. Jesse. The boy wanted her, too.

Perhaps if she had not been injured. If she had not been limited in her comprehension. She had seemed so close to loving him. She had welcomed his wedding ring and his kiss. Of that, he was sure. She would have welcomed his love, too, if only he'd had the chance.

He ran his fingers over the drawing. But even if she didn't love him, she certainly respected and feared him. A wife must first be obedient. "Sarah obeyed Abraham and called him lord," he quoted automatically.

One day, Ruth would be obedient to the truth … his truth. Why God had allowed her to run off, he would never know. Perhaps it was to purify his motives, make him work all the harder to accomplish his divine vision. But once Ruth was his again, she would not get another chance to wander, even if he had to break her legs. Better a cripple than a condemned sinner.

♩ ♪♪♫♪

Petter accompanied Haven on a visit to Professor Jaeger's house. He'd formed a picture in his mind of the tall, grey-haired lady who had figured so prominently in Haven's musical training and her restoration to her family. Haven had mentioned her concern that the professor would continue to hide in her house in the woods. But after meeting her, he thought the old woman seemed optimistic and full of life. Sitting at her kitchen table, sharing lunch with them, Anna described how her small church had embraced her, enjoyed her guitar playing, warmly drawn her into their community. At least, for the professor, church was a good thing. And it seemed to be a good thing for Haven, too. But it would never be good for him. Haven would have to come to grips with that.

He walked into the living room, taking in the grand piano, the professor's classical guitar, sitting on a stand nearby. It should have been a warm scene, except that, ten feet from the piano were the French doors Dade Colton, the carpenter, the kidnapper, had installed. The maniac had gotten that close to Haven.

Petter didn't know whether to shudder or growl his horror. He was spared either expression because Haven came into the room just then.

"First time I was here, taking care of Anna after her accident, I came over to the piano, wishing I could play and play and play." She put her hand on the curve of the piano and caressed the wood. "But I didn't even remember how I could do that."

He looked down at her lovely face, his heart agonizing at the thought of Haven having to run and hide in fear for her life. She had lived here, with the professor, without any memory of her loving family. How awful to lose one's memory. It was like losing yourself. A feeling akin to grief dragged at his gut. The only thing she had remembered then was Dade's abuse, and that he was still trying to find her. He couldn't comprehend the evil of a man like Dade who could harm a sweet, gentle woman like Haven.

"Well, kids, I'm going to take a little nap," the professor said as she shuffled out of the kitchen and toward the hall. Haven, why don't you take the doctor on a hike?"

"Okay, Anna. We'll be back by four. Have a good sleep."

They stepped out, breathing in the cool, pine-scented air. He followed Haven down the steep switchbacks that led to the lake. While they hiked, she told him in greater detail about her life in the wilderness after escaping Dade.

She stopped in a small clearing where a makeshift fire pit was still visible. "This is where I saw you and Pal when I was living in the cabin up the hill. He was fishing and you were sitting right here," she tapped her boot on the spot, "studying some thick notebook. The next morning, I came back to watch you. You were making coffee. Oh, how I wanted to ask you for help. But then you looked up and saw me. You said, "Hey, girl, are you all alone?" And I panicked. What if you turned out to be just like Dade?"

"That was you? You were so thin, and you looked so sad. And then you just vanished as if you were a ghost. For a long time, I wondered if I'd only imagined seeing you." Oh, if only she hadn't run from him. He could have helped her get back to her family. Dade wouldn't have found her again. Why couldn't God have helped her that very day?

They hiked farther west and Haven showed him the small hidden cabin, empty now and in disrepair.

"You lived here, all by yourself?"

"For six months."

Alone that long? It would have driven him crazy. And on top of that, she'd been constantly watching for Dade to appear. And here she was now, smiling, at peace, even though the bad guy was still out there. Amazing.

Her melodic voice broke into his thoughts. "It's the first time I've ever shared the extent of my despair … with anyone. Dad and Pal only know a little."

He couldn't answer, too moved by her transparency and trust.

"I was so desperately lonely," she said. "I felt like if I didn't find another human to talk to, I'd die. God answered my prayer and led me to Anna's place." She described finding the professor lying at the bottom of the hill in the snow and how she had dragged her back to her house and taken care of her until she recovered.

They turned back and crossed the stream where it was narrow, working their way downhill through the dense trees. He slowed to push his way through the branches. "Did you ever find out what happened to that man who wrote the journal, Haven?" he asked, thinking she was following him. Her voice surprised him, coming from farther down the difficult terrain. He swung his head around and caught a fleeting glimpse of her pale hair and blue jacket down the hill before she passed behind another tree. *Now, how in blazes did she do that?*

"They contacted me that summer after I'd gotten back to my family," she called back as she climbed over a fallen log. "Told me they were the family of the guy who used to live in the cabin." She waited for him to push his way down to the path. "My dad and I actually got to meet them and thank them for the use of Gregory's cabin. Really fine people. The son said that he'd come back to the cabin and taken his father home. Gregory died of lung cancer about a month later. He had made his peace with God and got to spend his last days surrounded by all of his family. I told them I felt like I had gotten to know their father through his journal and by living in a cabin he built himself."

He joined her on a ridge and they paused to look down over the valley, admiring the beauty of the land. "They'd been planning on coming up to the cabin after Gregory's death to clean it up and take all the stuff out. But months went by, and one thing or another kept preventing them from taking care of it. The next thing they knew my story was in all the newspapers."

She shook her head and laughed, eyes shining with joy and wonder. "Amazing, isn't it? I'm alive today because another person couldn't get to his housecleaning."

He studied her clear, untroubled eyes. Haven was an extraordinary person, thrust into an extraordinary set of circumstances that had saved her life and, as a result, led her to that snowy hillside just in time to save Anna's life. Were their individual stories of survival mere luck or chance? Or were they meant to live? He remembered his sister and was confounded by the inconsistency.

♩ ♪♪♫♪

Dade waited in the shadow of the trees outside Ruth's cabin. It was nearly dusk and a cool, dreary drizzle clung to his beard. He pulled his hat farther down. At last, his patience was rewarded by the sound of approaching cars. In another minute, the Sebring parked alongside the cabin, followed by the yellow jeep. Ruth gathered her satchel and purse and hurried up the porch steps. She unlocked the front door and stepped inside, and waved from the doorway. Immediately afterward, the deadbolt clicked firmly into place. Once she was inside, the driver of the jeep circled and drove back down toward the retreat.

Dade watched her through the window as she moved about, preparing dinner.

He hesitated on the porch just long enough to remove his hat, smooth his thick brown hair away from his face and ring the bell. Ruth opened the door. Pleasant aromas wafted past her shapely form and reached his nostrils. She smiled up at him and he handed her a bouquet of flowers. She took his hand, pulled him inside and led him to the couch. He sat down and watched while she placed the flowers in a vase. Ruth took a small pot off the stove and walked slowly over to him, smiling her shy smile. She knelt in front of him and, dipping a spoon into the soup, began to feed him. When he was finished she stood up and pulled him up with her. He took her into his arms. She welcomed his kisses. He sang in her ear, "My dove in the cleft of the rock, in the hiding places on the mountainside; show me your face, let me—"

A pine cone fell and struck Dade in the shoulder and made him jump. He drew back farther into the shadow of the trees, just yards from her front porch, heart still pounding from his desperate fantasy. Ruth passed close to the cabin window and paused to gaze outside. Then she drew the curtains shut.

How long would it take him to kick down her cabin door? A minute? Two minutes? If the door held long enough, she'd have time to use her cell phone. The entire Retreat staff would run up here to investigate. She'd look out the window and see him. The police would get involved.

Even if he could get to her, his car was parked down the hill on the shoulder of the highway. At least a quarter of a mile.

Without a fail-safe plan, he couldn't risk it. For all she knew, he had no idea where she was living. He meant to keep her ignorant. But if she needed an escort to her cabin every night, it was clear she also wasn't taking chances.

She was stupid, though. An escort up to her cabin wasn't going to be enough precaution. Sweet, helpless girl. A few more days—a week at the most—and she would once again be his. When the time was right. She wouldn't even see it coming.

And neither would anyone else.

♩ ♪♪♫♪

Petter came up with creative excuses for hanging out at Misty Mountain on his days off. The great room was a pleasant place to stretch out on the sofa and study a medical journal. The spot was made even more pleasant because the girl of his dreams spent time each afternoon sitting at the piano, making her magic on the piano keys.

She seemed so at peace. Yes, she'd been upset that he'd told her father about Dade and that the man had disappeared before the police could bring him in. But afterward, she had settled down and quickly returned to her usual state of contentment. He'd seen it before. Her kind of acceptance. And it always amazed him. He'd seen it happen to his uncle after Aunt Marthe died. A terrible struggle with grief. Then, a coming to terms. Finally, a newfound joy. This seemed to be Haven's story as well. She probably had no idea that it was her rare quality of joy, the noticing of daily blessings, and her extraordinary ability to focus on small daily wonders, that so dazzled him.

Passages of a Rachmaninoff Prelude broke into his thoughts. Haven's playing was magnificent. His sister had been a talented pianist. Would she have been this good if she had been allowed to live and keep growing in her own musicianship? He would never come to terms with Ture's death. She was only fourteen, gifted, and full of life. How cruel of God to take her. God had the power to save her. But He hadn't. Up until the night of Ture's death, he'd been a young man full of faith, full of prayer. But the next morning he stopped praying. God had chosen to allow chaos and suffering to reign in the world. He was no longer worthy of worship.

He had told Haven about his conclusions one day as they sat outside her cabin. But she had said to him, "Why are you even trying to attach meaning to suffering if you believe the world is nothing but chaos?"

And he had answered her with bitterness, "Better to expect chaos than to trust a God who's cruel."

"You think a God who would willingly die for others is

cruel?" she had asked, in amazement.

He had no answer and he could not argue with the evidence of God's mercy, sitting right next to him on the front porch of her cabin.

And now Petter had the daunting task of making sure Haven lived. Lived to fulfill her dreams, lived to keep bringing joy to her family, and to her God. And lived to make Petter the happiest man on earth, if she'd have him.

But how could he keep Dade from finding her? Even if the man were still in his Tacoma apartment, Petter couldn't have gone down there to threaten him. If he did, he'd have been the lawbreaker. But he could—

The music stopped. "What do you think, Petter? Do you think my Prelude is ready?" She was peering at him over the top of the piano's music stand.

"It's lovely." *And you are too, my Karita.*

Pastor Lauer wants me to do a recital this fall and I thought maybe I could do this piece. I've got some other Rachmaninoff pieces ready that would make a nice group."

"I can't wait to see you play there." Haven was a survivor. That was another extraordinary thing about her. She could have been pacing the great room, wringing her hands, wondering when the ax would fall. Instead, she forced her mind and will to keep on working toward her goals. "Rachmaninoff's one of my favorite composers."

She beamed at him. "And that's why I'm working on this."

Amazing that she cared for him.

♩ ♪♪♫♪

Haven smoothed back some stray hairs that had escaped her ponytail. Dinner was finally over. The guests had gone back to their cabins. Now, if she could just get these last few things done in the kitchen, she could go home and drop like a lead weight into her bed.

"Are you sure you don't want me to help finish up in here?" Petter asked, looking up from the medical book he'd been studying at the small kitchen table with a hopeful expression. "I'm really good at reaching top shelves."

She paused in her scouring just long enough to reply, her arms immersed in soapy water. "I'll be done in a few minutes. But thanks for the offer."

A stack of large, fancy serving dishes and fine china plates sat drying on the counter. She wiped them, one by one, and stored them in their various locations in the kitchen cupboards. She left the kitchen for a minute to store a stack of china in the dining hall cabinet. When she returned, Petter was just hurrying to sit down at the table again. He picked up his book, not even looking at her, and resumed his studies.

She had left the big serving dish, the one that belonged on the topmost shelf, for last. Then she would be done for the night. She felt unusually tired. Maybe she was fighting off a cold or flu. She picked up the dish. The step stool had vanished. How was she going to get that serving dish back on its shelf? She glanced over at Petter, but he seemed utterly engrossed in his book.

Now, where did that thing get to? She could have sworn she had just seen the stool sitting next to the door to the pantry. She looked over at Petter one more time but his nose was still buried in his book. She opened the pantry door. No stepstool. And it wasn't hiding around the corner anywhere.

"I must be going daft."

"What's that?" Petter peeped over the top of his book.

"Oh, never mind. Go back to your studying." Well, she could live without a step stool. She walked back into the kitchen, glanced up at the top shelf one more time, then clambered up onto the kitchen counter. Balancing on her knees, she reached down to pick up the dish. But before she could make contact, a man's hand grabbed the dish and Petter spoke near her ear. "Why didn't you just ask for my help? You don't need a stepstool when I'm around."

She turned to find his face just inches away. Unnerved by his nearness, she avoided meeting his eyes. "I didn't want to take you away from your studying."

He reached up and placed the dish on its shelf. She waited for him to step back so she could jump down off the counter.

"So, you're saying you'd rather break your neck than ask for my help? I hid that stepstool so you'd have to ask for help." He clucked his tongue at her, but good humor colored his voice. "You're a funny one, Karita." He put his hands around her waist and lifted her down.

When her feet touched ground, she was standing much too close to him. He was as tall as Dade and her nose was just inches from his chest. She should move back, but she couldn't make herself do it. Why didn't she retreat? He stood still also as if waiting. She couldn't take her eyes off his chest. He was breathing in a strange way. Attraction and fear warred within her. *Don't look up.* If she did, it would be his invitation to draw her into his arms and kiss her. And she was afraid, afraid first because her only experience with a man's love had been lust and selfishness, demonstrated by physical and emotional intimidation. What if she opened the floodgates of her heart and discovered that the feelings she bore for the doctor were more than she could handle? A kiss would lead to more kisses, and her heart would lead her to a commitment she shouldn't make, not when this man rejected her God.

She knew his eyes were boring into the top of her head, willing her to look up. But she would not. Better to keep the door of her heart shut and wonder about the size of the beast inside than to open for a look and have it burst forth and be trampled.

Finally, Petter sighed. "Is there anything else you need put away?"

She stepped back and finally looked up, eyes blurry with fatigue. "Just me."

Minutes later, as the Honda pulled up and stopped in front of her dark little cabin, she glanced at Petter. "Thanks for the lift." Before she could stop herself, she reached over and brushed his beard softly with the back of her hand. Then she escaped out of the car and hurried for her door. Once inside, she leaned up against her door and folded her arms across her chest. What had possessed her to do such an odd thing? She heard Petter's car drive off slowly.

"I'm such a fool." She pressed her fingers to her left temple as she walked over to the couch and slid down onto the soft cushions. "Haven, you're being unfair to that man. Don't stop him from kissing you and then caress his face like that. What must he be thinking?"

She sat forward and bowed her head. "God, I'm so sorry. Please give me wisdom. Please guide me. And please help Petter in spite of my mistakes."

Tired as she was, she did not sleep for a long time that night, thinking about Petter and wondering how she could possibly help him when she couldn't even help herself.

Chapter Fourteen

"Be joyful in hope, patient in affliction."
Romans 12:12

Petter didn't tell anyone about his appointment with Pastor Bernard. Now he sat in the pastor's book-lined office, feeling as if he'd just entered enemy territory. He gripped the armrests, far from comfortable under the gaze of the pastor's perceptive, dark eyes.

"Mr., I mean Pastor Bernard, I wanted to meet with you here because I'm not ready to come on Sunday mornings."

The pastor sat back in his chair and smiled warmly. "I meet with many people who aren't comfortable in a church setting. You don't have to come to church to talk about God."

Petter shifted in his chair. Maybe this appointment was a mistake. "It's just that I've recently met someone who's gotten me rethinking things."

Bernard waited quietly.

"We've both been through some hard things but she's come out of it with a different outlook. Different from mine."

"How do you mean?"

"She keeps saying that bad things happen but that God is good. That doesn't make sense to me."

"What doesn't make sense?"

"Just that," Petter said, a little irritated. "If God is good, then why does He allow suffering? You probably hear that question every day, in some shape or form."

"So, are you saying that God shouldn't allow suffering?"

"No ... no, not exactly. Not all suffering. I mean, some suffering is good, like pain that teaches you to stay away from danger. Or pain that means that the body is healing."

"So, which suffering should God weed out?"

Petter glanced sharply at Pastor Bernard.

"I mean that in all sincerity, Doctor," Bernard said. "I'm not trying to belittle your thinking." He leaned forward a little, and Petter was surprised by the distress in the man's face. "It is a question that I struggle with, too. Why do children die? Why did that tornado wipe out one house and leave another untouched?"

Petter relaxed a little. "I thought you were going to give me a pat answer to my question. Thank you for admitting your own struggle."

The pastor nodded.

"I thought I had it all figured out until I met Haven. But you can't argue with that kind of joy."

"Ah." Pastor Bernard said softly, nodding his head again. "You see it, too. There is no other explanation for her than God."

"Yes, I agree." Petter's own words jolted him. "But where was God, twelve years ago, when my car went off the road and pinned my sister in the wreck? I watched her life slip away while I pumped her chest and tried to breathe for her. No one deserved to live more than her. I prayed and pleaded for God to save her, to take me instead. But by the time the ambulance arrived, she was already gone."

He leaned over and put his head in his hands, trying to shut out the memory of that icy night, the rattling breaths of his little sister, the flashing lights and sirens.

"That night I screamed at God." His voice rasped through his fingers. "I told Him He was worthless, and that I'd never set foot in a church again. And I made up my mind that I'd never watch helplessly while another person died in such agony."

He struggled to keep his voice steady. "She was only fourteen. I couldn't save her. She'd still be alive today if she hadn't come with me that night. And so, I'm asking you, why?" He sat back up and eyed the pastor, hoping for an answer that he had never heard before.

The pastor looked down for a long moment before replying. "Dr. Eriksen, I know you came here to talk about the problem of suffering. But you see, I have had this discussion with many people and it rarely results in any great revelation as to the meaning of suffering or the will of God. No one can say why God heals or helps some, but not others."

He steepled his fingers on top of his desk. "I think that most people, when they ask this question, are really trying to figure out just who is in control. Do you control your life or does Someone else call the shots? And if it's that Someone else, can He be trusted? Will you be safe if you trust Him? Does He really care about you? That's the real issue.

"Your friend Haven has come to realize that God is God, and

that she is not. She has come to see, in spite of terrible things she has gone through, that God loves her in an indescribable and never-ending way. That is the source of her joy."

Pastor Bernard's gaze settled on him with a sad slant to his eyebrows. "I am sorry if I have disappointed you. I know you were hoping for something more. I hope that you will think about what I have said."

Petter stood up slowly. "No … no, you haven't disappointed me. It was a different answer than what I was expecting but you've given me some things to think about."

Bernard reached over his desk to shake Petter's hand. "I hope you'll come back and talk with me again. I appreciate your honesty and your questions."

Petter drove back to Misty Mountain, up the winding gravel road, through the trees and over the wood bridge, his only thought: see Haven. He jumped out of his car, cleared the porch steps and reached her door in two big bounds. He knocked and waited, holding his breath. There was no answer. He peered through the window. Her purse and music bag were sitting on the old sofa. She had to be around somewhere.

He ran down the path to the stream, checking to see if she was sitting on her favorite rock. Disappointed, he turned back up the path. He could wait in his car for a while or try to look for her at the lodge. He had just entered the clearing again, heading for his car, when he saw her coming around the corner of the cabin. She was carrying a basket filled with pine cones and various kinds of evergreen boughs. Her cheeks were flushed, she was breathing a little from climbing the hill, and her tousled hair cascaded about her face and shoulders. She beamed when she saw him and he had to remind himself to breathe.

"I didn't expect to see you today." She set the basket on the porch. "What brings you all this way from town?" She came around and sat down on the steps, and he joined her.

It took him a while to get his thoughts back in order. Her beauty and sweetness sometimes robbed him of articulate speech. It was embarrassing, and by the way she sometimes looked downward and smiled, he was sure she could read his thoughts.

He looked off for a minute as he tried to frame a question. Then he met her eyes. "Why in blazes are you the way you are?"

Haven sat up straighter, and her eyes grew wide in surprise and confusion. "Are you upset with me? Did I—?"

"No." He touched her hand. "I'm sorry," He made a conscious effort to ease his tone into something gentler. "That didn't come out right." He bent his head down and thought hard. "You once told me that God met you when you were living in that little place out in the forest. How do you know? You didn't see him." He raised his head and watched her. Would she get flustered by his question? Did he really want her to stumble now? .

"No, I didn't *see* Him. But He was definitely with me. I could feel His presence. I wasn't alone that morning."

"And you trust Him, even though this Dade guy might still be looking for you?"

"Yes." Her answer was quiet but quick and full of assurance.

He nodded slowly. She didn't doubt. Why couldn't he have her kind of faith? Why couldn't he let go of his own tragedy and trust God? "I've got to go to work now."

Her gaze followed him as he stood.

He put his hand on her shoulder. He wanted to keep it there.

He wanted to pull her into an embrace and never let her go, to bury his face in her soft, scented hair. He wanted—

No, don't keep on imagining. If she rejects you, it'll be that much more painful. "Thank you for answering my question." He left her there, still sitting on the porch as he drove off. Maybe, after he'd thought some more, he'd go see that Pastor Bernard again.

♩ ♪♪♫♪

Haven sat on her sofa and had just reached down to slip on her shoes when the shadow passed her front window. She jumped up, her heart pounding in alarm, sirens going off in her brain. She ran to the window. Maybe this time she'd catch a glimpse of her trespasser.

Third time this week. It wasn't her imagination. Creaking stairs. Fresh boot tracks going around the cabin. A creepy feeling she was being watched. She now double-checked the bolt on her door even when she was inside during the day, and kept the curtains drawn.

But this was not something she would be silent about. Most likely, her Peeping Tom was harmless. But, better to tell Erik and let him deal with the trespasser

That Dade could have found her was also a possibility, but she put that thought firmly from her mind. She moved away from the window. "You don't know anything yet. And you've been so careful. How could he know that you live here? He probably still thinks you're living somewhere down south."

She tiptoed into her bedroom and peeked through the curtains. No one. She didn't like to leave her place. What if someone was lurking outside? But she was expected in the lodge kitchen in ten minutes. Stuffing her music bag with everything she'd need for the day, she cautiously opened her door and scanned the area before leaving the safety of the cabin. Maybe this time it was just her imagination.

Minutes later, she pulled her car up to the lodge parking area and hurried inside. When she asked if Erik was around, Mrs. Graham informed her that he probably wouldn't be in all morning. He was out having breakfast with friends and then had several errands in town.

The older woman must have noticed something in Haven's voice. "Is there anything I can do, Haven? I can call him at the restaurant."

"No, it's okay, Mrs. Graham. It can wait." She smiled reassuringly and went into the kitchen to begin her prep work. She'd talk to Erik first, as soon as he returned. He might not want her talking about this with the staff before he had a chance to check things out.

She took out the fresh vegetables, gave them a thorough washing and prepared to chop them up for tonight's salad. Someone was using the gym equipment downstairs. She could hear the "clank, clank" of the weight machine. Who would be down there so early in the morning?

Just as she was storing the bowls of chopped vegetables in the refrigerator someone tromped into the kitchen. She started when Petter approached. He reached for a glass from the cupboard and filled it from the sink. "I didn't mean to startle you. Don't you usually come in here an hour later?" He took a big gulp of water, leaning against the counter,

He was wearing shorts and a sleeveless tee shirt and she had to force herself not to stare at his big muscles. Her cheeks grew hot and she was sure he noticed. "They've got some special activity going on this afternoon. Mrs. Graham wanted me to get the prep work out of the way so we wouldn't be bumping into each other later on."

Should she tell Petter about her prowler? Or would that add to his already stressful days?

"Are you okay, Haven? You seem bothered about something."

That was the second person to correctly read her mood this morning. "Is it that obvious?"

"Well, usually you have a smile on your face. Care to share what's on your mind?"

"Did you mean it when you said I'm not trusting you if I don't tell you about my problems?"

"Now you're worrying me." He steered her over to one of the kitchen chairs and seated himself, facing her. "Out with it. What's got you so upset?"

She hesitated. How would Petter react to news about a prowler? "Someone's sneaking around my place at night."

Petter's face clouded with concern. "Did you see anyone?"

Again, the thought of Dade made her body tense. "No," she said, trying to keep her voice from betraying fear. "I just keep hearing things outside, mostly at night. Although this morning I could have sworn someone was right outside. And I found boot tracks going around the cabin."

Petter thought briefly. "Do you have to go back there today?"

"No, I was planning on going straight to church after I finish here."

"Good." He looked relieved. "Don't even think about going back there tonight."

The intensity in Petter's voice should have made her feel anxiety. But instead, it brought her comfort to hand over some of her concern to him. All the same, she wondered if he was thinking about Dade, too, but didn't want to mention his name.

"You stay here tonight. When I get back from work I'll take your car and stay at your place." He was frowning in concentration.

"Just what are you planning, Petter? What if this prowler is dangerous?" She thought again of Dade.

His eyes narrowed. "I can handle myself."

And that was the problem. He'd handle himself all the way into a fight with a murderer who would have no trouble snuffing out his life.

She wanted to wrap her arms around him and hold onto him until he swore he wouldn't do anything dangerous. She couldn't risk losing him, not now. Not when he was becoming the most important person in her life.

♩ ♪♪♫♪

Petter stayed overnight in Haven's cabin, and when he visited the lodge the next morning, he told her, "Nada. Didn't hear anything, or see anything."

It was good news, and horrible news. Now, he'd probably think she was imagining things.

"Even so, I don't want you going back to the cabin for a while."

How would he react when she told him her plans? "Anna has

invited me to come down and stay overnight. And since tomorrow is my day off that would also give me a chance to go see a friend in Seattle."

Petter looked at her dubiously. "I have to work today and tomorrow so I wouldn't be able to come with you."

Good grief, Petter was as protective as her father. "I'll be fine. The car is all gassed up. I'll drive straight there—won't even step out of the car. What could happen?" *A lot.* But she wasn't going to show him she was afraid.

He still looked uncertain.

She sighed. "Look, I can't keep hiding here, wondering if and when Dade will show up. And anyway, now that the police are looking for him, he's probably in Mexico … or Canada." She wished she believed that.

She left that afternoon, looking forward to spending a quiet evening with her friend. She brought her guitar just in case she and Anna got a chance to play some duets.

On her way down south on I-5, Petter's attractive singing voice popped into her mind. "From Banbridge town in the County Down, one morning in July," he'd sung the other night while she played the piano. Standing behind her, looking over her shoulder at the music, the heat of his body had penetrated her back. His nearness made her breathing get so shallow, she almost couldn't sing. He—"

No. She had to get her mind off Petter and think of something else. "God help me. I'm falling in love with Petter and I can't stop."

Lately, he was all she thought about, and it disturbed her that she enjoyed the thrill of seeing how her nearness affected him.

That made her feel guilty, but she wasn't exactly sure why. Why should she feel guilty because a man cared for her? He'd never done anything improper and she'd never encouraged him, either.

But it did bother her, nevertheless. They could never have any lasting relationship, the way he felt about her faith. She'd just get frustrated trying to share thoughts and feelings with him that he could never understand. "Oh God, how can I stop loving him? Help me do the right thing, whatever that is."

It was the first day she had used the word "love" when she prayed about Petter. She'd said it without thinking.

He had won her by his gentle ways, this man who looked so much like that other man. No wonder Pal had spoken about his cousin with so much admiration. It wasn't hard to love a man who loved caring for others. She was beginning to see why she had been called to "help the doctor." He was the kind of man she wanted to help.

♩ ♪♪♫♪

Haven slid her guitar case onto the back seat of her car, followed by her overnight bag. Anna leaned on her walker, Beau at her side. "Bring your guitar next time you come and we'll go over some of those new pieces."

"I will." She bent and hugged the big, black dog, kissing his grizzled muzzle. "Beau, take good care of your lady, okay?" The dog waved his tail slowly.

"Thanks for the visit, Anna. I love you." She hugged her friend, climbed into the driver's seat and rolled down the window. "I'll be in Seattle for a couple of hours, but I'll call you when I get back home."

Later that afternoon Haven parked in a garage a few blocks up from the Pike Place Market and hurried to find the café where she and Jesse had agreed to meet. She turned the corner and saw him halfway down the block, shading his eyes, looking for her. He waved when he recognized her. She gave him her customary hug and he ushered her inside the café without speaking. They found a table and she studied Jesse's face. His expression told her this was no social visit.

"Jesse, when you called the other day I thought we were just going to catch up on each other's doings. Something tells me you've got bad news."

"Are you likin' yer life at that retreat place? Do you have lots of friends hangin' around you?"

What was he hinting at? Why couldn't he just say it? She nodded in response to his questions, drumming her fingers on the table.

"I … I gotta apologize for something."

She stopped drumming. "Apologize?"

"I think I'm the reason Dade got away from the police."

Haven sat forward. Instantly sickened, she fought the urge to retch.

"I-I went to see him."

"Jesse, you told me you never wanted to see him again."

"I know. But I had to know what he was thinkin'." Jesse shifted in his seat, hardly looking at her. "I had to know what he was planning. And I found out.

"Funny, when I visited him in prison he didn't seem so big as I remembered. I guess when yer sittin' separated by a big glass wall, you feel a little safer." He laughed humorlessly and shook his head. The waitress brought their coffee and Jesse waited until she had moved out of earshot.

"I went and talked to him. Made up a story about how I'd repented—about helping you git away—and wanted to start following the true way again. He was real suspicious at first. But I laid it on thick, crying, almost gittin' hysterical. Told him you belonged to him and I'd prove I was telling the truth by helping him git you back."

"Jesse!" His name exploded from her mouth before she could stop. She looked around the café. Fortunately, no one near seemed to have heard her outburst. "What were you trying to accomplish?" she whispered.

"Don't you see?" His eyes seemed to plead. "It was the only way I could find out if he's still hunting you."

He shook his head. "You wouldn't believe what his apartment looked like. He had drawings of you tacked up all over his walls. He had piles of boxes stacked up in his living room … looked like all food and supplies. And he didn't even try to bluff me about how he still wanted you back. He's got someplace he's stashin' all those supplies. I tried to git him to tell me where it was but he wouldn't say."

"Maybe he was just making it all up," she said, trying to convince herself. Her pulse throbbed in her scar. "Maybe—"

"No, Haven. I came back the next morning and watched the apartment. He came out and loaded those boxes in his truck. I followed him all the way out of town, onto a highway and out toward Mt. Rainier. Then he got off onto some dirt road. After a few miles, the road got so rough I couldn't follow him anymore.

So, I didn't actually see the place, but I know it's out there. Probably well hidden in the trees."

Haven wrapped her hands around her coffee mug so tightly that her fingers turned white. The sickness she always felt when thoughts of Dade invaded, had returned. "I can hardly believe you went and talked to that man."

Well, I'm apologizing 'cause he musta seen me watching him the next morning at his apartment. That's probably why he moved out suddenly. Haven, it's time for you to go into hiding again. I think he might already know where you are. Dade's got a plan and he's smart enough to carry it out. And if he even suspects that I know where his secret place is, he could take you and disappear, who knows where."

"Dade's not going to get anywhere near me with the police being on the lookout." She placed her hand on Jesse's. "That was a very brave thing you did. And I'm grateful. But I hope you don't ever see him again."

Jesse shrugged. He reached into his pocket and pulled out a sheet of paper. "Here, take this. I wrote down the make and model and color of Dade's truck. And his license plate number, and anything else I could remember. The police probably already have this stuff, but he's smart enough to ditch his truck and use somebody else's."

He stood. "You should get home before it gets dark."

He walked her around the corner of the block and up the street to her car. "I'll call you if I can find out anything more. And remember, don't go anywhere alone."

She drove home through heavy traffic, constantly checking her rearview mirror. She needed to tell Petter everything Jesse had told her.

Chapter Fifteen

"A wife of noble character who can find?
She is worth far more than rubies."
Proverbs 31: 10

Both relief and guilt alternated in Haven's chest at the thought of Petter continuing to switch places with her, staying in her cabin each night. He had to attend a couple more evening seminars, but afterward, he drove to the retreat and traded cars with her. By the end of the week, he looked visibly fatigued when he returned to the lodge at night. She begged him to go back to his own apartment for a good night's rest.

"Not until I catch this creep." He folded his arms across his chest. "I heard some things out there last night."

"You can't keep going on like this, working and not sleeping. You'll make yourself sick." She didn't say what she feared even more, that Dade was watching her place. And, if he were really out there, what if he saw Petter? What if he had a gun?

"Why don't we just call the police?"

"That'll just scare him away for a while," he said, picking up her car keys.

She followed him to the door, feeling helpless to convince him, and awful for drawing him into her problem.

"Good night, Haven." He wouldn't look at her, slipping out quickly before she could argue.

That night, Haven dreamed of sirens and flashing lights. She woke suddenly and glanced over at the clock. Just after two thirty in the morning. Sounds came from downstairs, something like drawers opening and shutting and a man's footsteps on a tiled floor. She slipped out of bed, pulled her robe on and picked up the rock she always kept on her nightstand. She moved noiselessly down the hall and down the stairs, hardly breathing.

Whoever was in the kitchen, he certainly wasn't trying to be stealthy. She had her rock ready, just in case as she nudged the kitchen door open a couple of inches.

He saw her immediately and motioned for her to come in and keep quiet. "Would you take my keys and go outside to my car and get my medical bag? It's in the back seat."

She left without a word to carry out his request. When she returned, Petter was sitting on a stool, bent over the sink, soaping his arm under the tap. There was a three-inch gash on his right forearm, ending just above the back of his wrist. The wound looked nasty.

He glanced over at her. "How are you doing, Haven?"

"How am *I* doing?" Hushed concerned made her voice tremble. "You're the one with the war wound. What can I do to help?"

"How would you feel about doing some minor surgery,

Doctor?" He watched her reaction.

She gasped. "Why don't I just drive you down to the hospital?"

"Nei, I'm sure you can do this little job."

She looked at him in alarm. "Just as long as you realize I can't be sued for malpractice."

Petter chuckled. "First, wash your hands."

She joined him at the sink, turned on the water and soaped up her hands. "Do I need to do my forearms, too, like they do in those medical shows?"

Her question was sincere, but Petter's grin told her he thought she was joking.

"Now what?"

"Use a paper towel to dry with." He rummaged through his medical bag. "Good thing I just had a tetanus booster." He pulled out something that looked like a tube of glue. "Here, this should work just fine. And after it heals, I'll have a scar, but that'll impress my patients."

"I can't believe you're joking about your arm being all slashed open, Petter. You could've been killed."

"What?" He raised one eyebrow and studied his arm. "This is nothing. Want me to tell you some truly gory ER stories?"

"Uh, no." Normally, she liked to watch real-life medical emergency shows on TV. And even though those doctors and nurses sometimes had to subdue out of control patients, it was hard to imagine the calm and logical Petter having to use his size and strength to wrestle an unruly patient.

"All right, Florence Nightingale, I'm going to hold my arm really still. All you've got to do is run this goo along the wound.

That will hold it until it heals." He paused and examined her face. "Are you ready to do this?"

Haven took a deep breath. "As ready as I'll ever be." She'd never done anything more than put a bandage on her father's heel to cover a blister. Gluing the painful wound of the man she loved was way more intimidating.

Afterward, he held up his arm to inspect her work, nodding at the satisfactory result.

"Now, will you please tell me what happened tonight?" She planted herself directly in front of him.

"I got tired of waiting for this guy to get close enough for me to grab. So," Petter hesitated as he watched her face, "I decided to put out some bait."

"Huh?"

He smiled sheepishly. "I left one small light on, coming from the bathroom. Then I put some pillows on the bed and covered them with a blanket so it looked like you. I left the front door unlocked. Then I went and hid behind the couch."

"Evidently," he went on, "he wanted a closer look. He got the surprise of his life when he found me waiting for him and not some cute little blonde."

"Who was it? What did you do?" The suspense made her breathless.

He put his hand up. "Hold your horses. I'm getting to the end."

"He turned out to be this little squirrelly-looking man who smelled like dirty clothes and liquor. When he saw me he tried to run, but I jumped on him and pinned him down. That must be when I cut myself. He tried to fight but once he saw he wasn't going to get away he started crying. He kept saying he was just looking for a warm place to sleep. Finally, he admitted he was the one who'd been hanging out around the cabin all these nights. He seemed like a pretty harmless bum. I almost felt sorry for the little guy. Almost. Still, I didn't believe him about just needing a warm place. So, I told him if I ever caught him anywhere on Misty Mountain property, I'd tie him up and turn him into a steer."

"You said that?" She was aghast.

He avoided her gaze. "Well, I didn't exactly say it in such polite words."

She stared at Petter. This was a side of him she wouldn't have suspected. "So, what happened to him? Did you just let him go?"

"Nei. He was hungry, so after I called the police, I gave him a hunk of your homemade bread and some left-over soup. Funny little guy. When the police arrived, he told them what he'd done. We talked as they gathered evidence. Then they took him away."

Now that his story was told, Petter's eyes softened and he sighed in relief. "I was sure it was going to be Dade. I had myself all ready for a real fight." He looked down to find Haven's eyes filling with tears.

Her lips trembled and she struggled not to cry. She had just finished gluing Petter's skin back together, heard how a homeless drunk broke into her cabin, discovered that her prowler wasn't Dade, and realized that Petter was no longer in danger from Dade's gun or fists. Overwhelmed with relief and thankfulness, she did not try to stop him this time.

He drew her into his arms and pressed his lips to hers. "You know I'm in love with you, don't you?" He searched her eyes.

She nodded. How wonderful it felt to be held by this beloved man and to taste his kiss.

"Do you think," he asked tenderly, "that maybe you might have a little bit of love for me, too?" His green eyes crinkled with gentle humor.

"You know I do," she whispered, looking down. She'd never been in love before and didn't know what to do with the strange and wonderful feelings coursing through her chest.

"Do what?" Petter teased her. He lifted her chin, making her meet his eyes, making her say it.

"Love you," she whispered fiercely. "I love you, Petter." She wrapped her arms around his neck and kissed him again. Then laid her head against his chest, not trusting herself to kiss him again.

♩ ♪♪♫♪

Petter finally had some free evenings and he spent them all with Haven. He and Erik had agreed that, as long as the uncertainty existed about Dade's plans, it would be better for Haven to stay at the lodge. She hadn't seemed happy about moving out of her quiet cabin but admitted that she saw the logic in staying surrounded by people all the time. And after he told her how tortured he'd been about the whole Peeping Tom affair, she'd said that she wanted to spare him any more sleepless nights.

It had become their routine that, any time Haven had a late afternoon or evening rehearsal, she'd be dropped off and picked up either by him or Erik at the church's office. She was getting close to the children's last presentation of the summer before the kids took a break, and some of her rehearsals lasted a little longer than usual.

Petter didn't mind. It gave him a chance to visit with Pastor

Bernard, who was usually just finishing up for the day in his office.

One evening, as he and Haven drove home, he said. "I like Pastor Bernard. He doesn't give me any condescending looks just because we don't see eye to eye on things."

"What things?"

"Oh, just our observations about life."

"Hmm." She turned to look out the window, but not before he caught her smiling mischievously.

"Just 'hmm?' That's all you can say? You're not even curious?"

"It's none of my business."

She wasn't even going to give him the satisfaction of a discussion. He was tempted to pull the car to the side of the road and kiss her passionately until she agreed to spill her thoughts.

"I'll just say this," she said, a little teasing curve on her lips. "With Pastor Bernard, you may have finally met your match in the brains department. Just take comfort in the thought that when you come home, licking your wounds, I'll be around to glue you back together."

He grinned in amusement, drinking in Haven's sweet face. What a woman. And she loved him—a big, shy oaf of a man, more than twice her size. Amazing. What in blazes did she see in him?

"I'm going to see Bernard first thing tomorrow," he said. "But then I was hoping we could spend the afternoon together. Are you free?"

They pulled up alongside the lodge steps and Haven gathered her music bag and purse. "I only have a bit of kitchen work in the morning."

He took her hand and brought it up to his lips.

Haven laughed. "What are you doing?"

"Trying to behave myself. This is nice," he said, looking at her hand, "but not nearly so exciting as kissing you."

"Uh, I see." She pulled her hand away with a nervous giggle and hurried to climb out of the car.

"Haven, I can't stay," he called out the window. "Got to do some things at the hospital tonight. See you for lunch?"

She nodded.

He drove off. Was his visit with Haven tomorrow premature? His next meeting with Pastor Bernard would answer that question.

♩ ♪♪♫♪

"You look tired, Doctor. Long night in the ER?"

Petter was back in Pastor Bernard's office the next morning, a little bleary-eyed, but smiling. "It's been a very interesting fourteen hours since we talked yesterday."

They sat in their usual places and the pastor raised his eyebrows expectantly.

"Last night I was taking care of some paperwork. It wasn't my shift and I thought I'd get some work done without any interruptions. Around midnight all these cases came in and suddenly there wasn't enough medical personnel to go around. I went in to help. They'd brought in this teenaged girl who was right in the middle of delivering a baby. She was doing just fine, but she didn't have any family with her. And she kept crying, 'Doctor, don't leave me! I'm scared.' We finished the delivery and just as I was putting the baby on her chest the strangest feeling came over me. I felt like I was floating above the scene, watching myself work. Then I heard a voice in my head. It said, 'I've blessed you so you might bless others.'"

"Some blessing, Pastor." He shook his head. "Taking my little sister, then letting me live with guilt for the last dozen years."

He looked at the pastor to see his reaction. But Bernard merely said, "And what happened next?"

Petter swallowed. "I got home about two in the morning. I had this feeling that it wasn't over, that something else was going to happen. It was eerie, Pastor, like I wasn't alone."

He glanced over at Bernard, half expecting him to look skeptical, but the pastor watched him calmly.

"I went to bed, but I couldn't sleep. That never happens. My whole body felt like it was attached to an electric current, and I had to keep getting up and moving around. I went into the kitchen and poured myself some milk, thinking that would calm me down. Just as I was coming back into my bedroom I heard the voice in my head again. This time, it—I mean He—said, 'Petter, come back home.' I fell flat on my face and shook like a leaf."

"Did you know Who was speaking to you?" The pastor's voice quivered with emotion.

"*He* was in the room. Pastor Bernard, I'm not crazy. I'm not the emotional type."

"I believe you." Bernard came around the desk and put a hand on his shoulder, as he had done the night before. "What did you do next?"

"I cried like a baby. I haven't cried like that since Ture died. For a long time, that's all I could do. But it was a wonderful kind of crying.

After a while, all that strange feeling went away. I thought about my little sister and knew for the first time in twelve years that she's okay. She's okay, Pastor!" He slumped over his knees and his shoulders shook with silent weeping.

"All those years. Wasted" He straightened, collecting himself

Pastor Bernard's voice came as if through a fog. "Not wasted. God never wastes our experiences … or our pain. It led you to medical school. Then it led you here. Think of all the lives you've saved."

"It's God I'm talking about. I shook my fist at Him for years. I thought He hated me as much as I hated Him."

Pastor Bernard murmured, "How could He not love His own child?"

"Even now it's hard to believe."

"Are you ready to make a change?" The pastor straightened and took a deep breath as if preparing for some athletic competition.

Petter raised his head and studied Bernard's face. "I already have. And the first person I'm going to tell is Haven."

Petter borrowed one of the Misty Mountain jeeps and drove Haven up to Mt. Baker Wilderness. He had much to tell her and he didn't want any interruptions. They wound up the narrow highway, savoring the beauty of the snow-capped peaks and the brilliant blue sky. He turned off onto a dirt road leading to a trailhead and pulled over to park. They got out and stretched their legs, breathing the cool, balsam-scented air. He took Haven's hand and led her down a path toward the river. They found places to sit by the water and still he hadn't figured out how to begin his announcement. He wouldn't let go of her hand, gazing at the water with a determined expression, and Haven watched him curiously.

"You've got news for me and you don't know where or how to begin, right?"

That startled him "How did you know?"

"It's like you're a bubbling pot with its lid about to blow off." She squeezed his hand. "You've been like that all day and I'm getting mighty curious."

"I was thinking," he said slowly, looking across the water at the line of dense firs growing along the banks. "Today's the first day since my sister died that I haven't felt this cloud of guilt hanging over my head. Last night, I saw her. In my mind. She was …" His voice turned raspy again. "She looked … beautiful."

Haven stood up and came behind him. Leaning into him she stroked his hair. "God gave you a rare gift. A glimpse of life beyond the grave."

"I didn't deserve it."

"No," she murmured, "but that's how God is."

"He's hounded me for twelve years, and I've finally stopped running."

He grasped her hand and pulled her around and onto his lap. It was a moment to be savored and he cradled her for a long time, her head resting on his shoulder

"You're so quiet, Haven." He lifted her chin and gave her a soft kiss. "What are you thinking?"

"Mostly, I'm trying not to distract you from thinking about all that's happened today." Her eyes penetrated his with such tenderness that he saw in them a reflection of God's love.

"I'm sorry I've been so hard on you," he whispered. "I don't know why you've put up with me and my anger."

Her eyes flickered in surprise. "You've never been anything

but honest about your thoughts. That's one of the reasons I love you."

"Really?"

"Really."

"And you don't regret that I'm not some suave, sophisticated, music-educated, normal-sized, good, ol' American boy?"

His heart nearly overflowed when Haven laughed and wrapped her arms around his neck. "I love every long foot of you."

"You'll put up with my long hours at the hospital and my gory stories?" He held her tightly.

"Um-hmm."

"And you'll keep singing for me when I've had a hard day?"

"Yes."

"Even when our children are grown and my hair is thin and grey?"

"Even then."

They held each other quietly.

Haven raised her head and held his gaze. "You *are* asking me to marry you, right? This sounds like a proposal. But it would be awkward if I say 'yes' and I got it wrong."

Petter lifted her from his lap, dropped to his knees and took her hands. "Haven Ellingsen, I didn't think I'd be proposing today, so I don't have a ring yet. But if you give me your hand in marriage, I promise to love and honor you the rest of our lives. And give you the most beautiful diamond ring you could ever imagine."

Her mouth trembled and tears filled her eyes. "Oh, Petter, I couldn't imagine life without you."

He started to rise but she stopped him.

"There's just one thing, Doctor."

"What's that?"

"The man I marry needs to first ask my father for my hand."

Petter sighed as he stood. "I'd better take you home, then." In one swift motion, he lifted her like a groom carrying his bride and trotted her over to the jeep. Depositing her, laughing and squealing in the passenger seat, he ran around and started the motor.

When she caught her breath, she said, "Dr. Eriksen, just what are you planning?"

"If I leave right now, I could be in Portland in time to have dinner with your father."

Chapter Sixteen

"In You, O Lord, I have taken refuge; let me never be put to shame; Deliver me in Your righteousness. Turn Your ear to me, come quickly to my rescue."
Psalm 31:1, 2

Erik dropped Haven off at Fairhaven Community Church's main entrance. "Petter asked me to tell you he might be a few minutes late and to be sure you just wait for him in the office."

She smiled tolerantly. She had to get used to the reality of Petter guarding her for the rest of their lives. "I think he's afraid I'll try to walk home again like I did in the thunderstorm."

"Just humor him, Haven. He loves his fiancée very much." Erik's tender eyes crinkled.

"Okay, Papa." She squeezed his hand. "See you tonight."

She went down to the choir room and unlocked the back door for the children. This would be their last rehearsal of the season. Saturday, she and Pastor Gary would take both of her elementary choirs to Cascade Spring's Assisted Living facility to present their music and skits. The next morning, they planned on performing the same material for the Sunday service at Fairhaven.

She pulled down the boxes of props and costumes and began setting them out for the children.

Pastor Gary poked his head in the room. "Hi. I'm just getting the sound booth and the stage set for the kids. Anything you need?"

"Not that I can think of. We'll warm up in here and get our costumes on before we come up."

Just then, the children began to arrive and she turned her attention to greeting them.

Two hours later, tired and over-stimulated from an energetic work-out, Haven and the children returned to the choir room.

"Emily, leave your costume on the chair here."

"Miss E., my head-piece itches. Do I have to wear it?"

"Only for the first skit, Katelyn. Then you can take it off. Josiah, where's your armor? Did you leave it on the stage?"

"I put it in this box, Miss E.," Josiah answered, showing her. "My sword's in here, too."

"Thanks for helping me, Josiah. I really appreciate it." She bent over and hugged the small boy.

Parents began to arrive, greeting her, asking how they could help on Saturday. Children swarmed, tugging at their mother's elbows excitedly, telling them about the party planned for Saturday afternoon after their performance. She handed out directions to the Assisted Living Home, speaking loudly over the cacophony of children's voices.

After the children and parents had driven off, Wendy and Gary backed their van up to the choir room's steps and the three carried boxes of props and costumes outside, loading them into the back.

"Okay, that should do it." Gary slammed the back doors of the van. "See you Saturday."

Haven followed Wendy to the front of the van.

"Are you excited about this weekend?"

"Oh, yes. But I'm also a little sorry that the season is ending. I always miss the kids during break."

Wendy climbed into the front seat and leaned her head out the window, grinning. "I doubt you'll have much time this summer to miss the kids, with a wedding to start planning."

Haven smiled and her cheeks warmed at the thought of Petter in a tux, waiting for her to walk down the aisle and join him in saying their vows in front of Pastor Bernard and hundreds of witnesses. "I'll guess I'll find out." She walked back up the steps and stood at the back door, waving as the van slowly pulled forward. The tail lights receded into the gloom of dusk.

Going back inside, she shut and locked the door, expelling a sigh of fatigue. It had been a long day and sinking into her bed with a good book and a hot mug of herbal tea was going to feel heavenly. She was just moving over to the prop table to collect her things when the piano bench creaked.

"Ruth."

Only one word. Spoken in a deep rumbling bass. For a second she thought it was Petter, but the character of the voice was not gentle. It was more like—

She turned toward the voice. Like a punch to the gut, all her breath left her. She willed herself to scream. Her chin trembled, she opened her mouth, but nothing came out.

Dade stood up and moved around the piano. He slowly approached her, eyes fixed on her with the same hypnotic, catlike stare that haunted her nightmares.

The shock of seeing the big man again robbed her arms and legs of strength. Her vision darkened, and nausea flooded her stomach. But fainting was not an option. She needed to stay awake and alert.

"What do you want, Dade?" She'd forced herself to say his name, to look strong. She stood straight and met his eyes.

"What do I want?" The hard sound in his voice resurrected awful memories. He came very near and towered over her as if trying to make her flinch or show fear.

Her cell phone, sitting on the table by the piano, rang. Dade started. Both of their eyes darted toward the phone. She made a move to answer it, but Dade seized her wrist.

"If I don't answer, someone will come down from the office.

Dade opened his jacket revealing a gun in his belt. He walked her over to the telephone. "Anyone comes down here ..." He pulled the weapon out and gripped it at his side.

Her hands shook as she picked up the phone, her eyes never leaving Dade's face. "Hello?" she said, sounding ridiculously calm. "Yes, I'm just about done, Lucy. I'm straightening up in here. Please tell him to wait in the office. No, I don't need his help. I should be finished in just a few minutes. Tell him to wait upstairs. Okay, bye." She hung up and Dade slid his weapon back in his belt.

He gripped her arm and hurried her to the back door. Unlocking and opening the door, he scanned the empty parking lot. They went down the steps like lovers, his arm slung around her shoulder. He walked her quickly across the lot in the direction of a truck parked along the street.

♩ ♪♪♫♪

Petter paced the room next to Lucy's office. The small box in his blazer pocket seemed to burn a hole straight into his heart. He'd made reservations at Haven's favorite fancy Chinese restaurant and he didn't want to be late. He had not told her about the dinner plans or his other surprise. And he couldn't wait to see her face when he presented the engagement ring. A one and a half carat marquee diamond surrounded by smaller diamonds and sapphires.

He took out his cell phone and called her number, but there was no answer. "Wasn't Haven just cleaning up?" he asked Lucy, who was shutting down her computer and preparing to go home. "I think I'll go help her."

He went out the office door, down the hall, down the stairs. The choir room door was closed and he heard no sounds inside.

"Haven," he called. He opened the door. Her music bag, cell phone, and purse were sitting on the table and everything appeared to be in order. Maybe she was in the ladies' room. He went down the hall and knocked on the restroom door, calling her name. He nudged the door opened a couple of inches. The lights were off. He hurried back to the office, thinking that somehow, they'd missed each other.

"Lucy," he called, "did Haven come up here?"

Lucy was standing outside the office door with a stricken look on her face. A little boy and his mother pushed past Lucy and approached.

"Are you Dr. Eriksen?" the mother asked. Her voice quavered.

He nodded, and the look on the woman's face made his stomach tighten

"I'm Mrs. Weston. We just came back because Josiah forgot his bag. As we were driving up we saw Haven walking away from the church with a man. From the way she described you, we thought it was you."

Lucy broke in. "I've already called the police."

"All of a sudden," Josiah's mother panted, "Haven started running toward us. I was too far away to hear most of what she said. All I heard was 'the police!'"

Mrs. Weston gripped her handbag to her chest. "That man ran after her and yanked her back. She screamed and tried to get away, but he hit her. Then he picked her up and shoved her into a pickup truck and drove off."

Dade hit Haven. Took her. Every nerve in Petter's body seemed to fire simultaneously. He didn't have time for rage or fear. He had to think fast. His voice turned hoarse, but his Emergency training kicked into high gear. "Did you get a good look at the guy?"

"He was very tall, had brown hair and a beard, wearing a dark blue or black jacket."

"Ma'am, which direction did they go? Could you see what kind of truck?"

"They went east. That's all I noticed. I didn't have my cell phone so I ran in here to tell Lucy." She shook her head helplessly.

Petter swiped his hand across his jaw. Every instinct told him to jump into his car and pursue. But the police would be at the church any second. They needed him. They'd—

"Excuse me, Mister." the boy tugged at Petter's sweater. "I'm Josiah. I saw them. I saw the truck. I can tell you about it."

He crouched down and looked the little boy in the eyes

squarely. "Now Josiah, this is important. What can you tell me about the truck?"

"It was a 2012 Ford. Just like my Dad's, 'cept it was green. I think I can remember the license plate number, too."

♩ ♪♪♫♪

Haven concentrated on praying during their flight south, thankful that Dade said nothing to her. Jesse had already given her all the information on Dade's truck and everything else he could think of that might be pertinent, and she had handed over this information to Petter. By now Petter would have called the police and they'd be looking for her. Had Petter tried to find Jesse? If Dade took her to his hiding place, Jesse could show them right where it is. *Please, Lord, please keep Petter safe. I'm so afraid he'll come after us and do something to get himself hurt. Please keep him away from Dade.*

But just then Dade exited the interstate. She rubbed the sore spot on her cheek where he'd struck her. "Where are we going, Dade?"

His tone came out harsh. "You don't need to know anything, little girl. Just trust me to take care of you."

She tried again in a calmer voice. "The police know about you. Wouldn't it be better to just let me go before—"

"Shut up! Just shut up!" He raised a fist as if he were going to strike her again. "You stupid woman. You've caused me enough trouble. I don't want to hear another word out of you."

He turned onto a dark country road, pulled the Ford over and shut the motor. Reaching into the glove compartment, he pulled out a small plastic bag and fumbled in the dark. She saw the syringe a split second before he plunged it into her shoulder. She yelled and clutched her shoulder. Then she stared at him wordlessly, watching him watching her. He smiled, but his eyes were hard. His face came closer, like a predator checking for signs of life in its victim. She launched her fist like one of her rocks at his toothy grimace, but he caught her hand just before it connected. He laughed and his breath batted at her face as he pinned her arms back. "Not this time, Ruth."

♩ ♪♪♫♪

This is exactly the spot I followed him to." Jesse's voice rose in anger. "I swear it."

"Maybe he turned off farther down the highway." Detective Butler looked skeptical. He shone his flashlight down the road. "The roads all pretty much look the same in—"

"Not a chance," Jesse interrupted. "I wrote it down." He pulled his wallet out of his back pocket and thumbed through several slips of paper. "Here it is." He might not be in law enforcement, but that didn't make him stupid. He shoved the paper into the detective's hand.

A K-9 officer approached. "The dog isn't picking up anything, Doug."

Dr. Eriksen shone his flashlight on the paper the detective was inspecting. "Jesse, are you sure Dade didn't see you following him? You said he's a smart guy. Maybe he was just making you think this is where his place is."

Butler's radio crackled and the detective hurried over to

respond.

"Think hard, Jesse," Eriksen pressed. "When you went to see Dade at his apartment, did he say anything, anything at all about his secret place? Did you see anything?"

Jesse wanted to punch the doctor. Did the man think he was the only one who was crazy with worry about Haven?

Butler called and motioned for his team to come over. He turned to the doctor. "Doc, we've got some guys at Colton's former apartment. They're talking to the apartment manager right now."

Jesse stood off by himself, rubbing his forehead in concentration. Suddenly, he froze, then pounded his fist into his other hand. "Listen!" He rushed back over to Dr. Eriksen and the group of officers. "This could be nothing, but it's worth looking into. When I was in Dade's apartment last month, I noticed a stack of receipts sitting on a shelf by the door. I got a chance to get a quick look at them when he answered the phone. At the time, I was hoping to see something that would link him to Cascade Springs so I could warn Haven. The top two receipts were both from businesses in Clear View, off I-90. One was a tire place and the other was a motel. I forgot about it until now 'cause it didn't seem to fit with what I thought he was planning."

"Let's head back toward Tacoma," Butler said. "We can check out those leads while we're driving.

♩ ♪♪♫♪

When Haven woke she was lying on a mat in a dark room, covered by a blanket. Her wrist was sore and she tried to bring her arm up to inspect it. It would only come so far. Her wrist was tethered with duct tape to the leg of a ratty old upholstered chair.

One small beam from a flashlight danced up and down the walls. A shadow and footsteps approached. Dade leaned over her. She shut her eyes. His steps retreated. Dade settled onto the only other piece of furniture in the room, a straight-backed wood chair near the window. He rested his rifle across his thighs and leaned forward to stare out the window. A dog yipped. Dade jumped up and peered out the window. He listened for a long time. "Probably just a coyote," he muttered. He sat down again. Whenever he turned his head to check on her, she shut her eyes and pretended unconsciousness.

She "slept" for the remainder of the night. What would she do in the morning?

♩ ♪♪♫♪

Petter insisted that Jesse come along with him when he accompanied Detective Butler to the Woodlands Apartments where Dade had lived recently. When they knocked on the manager's door, the man opened and regarded them warily. It took all Petter's restraint not to grab the manager by the throat and demand more answers.

In response to Butler's questions, the manager said, "I told you, he didn't leave any forwarding address. Wait a minute." He stomped inside his apartment, returning seconds later, holding an envelope. He handed it to Detective Butler. "This is the only thing I got that has his name on it. It got put in the wrong mailbox and I forgot to give it to him before he moved."

Petter and Butler walked back to the squad car. Jesse jumped out and came over. The three of them hunched over to study the envelope by the light of Butler's flashlight. A feminine hand had penned a single name on the outside of the envelope. "Dade." Butler slid his thumb under the envelope flap and pulled out the single page handwritten letter. Petter leaned over and read the message out loud.

"Sir, I know you don't ever lie. I know now I can believe you that I am beautiful. I am ready to work hard and do whatever you ask to make your kingdom come. I want to belong to you. I will wait for you to come back. I love you. Fiona"

Included in the envelope was a photo of a sad-faced, plain young woman standing behind a restaurant counter. Turning the photo over, a hand-printed caption read, "Remley Pub."

"Remley?"

"That's just up the road from Clear View," Jesse said.

For the first time in hours, Petter felt his heart lighten with hope.

"You been there?" Butler asked. "What's it like around there?"

"Lots of dirt roads going nowhere, mountains … real undeveloped," Jesse replied excitedly.

The detective squinted at the photo of Fiona. "Thanks, Mr. Garson, we'll go check it out. You can go home now."

"But, I can help. I know Dade. You need me!"

"What we need is for you to not get hurt. Odds are we'll get Mr. Colton, and we need you safe and sound to give your testimony in court," the detective replied, testily. "Go home, Mr. Garson … wait." He reached into his pocket. "Here's some cab fare."

Jesse stormed away, his face grim.

"Come on, Doctor Eriksen." The detective gestured toward his car. "We can be there in a little over an hour."

♩ ♪♪♫♪

It hadn't taken Jesse long to get back to his apartment in Seattle, stash a rifle in the trunk of his car, then head east again. Remley was so tiny a town that it hadn't been hard to find the three police cars pulled up alongside Fiona's place. And it was the only house with its lights on inside. He parked his car halfway down the block from the house, got out and moved stealthily up the road. He hid across the street behind a fence and hedge. Once in a while, a shadow moved across the curtained front window. They'd been in there for two hours and in another half hour the sun would come up. Then he would have to move back to his car and park somewhere else.

What was taking them so long? Dade must've really gotten under Fiona's skin. Jesse pictured the police trying to convince the girl that Dade wasn't all that he seemed. He was tempted to go knock on her door and tell her a thing or two about the man. Some women just couldn't look at things the way they really were. Dade had Mama convinced he was some great spiritual giant. Even when he was knocking her around she still couldn't see how bad he was. And now he'd gotten some other poor, needy woman looking at him the same way. He shook his head. *I don't get it.*

It was nearly light when he returned to his car, still pondering about Dade and his women. But Haven wasn't like those other women. She was never impressed by his preaching or his big muscles. *She's sweet but spunky, and she'd never put up with a man hitting her.*

Dade *would* hit her. The thought made his stomach clench. Maybe not today or next week, but someday. She'd disobey him, or do something to make him feel disrespected and he'd hurt her. Not the lashing out that most people think of when they imagine an abuser. No, it would be the kind of punishment that Dade had thought about and planned for hours. The kind of punishment you knew was coming, but you didn't know when it would happen. That was part of the torture. His jaw gritted when he remembered the slaps and punches, usually where it would be hidden by clothing, the cruel grip, the metal tip of the belt tearing into his back. The scars.

"That's never gonna happen again, Dade. Not to me or Haven or anyone else." He folded his arms across his chest and settled himself to watch Fiona's house.

♩ ♪♪♫♪

The first rays of dawn stole into the room. Dade's head had slumped to the side and he snored softly, still seated at the wood chair by the window. Haven had worked on the duct tape the rest of the night, stopping whenever there was a pause in his snoring. Still, she had only managed to fray about a third of an inch of the strong stuff. If only she could move close enough to get her teeth up to the material. When she tried to slide her body toward the edge of the mat, Dade stirred immediately.

"What are you doing, Ruth?"

"I need to get up, Dade. Where's the bath?"

Dade rose, reached into his pocket and drew out a pocketknife. He cut the tape and she stood, rubbing her wrist.

"Come on." He took her arm and led her through the bedroom door, into the main living area. She glanced around quickly. The layout was similar to the old, dark cabin where she'd been imprisoned. Whose cottage was this? The furnishings were sparse, as though no one lived here. They went through a back door and out into the cold dawn. Dade waited outside the outhouse for her to finish. When she emerged, she was bent over slightly, clutching her abdomen, whimpering in pain.

"Do you have any aspirin or something? It's really bad this time." She hobbled past him.

Dade's eyes narrowed.

"Really bad cramps. Hurts so bad I feel like I'm gonna throw up." She avoided his eyes.

Dade scowled and followed her back inside. She sank down onto the kitchen chair and moaned. He went over to the pantry.

"Here, this should work." He came over and handed her a bottle of pills and a glass of water and put a big paper bag on the table in front of her. "And there're all the other things you might need."

She peeked into the bag, seeing an assortment of feminine products. Looking up, she caught his awkward expression. How silly that men got so embarrassed by a woman's period. Like it was somehow shameful. She remembered her imprisonment in his cabin. Dade would sleep on the floor in the living room for a few days each month. He wouldn't even touch Mama during that time. Maybe her ruse would keep him away for a day or two.

"Are you going to need the outhouse again?" He watched

while she swallowed a couple of painkillers.

"Yes, Sir." She forced a grateful expression. "Thank you for the pills."

Dade nodded, looking gratified by her sweetness and respect.

She stood up, holding the bag, and moved toward the back door again. Dade followed her out and stood guard again outside the outhouse. When she was finished she followed him back to the bedroom. This time he did not wrap the duct tape so tightly around her wrist. As he was securing the tape around the chair's leg she looked up and met his eyes.

"Thank you for being considerate. I know you could have been a lot rougher with me. I appreciate it, Sir."

He leaned over her with a look she remembered from her first imprisonment. Alarmed, she flipped over on her side, curled her body and moaned in pain. Dade hesitated, then turned and walked out of the bedroom.

Chapter Seventeen

"Many are the woes of the wicked,
but the Lord's unfailing love surrounds the man who trusts in
him."
Psalm 32:10

Petter and the detective came out of Fiona's house. "That girl is completely under Dade's spell," he muttered as they got into the Butler's squad car.

"I know, Doc. But she didn't say anything to implicate herself in the kidnapping. We're just going to have to watch her house and see if she goes anywhere."

He watched for any sign from Butler that he was keeping anything from him. "What does your gut tell you, Butler?"

The detective thought before responding. "My gut tells me that Fiona knows where Dade's place is. Whether Haven is even there I don't know. Dade might have stashed her somewhere else." He started the motor and pulled away from the curb. "In the meantime, we can start getting Dade's phone records, credit card receipts, talk to anyone who knows him."

"That could take a while," Petter exclaimed. "Dade thinks he's married to Haven. There's no telling what he's already done to her." He'd kill the man himself if anything had happened to Haven.

"I know, Dr. Eriksen. But we're making progress. We'll get this guy."

They turned the corner onto the main street through Remley and the detective added, "We got an undercover man watching Fiona's house. If she comes out, he'll let us know right away."

Butler pulled over to park. "I gotta get some coffee before I pass out, Doc. There's a vending machine at the gas station down this street."

They got out and he followed Butler to the machine, fatigue and worry making him weak. *Lord, please keep her safe. Bring her back to me. Keep her alive.*

♩ ♪♪♫♪

Dade made breakfast that morning. When it was done he came into the bedroom and looked down at Haven. Her eyes were closed and her breathing was slow and regular. His eyes swept over her, taking in her hair, her beautiful face, the shapeliness of her form. *"This is now bone of my bones and flesh of my flesh,"* he quoted from Genesis. She was his promised fruitful vine. God had rewarded his diligence.

It had been a tense night. He cursed inwardly when he thought about the woman and child who'd witnessed the kidnapping. But, anyway, it didn't matter. He'd gotten away quickly and cleanly. During his drive to the cabin, he'd seen no police cars. No one had a clue where they'd gone. Certainly not Jesse. He almost laughed when he remembered leading Jesse out of town and onto those winding county roads. He'd finally lost him on a particularly rough dirt road. Jesse's old sedan couldn't handle the ruts and rocks. He'd waited for an hour, making certain Jesse had given up and driven off, then returned to the county road and proceeded back onto the highway, heading for I-90. The police would be searching fruitlessly miles away in the shadow of Mt. Rainier. There was nothing to trace him to this area. Unless. Unless Ruth knew more than she had let on. That's what had kept him up all night. That she-devil had a way of knowing his mind.

But Ruth was already softening toward him. She'd thanked him for thinking about her needs and for not hurting her. He could have roughed her up good. He'd been gentle, even when she was unconscious. Even when he had grabbed her back in Cascade Springs, it didn't seem that she had struggled too hard. Maybe she just had to give a good show in front of that mother and boy.

Those foreign men at the retreat—the men at her church, and especially that big doctor, sniffing around Ruth like she was female dog—they'd never get to feast their eyes on her beauty anymore. He had rescued her from their lustful plans. From now on she'd look only at him. "The Lord has dealt with me according to my righteousness; according to the cleanness of my hands He has rewarded me," he murmured while gazing down at Ruth. It was almost as if the time between their betrothal and the present had simply slipped away, transporting her back to that sweet, shy love she had once shown him.

Haven opened her eyes.

"Ruth," he said. "You are my wife."

Ruth threw her arms out to keep him away. Her mouth gaped wide, and her blue eyes filled with terror. She gasped as if she were going to scream, but no sound came out.

He scowled. Ruth feared his touch. Nothing had changed in a year's time. She had not learned to desire him during their separation. Maybe she wanted that big blonde man at the retreat instead.

His hands balled into fists. Her fear and rejection made him want to hit her. He stepped closer. Maybe he would.

But the terror in her eyes' blue depths suddenly melted into an expression of wonder and then, peace. She looked past him, at the ceiling. Her mouth relaxed and she drew a deep breath. "Thank You," she murmured, still staring past him.

He jerked around, eyes darting around the walls, half expecting to see a police officer standing in the doorway. But there was nothing.

The batty woman. Her palms turned upward as if in worship. "I trust you."

He glanced up at the ceiling, just to make sure. But there was nothing there. Just rough cabin walls. Beamed ceilings. The woman was crazier than he'd remembered. Seeing things that didn't exist. Talking to someone who wasn't there. Must be the brain damage.

But it pleased him that she had thanked him. She knew he had the power of life and death over her. Ruth would come to love him. "I made some breakfast, Ruth."

She held her tethered arm up and he took out his pocketknife.

♩ ♪♪♫♪

The slender young woman stepped out of her front door and turned the key in the lock. She had draped her shawl over her hair and part of her face and now she walked briskly away from the house. She noticed the man sitting in his car, three houses down, pretending to read a magazine. She reached the street corner and turned in the direction of the Remley Pub "It'll work. It's got to work," she murmured to herself several times, trying to speak courage into her faltering heart. As she turned the corner she quickened her pace and glanced over her shoulder several times. Just as she crossed the street, one block away from the Café, she looked back one more time. The undercover officer had taken the bait and was walking nonchalantly in the same direction. If she slowed down, he wouldn't lose her. He was only half a block away when she reached the restaurant. She entered and took a seat, facing the door. She unwrapped the shawl and let it fall back over her shoulders. The undercover sauntered in seconds later. But when he saw her, he started visibly and his face turned pale. She smiled.

♩ ♪♪♫♪

Fiona inched her front door open and scanned the area. The undercover had taken the bait, following her sister into the business district. Fiona slipped out, hurried up the street and turned the corner, going the opposite direction. She climbed into an old, beat-up VW van and pointed the car out of town, going northwest. After a long mile, she turned onto an unmarked dirt road and slowed, looking for the fork in the road. She turned right and started to climb steeply. After a couple hundred yards the road ended. She backed the van behind a thick tangle of downed tree limbs and vegetation, next to Dade's green truck, and shut off the motor. She hurried up the path through the trees. After three minutes part of the cottage roof peaked through the trees. She hesitated. How would Sir react? He hadn't summoned her. Didn't matter. She mounted the steps and banged on the door. Through a slit in the curtains, she saw Dade spring to his feet. He snatched up his rifle hanging on the wall. Leveling the weapon, he called out hoarsely, "Who is it?"

"Fiona," she cried, "Let me in!"

Dade unlatched and opened the door, still holding the rifle. Seizing her arm, he yanked her inside and slammed the door shut. "What are you doing here, girl?" he thundered. He looked out the window. When he turned to face her, his eyes threatened violence.

"You said I should warn you if anything happened. I was just—"

She stopped and stared hard at Haven, sitting at the kitchen table,

Haven jerked to her feet. "Fiona! How did you … what are you doing here? Do you know this man?" She ran over and grabbed Fiona's hand. "Please help me. He's kidnapped me."

Fiona pulled her hand away. "Let go of me." Her lips drew back in disgust. She turned to Dade. "Then it's true? The police were telling the truth about Haven?" She didn't want to believe them. It couldn't be true. Why would Dade still be thinking about this stupid rich girl? She thought she'd seen the last of her in Issaquah.

Haven tried to put her hand on Fiona's arm. "Fiona, please. Listen to me. He—"

"Shut up, girl." Dade lurched toward Haven, his fist raised to strike her. She ran back and hid behind the table.

"Sir … you … that girl …" Dade wouldn't lie to her. Fiona was the only girl he loved now. But now, here she was again, standing between her and Dade, threatening her special position.

Dade glared at her. "That girl is my wife," he roared. "Nobody, not even the law, comes between me and her."

He peeked through the curtains. "Whatever you heard from the police, they're wrong. Why are you here, Fiona?" He took a step toward her and she recoiled. Was he going to strike her?

She looked over at the girl she hated. "They talked to me all last night … the police. Tried to get me to tell them something."

"What?" He lunged toward her and seized her arm, gripping it so hard that she squealed. "B-but I wouldn't tell them anything, Dade. I-I protected you." She started to cry, fearing his fist and at the same time feeling betrayed. Would he have ever broken the law to keep her for himself, like he had Haven?

"Where are they now?" Dade hissed, looming over her, his eyes frightening.

"In town," she whimpered. "But they don't know anything. I got away. Dade, I can help you. Just leave her here. Come with me before it's too late."

♩ ♪♪♫♪

Dade had ordered Haven to stay put at the kitchen table. She watched Dade and Fiona. They'd been standing face to face, whispering at the other end of the cabin for almost fifteen minutes. The time seemed to pass in slow motion. But from that distance, she couldn't understand their conversation.

Fiona. It couldn't be true. The same girl she'd rescued from her abusive boyfriend. The same one she'd befriended. How long had she known Dade? The coincidence—if it was one— was too horrible to think about. How could this girl care for Dade? Didn't she know he was a monster?

Dade left Fiona, paced, and looked out the front window from time to time. He seemed to be weighing his options. He glanced over at Haven and for the first time she could ever remember, his face showed fear.

Fiona followed him into the main room. "We still have time to get away," she whispered urgently. "Please, Sir. I don't want you to get hurt."

Fiona turned and glared at Haven. Hatred pinched her thin, colorless lips.

Haven dropped her gaze. That Fiona was in love with Dade.and murderously jealous could be worked to Haven's advantage. Fiona wanted her to disappear. What if Fiona could convince Dade to leave her here and the two of them could run?

If they stayed in the cabin and the police showed up, she would become a hostage. Dade had obviously been planning her kidnapping for a long time. But now that he had her, even if the police discovered their hideout, it was unlikely he would surrender her alive. And what if Petter came with the police? What if he got shot?

Being a hostage was the worst-case scenario. Outside the cabin and on the run, she might have a better chance of escaping.

She jumped up, ran to Dade, and grasped his arm. He looked down at her and his eyes communicated indecision. "Dade, let's run away quick … before they come here. Please."

Dade's eyes narrowed, looking from her to Fiona, and back. Then he strode over to the kitchen cabinet. Reaching up high, he pulled down the handgun he'd used the night before. He handed it to Fiona.

"The cabin's the best place to hold them off."

Chapter Eighteen

"A man who remains stiff-necked after many rebukes
will suddenly be destroyed—without remedy."
Proverbs 29:1

Jesse had followed Fiona's car until she'd taken the right fork up the steep, rutted road. He parked and jumped out. Following the trail of dust her van had made, he found it parked next to Dade's truck. He ran up the path and hid himself just in time to see Fiona bang on the cabin door and see Dade's angry face as he opened the door and pulled her in. Satisfied, he circled the cabin, noted its back door, then ran back down the path and got into his car. Putting it in neutral, he coasted down the hill. Once out of earshot his tires spun dust all the way back to the county road.

He found Petter sitting in the police station's front office, his head slumped over in exhausted sleep. He woke the doctor and told him what he'd seen.

Petter grabbed him by the shoulders. "Did you see Haven?"

"No, but if Dade's there you can be sure she's there, too. He wouldn't let her out of his sight."

"Where's Butler?"

"They're in the back questioning that girl," Petter said.

Just then, the locked door leading to the offices and jail opened and the detective poked his head inside the room.

Petter rushed forward before Butler could speak and gave him the news. The man's jaw dropped at Petter's announcement.

"You sure it was him, Mr. Garson?"

He scowled. "Do you think I'd forget my stepfather's face?"

"Was he armed?"

"Carryin' a rifle. . . and he's a real good shot. Look, Detective Butler, Dade's got some strange religious ideas about Haven. He thinks she's supposed to be the mother of a whole new religious group. He's never gonna let her go. So, don't go thinkin' you kin just surround the place and make him surrender. If Haven's gonna come out alive yer gonna have to sneak up and snipe him."

Petter's face went pale at his words. "Wouldn't it be better then, to just wait until he shows himself ... comes out to town or something?"

The detective seemed to consider the doctor's suggestion. "I don't know, Eriksen."

"We can't just storm the place," Petter exclaimed. "If he's got a gun, there's no telling what he'll do to Haven!"

"We're not going to do anything yet, not until we talk this thing over with the guys down the hall," Butler replied quietly. "Mr. Garson, how's Dade's cabin laid out?"

Finally, they were talking to the right man.

♩ ♪♪♫♪

Petter wanted to jump into the squad car and drive immediately to Dade's hideout. But the detective called for back-up. Half an hour later, six squad cars snaked down the county road. They parked at the fork in the road and Petter waited while Jesse showed the detective and the officers the way up to the cabin. Then Butler sent Jesse back with the order to stay inside the vehicle. But as soon as the detective and officers left, they both climbed out and followed. The Clear View police fanned out, moving uphill, staying behind cover. Detective Butler had mentioned the need to surround the cabin before trying to contact anyone inside. But what if Dade could see the police moving into position?

Without warning, two shots, fired from the cabin, shattered the front window. Butler and the police officers accompanying him dropped to the ground. Petter and Jesse weren't much farther behind the police. They crouched and hid behind thick bushes.

Butler raised a bull-horn to his lips. "Dade Colton, drop your weapon and come out with your hands up. The police have your cabin surrounded." Another shot rang out, coming from the same window.

The detective gestured for his officers to start moving around to the back of the cabin.

Butler waited for them to safely maneuver into position. "Dade Colton, we don't want to hurt you. Please let your hostage go." Silence followed.

Butler raised the bull-horn again. "Dade Col—"

A fourth shot rang out. Seconds later, men's voices shouted, followed by the sounds of boots rushing about inside the cabin. Another shot sounded, this one more muffled.

The front door opened and an officer poked his head out,

keeping his body hidden behind the wall. "Stand down," he shouted. "Premises secure. One woman in here, wounded. No others in the house."

Butler jumped up and rushed forward. The same officer came out onto the porch. "We need the doctor, quick."

Petter vaulted from cover, followed by Jesse. They raced uphill, and into the cabin. Petter's pulse hammered in his ear. An officer crouched over a small, slender form, lying on the floor. Her face was hidden by the officer's back. *Oh, God, no!* Petter flung himself onto his knees next to the injured woman. Her arm shielded most of her face. He gently moved it aside.

"Fiona!"

♩ ♪♪♫♪

Haven stumbled and fell, gasping for breath. Dade had been dragging her steadily uphill at a grueling pace for an hour. Did he ever tire? He cursed when she fell and yanked her back to her feet. He'd tethered her wrist to prevent her from escaping and kept a firm grip on the other end. They'd clawed their way through dense forest, their hands and faces whipped and scratched by pine boughs. But Dade seemed to know exactly where he was going. Even though they had to constantly climb up and down ditches or ravines, he always readjusted his direction. He stopped every few minutes to listen and catch his breath. Then, apparently satisfied that no sounds of pursuit met his ears, he pulled on the rope and trudged onward.

Dade had threatened to strike her if she made a sound. But even if she'd wanted to, she was too out of breath to speak. Any time he stopped she tried to glance backward and get her bearings. But after several ridges, it was impossible to tell where they'd come from. They were heading north, that was clear by the direction of the sun. At mid-afternoon, clouds began to build and the sky to darken. Just when they made it to the top of another high ridge the first raindrops fell.

Where was Petter? Was he with the police? They had to be searching for her.

Dade rationed the water from his canteen, giving her just enough to keep her on her feet. Having climbed for most of the morning and afternoon, they now began to descend into a dark valley. A cold breeze carried the rain straight into their faces, and the way down turned slick. Lightning flickered in the west, moving ever closer. What was once a distant rumble of thunder had crescendoed to a ground shaking, ear-drum-shattering display. Dade scanned the area for shelter.

They made it halfway down the ridge when she saw a downed tree and pointed. They climbed through and under the branches of the fir. Dade dragged his rifle and pack with him. He took out a tarp and the two huddled under it. Even as their cold breaths swirled in a fog about their faces she tried to imagine what Petter might be doing at this very moment. *Please help him, Lord. Please give him and the police an idea of where I might be.*

♩ ♪♪♫♪

He cursed the rain. It pelted the tarp and ran down its sides. Clouds blew across the ridge they'd just descended. Had the police found his cabin? And if so, how long could Fiona have held them there with his gun? Not for long. Once they got inside they'd realize he and Ruth had run. They'd launch a man-hunt. They'd probably use dogs, too.

They had to get moving again, to cross the west fork of the Tennyson, then head north, following the middle fork. The rivers were still swollen after a long, wet winter. Crossing might be difficult. They might not make it today.

As soon as the lightning and thunder moved east, he pulled Ruth with him out of their temporary shelter. He shouldered the pack and rifle and grabbed onto the end of her tether. He led her downhill, listening for sounds of pursuit, and into the thickest part of the trees. The air chilled and the sun sank behind the tall firs.

♩ ♪♪♫♪

Haven had remained silent during their flight. What use was it to ask Dade questions? He'd probably hit her again if she did. The tense, desperate movements of the big man warned her not to ask questions or express fatigue. Her wrist throbbed from the tight tether, and every muscle in her body ached for rest. She struggled to keep pace with Dade's long, untiring stride. He searched for and apparently identified familiar landmarks, then adjusted his direction accordingly. Where were they going?

The sun had sunk and it was getting hard to see her footing. Just when she was tempted to say something about holing up before they were surrounded by blackness, Dade found what he was searching for. He lowered his rifle and pulled off his heavy pack. A rocky outcropping perched at the top of a steep descent to the river. A cleft between two rocks was just wide enough for a man to fit through. He ordered her to crouch and climb through. Inside, she found a sheltered space with dry ground, padded with pine needles.

"Lie down and be still," Dade growled. His steps crunched about the outside of the shelter. Then it was quiet. She waited for a long time. He could have been near but no sounds alerted her. *Get out. Do it. Now.* If Dade had gone somewhere, this could be her one opportunity for escape. She made it past the entrance, rose to a crouch and scanned the area. Where was Dade's rifle? Did he leave it somewhere around? She crept around the rocks. Her heart sank. No, it was gone. Would she have time to make a dash for freedom? Even if she did, it could be dangerous running about in the dark, risking injury, without any supplies or extra clothing. And if he caught her? Well, she wouldn't think about that. She took a step, then another. Adrenaline shot through her muscles as she tensed for a burst of speed.

Dade came around the corner, carrying his canteen. "Ruth."

No! No, God.

His face turned dark, the way it had when he'd roughed her up a year ago and threatened her. "Didn't I tell you to wait inside the shelter?"

He strode toward her, a snarl twisting his lips. But she ran to meet him, and threw herself onto his chest, hiding a face tense with frustration and defeat. "Where were you? I was afraid. I thought you'd left me." She trembled. *Please don't beat me.*

The man's angry energy calmed. He held her, and when she looked up, he seemed surprised and pleased.

"I told you to stay put. You're going to have to learn to obey me, Ruth, and not ask questions." His voice actually sounded gentle.

"Go back inside," he ordered. She scrambled back under the rocks. When he followed, he was dragging the pack, the rifle and his freshly filled canteen.

He spread out the tarp and they sat on it and ate jerky and sipped from the canteen. Later, he kept the flashlight on just long enough for them to climb under a wool blanket and settle in for the night. Then it was terribly quiet and dark.

Dade slept fitfully. His body jerked awake at the slightest sound. She lay completely still and listened to his breathing. He'd wake for sure if she tried to sneak out. Her gaze roamed about the blackness of their shelter. So far it had worked. Dade saw her silence and obedience as evidence of her willingness to follow him anywhere and submit to his magnificent plan. Clever as the man was, he could not see beyond his delusion. And she had known, having spent the year recollecting her imprisonment, and analyzing Dade and his strange ways, that reasoning, or rebelling, or allowing herself to break down in front of him would all have been counterproductive. She had escaped him because she had managed to appear entirely submissive. Had she not, most likely by now she would have been a defeated, broken, terrified, slave-wife. Or dead.

But, had he forgotten how she nearly broke his leg, six months after her escape, when he tried to re-capture her? Was that still in his mind? Or had he conveniently rationalized her throwing lethal rocks at him? No way to know.

Where would they go in the morning? She'd glimpsed the river. Would they have to cross it? Most likely. She shuddered. At this time of year, the water would be high and swift. But the very danger of the water made escape a possibility. She'd have to think long and hard about that.

♩ ♪♪♫♪

The rain had been a disappointing setback for Petter and their search plans. But, as Butler had told Petter, Dade could not get far on foot—and with a woman—in this terrain. After arranging for a helicopter and dogs, the exhausted detective had sacked out at the station for a few hours of sleep.

Petter waited at the station, wondering where Jesse had gone. He had already contacted Guy in the early morning after the kidnapping. Guy had raced up and met him at the police station.

"When are they going to get started?" Guy paced about the small lobby like a lion in a cage, rubbing his unshaven chin, his eyes staring.

Petter tried to sound in control of his emotions. "They said as soon as it's light enough to see anything. A helicopter's going up in the morning. They've got a tracker and a dog and I've already given them Haven's sweater. They said the dog should be able to scent her even after the rain. They'll be starting right from Dade's place and they'll go wherever the dog leads them." Would it lead to Dade and Haven? It had to. *God, help us.* It had to.

"So, what can we do?" Guy's eyes glittered with the kind of spirit Petter had seen in Haven's face when she spoke about Dade. "If they think I'm just going to sit here and wait for them to find my daughter, they've got another thing coming."

"I've been studying this topographical map all afternoon." Petter spread it out on a small table and ran his finger to the spot where Dade's Remley cottage sat.

Guy came over and bent to look.

"Dade went up this ridge—we know that much—and headed straight north. If he turned west he'd run into the lake and the possibility of being seen by people. Same thing if he headed east. Detective Butler and I both think Dade will continue to go north, but then he'll have to cross one of the Tennyson forks. I doubt that he's made it that far yet, especially having to drag Haven along with him. She's athletic, but even she'd have trouble keeping up with a giant woodsman unless he slowed down."

Guy examined the map, his jaw set in grim determination. "I'm going to be on that helicopter tomorrow morning."

"Good." He met the father's eyes. "And just in case the police lose Dade's trail I'm going to head along the lake and then go over the ridge and watch the river. But first I'm going to get some supplies."

"You look like you haven't slept in days."

"After I get my pack filled we can get some sleep at the Inn."

"I'll drive." Guy pushed his chair back and they walked out the station door.

Chapter Nineteen

"Many waters cannot quench love,
neither can the floods drown it."
Song of Songs 8:7

They woke early. The sun had not yet risen over the eastern ridges and a dense mist shrouded the trees. Haven did not know Dade's plan but reasoned they'd have to cross the river she'd glimpsed the day before if they were to continue to head north. Back at Dade's place, there had been no information—no newspapers, no maps, no mail—that would have given her a clue as to their location. Not even the brown paper bag or any of the feminine products in it that Dade had supplied her with had suggested any particular supermarket.

Jesse had mentioned Mt. Rainier. But she had not seen any mountain that resembled that enormous peak. They'd been hiking due north. But into what? Mt. Rainier had roads crisscrossing its wilderness. So far, they had not even crossed a logging road.

Dade opened a package of granola and gave her a handful. She downed it hungrily while studying him. What would his next move be? She helped him roll up the blanket and pack up their supplies. If only Dade would talk or give her permission to speak. Where were they going? How would he evade the police? Did he think they could hide indefinitely in the wilderness? Did he have other followers like Fiona who might come to his aid? If only she could get some information.

Where was Petter? Suddenly she thought of her father and almost gasped. Did he know what had happened to her yet? Knowing him, nothing would stop him from becoming part of the hunt for her. But why hadn't she heard any sounds of pursuit? A sudden, irrational thought pushed its way into her mind. What if no one was looking for them? What if Fiona managed to convince the police that she and Dade were hiding somewhere else miles away?

She had to stop wondering. It would only make her grow more and more anxious. The police were smart. They were trained in interrogating people and hunting down criminals. They'd find her. And Petter wouldn't ever give up looking. He'd think of something. Dade might be smart, but he couldn't come close to Petter's brain-power.

Dade crawled out from under the shelter and motioned for her to follow. They scrambled down the steep hill to the river. When they reached the south bank, she was disappointed to find a narrow, easily fordable stream. Two large, flat rocks evenly divided the span. They would not even need to get their feet wet. After they crossed, they followed the stream until the banks rose sharply and they had to clamber up to higher ground, grabbing handfuls of moose berry, ferns, and grasses to keep their footing.

She stole backward glances any time Dade wasn't looking. Twice she thought she saw movement up the ridge. Maybe the police were trailing them after all. Had Dade seen it, too? More than once he stopped and looked behind, nervously scanning the area they had just passed through. And when he stopped, he listened. He let go of her tether just long enough to take his rifle in hand.

Even Dade looked tired and she wondered how a man his size could survive on the small amount of food they'd consumed. He was stopping more often now, catching his breath, taking sips from the canteen and handing it to her afterward. They had begun to climb another ridge when the first of the sun's rays penetrated the shadowy forest. Her heart stirred and fresh hope flooded her soul. Surely now the police would be searching. *Lord, I know you see me. I trust you. Please protect Petter … and my dad.*

♩ ♪♪♫♪

Petter examined the river and the surrounding areas. Dressed in camouflage gear, he blended into the grasses and deep greens of the Douglas firs. He'd studied the topographical map closely and had a good idea about where Dade and Haven were likely to come down the ridge and attempt a crossing.

The Clear View police had provided him with a two-way radio transmitter just in case he spotted Dade. He hadn't heard from the police yet and wondered just how far they'd gotten, following Dade. Now, he hiked the southwest banks of the river, studying the current and looking for fordable spots. He traveled half a mile in either direction. It was all deep, swift and hazardous, and the thought of Haven being forced to cross anywhere along the stretch tormented him.

Farther east he encountered a narrower section where the water slammed into high rocky banks and careened eastward. Just beyond this stretch, a large, thick Douglas fir had fallen across the water, the last ten feet of its length resting on the opposite bank, disappearing into tall ferns. He climbed down to the water's edge and examined the tree. It had probably been there at least a year. The branches were dead and in places on the trunk the bark was soft. He stepped up onto the trunk to test its strength and slid his foot up and down between the dead branches. Then he jumped up and down a couple of times. The tree would definitely support a big man and a small woman. He jumped back down onto the bank. If Dade and Haven planned to cross the river, the tree would be their only safe means. But one misstep could be deadly. He looked down at the icy, clear water. *Lord, please take care of Haven.*

Dade and Haven would have to cross at this point. Farther east the river turned into rapids, and then a waterfall. And back where he'd just explored, the river was too wide and deep to ford.

He hiked up from the river and settled himself in a thick cover of vines. Transmitting his position, he described the location around the river. Then he waited.

♩ ♪♪♫♪

Dade ordered Ruth to stop. The girl couldn't go on much longer. They had reached the top of a ridge, and Ruth was gasping for air. He took a swig of the water from his canteen, then gave it to her to finish the last couple ounces of water. The sun had begun to warm the air and the mist was dissipating. He had left the trail when it wound into the open, opting to stay under cover. The Tennyson was just at the bottom of the ridge. He replaced the canteen and grabbed Ruth's tether again.

They zig-zagged down the steep, north face of the ridge. Once or twice he thought he'd heard the distant roar of an airplane or helicopter. And once, when he glanced backward, he thought he saw the shape of a man at the top of the ridge they'd just crested minutes earlier. He yanked Ruth's tether so hard that she winced. He was tempted to ditch the backpack and just throw her over his shoulder so he could move faster. But they were still a day and a half away from the bunker, and if the weather turned he'd regret not having his supplies.

Once down the hill, it was only a couple hundred yards to the dead tree that spanned the river. That would put them in plain sight of any searching helicopter. He would have to be very careful before they climbed up into its branches for the slow crossing.

♩ ♪♪♫♪

Haven stumbled, trying to slow Dade's progress down the hill. Dade cursed her clumsiness under his breath and yanked her forward. The trees were so dense that she couldn't see the river, but she could hear its roar. Were they going to attempt a crossing? Dade did not even hesitate. When the river became visible, he turned confidently toward the west as if following a path visible only to him. The ground leveled nearer the water. A thick tangle of berry bushes and vines grew near the water. To get to the water, they were going to have to walk right by the thorny wall.

If ever there was the perfect spot for an ambush that would be it. It was the first time she had even considered the thought that the Law might actually be ahead of them, waiting to cut them off.

Dade must have had the same thought because he slowed his pace and his sharp eyes moved back and forth, up and down, as if trying to probe the depths of the undergrowth. Then he pulled her forward and quickened his pace once more. They were almost past the vines, maybe ten more paces to the water's edge when she saw something in the bushes, out of the corner of her eye. It was only a hint of color that didn't seem to belong in the tangle of vines. A patch of gold hair, then a human eye, caught in a slim beam of sunlight that had somehow penetrated to that exact spot. She stifled a gasp. Petter!

Dade stopped and let go of Haven's rope. Had he seen what she'd seen? She worked to keep her eyes away from Petter, focused only on Dade.

No. Dade hadn't noticed anything. His eyes were focused on the downed fir. He slipped the backpack from his shoulders and lowered his rifle.

Her eyes flicked back to the vines where Petter lay hidden. Here was her chance. She caught up with Dade and grabbed his arm. "Dade, look! I think I saw someone. Over there." She pointed northward, to a spot across the river. Dade grabbed his rifle, crouched and scoped.

Petter launched himself from his hideout, covering the distance to Dade with a speed Haven didn't know a man possessed, and threw himself on Dade. Dade fell underneath him, landing hard on his side. Petter kicked the rifle far from Dade. They rolled in the grass and grappled for control.

Dade sent a fist flying but Petter deflected the punch.

"Grab his rifle, Haven!" Petter shouted.

She crawled over to get to the gun but was knocked down when Dade and Petter suddenly rolled her way. She scrambled safe from the men's flailing fists and lethal boots, crouched and waited for another chance to go for the rifle. Dade sent an elbow into Petter's ribs, then flipped, catlike, onto his knees. He jumped up and shot out a booted foot to kick Petter. But Petter was too quick. He grabbed Dade's boot and twisted it. Dade fell backward, snarling in pain and anger. Petter fell on Dade again and pinned him on his back. Dade tried to get his hands around Petter's neck. He gripped the collar of Petter's jacket and twisted the material like a tourniquet. Strangling, Petter raised his fist and desperately landed one powerful punch to the older man's jaw. Dade stopped struggling.

Coughing and catching his breath, Petter remained on top of Dade. He watched the man's face warily. Dade's rifle lay partially buried under his long legs. Petter reached under Dade's thigh to pull it out and push it over to the side.

"Haven, get into his pack and see if there's any rope in there."

She ran over to the backpack and pulled out its contents. Petter leaned forward to check the unconscious man's breathing and pulse.

"Is he still alive?"

Petter sat up, straddling the big man. "He'll live." He climbed off and crawled nearer Haven.

She looked up momentarily and met his eyes, her own blurry with exhaustion and tension. She'd found the rope and was just handing it over to Petter when her hands faltered. Dade's head reared up behind Petter. She screamed. Petter didn't react fast enough. Dade sent the butt of the rifle onto Petter's skull. He slumped to the ground.

"No! No!" She threw herself over Petter and tried to shield him with her body. Dade seized her by her hair and hauled her up, his bloodied face dark with rage. Reason and restraint left her. She threw herself on Dade and pounded his chest, screaming, "You monster! I hate you." She kicked him repeatedly, trying to hit his groin. Dade grabbed her wrists and slapped her so hard she fell backward several feet, landing with a hard thump. He stomped over to his backpack and stuffed everything back inside. Then he took the rifle and the pack and came and stood over her.

"Get up, you devil!" He kicked her savagely and she pulled herself up and stood unsteadily. He seized her arm, dragged her over to the fallen tree and shoved her toward the trunk. "Get up there!"

Haven took one last look at Petter, lying very still, twenty feet away. *Lord, please help him.* Then she climbed up onto the dead tree.

The movement of the water over the rocks was just a blur, like the blending and blurring of watercolors, or a camera shot that couldn't quite capture the speed of movement. It was a world of sky turned upside down, racing to meet the horizon. A world of churning, bubbling, swirling, frolicking icy molecules. A world where Dade could not, would not follow.

She gazed down at the water. Images and voices from her memory crested and fell like crashing waves. She was a little girl again, standing on the high diving board. *"C'mon, Haven,"* her *mother shouts from the bleachers. "You can do it. I'm going to count to three and then you jump."*

"Move, girl!" Dade had climbed up and was weaving through the dead branches toward her.

Haven snapped back to reality.

Her steps had carried her to the middle of the river, to the deepest part. She could take this dive. Maybe. The water moved fast. Maybe too fast.

It didn't matter. Anything was better than being Dade's prisoner.

"When you pass through the waters, I will be with you; when you pass through the rivers, they will not sweep over you." [i]

Did she have the courage?

Dade came up from behind and snarled at her. Carrying the rifle over his shoulder and balancing the pack in front, he yelled, "Get moving, woman!"

She balanced precariously, muscles twitching. "I'm not going any further, Dade." She stared downward. "I'm going home."

♩ ♪♪♫♪

Petter came to. What seemed to be the roaring of his throbbing head morphed into the roaring of a river. He reached back and felt the lump on the back of his head. His hand came away with blood.

Then he remembered. Haven. She was gone. Dade had taken her. Petter raised his head and waited for his blurry vision to clear.

Two figures came into focus. A big one, and, farther away, a small one. They were on top of the downed tree. About midway.

He pulled himself up. Stood. Moved like a drunk toward the tree, fighting to stay conscious.

River spray wet his face, reviving him somewhat. He had maybe ten seconds to get up on the tree and take that maniac down. It wasn't as hard as it looked. His balance was coming back. He put a boot on one of the tree roots. It held firm. Another boot. He was on top. And Dade was fifteen feet away, shouting something at Haven. Haven turned to face Dade. Said something back. Petter couldn't hear.

Then Haven swayed. Horror slashed Petter's gut like a sword. She was going to jump. Haven leaned far forward. "Haven, don't! The river's too strong." She didn't hear him. Didn't see him. She took the dive, her body slicing through the frigid water. Dade stood as though frozen. They both watched her slender form rise to the surface and glide swiftly away with the current. Petter let out a kind of unearthly howl. Anguish mixed with rage. Dade turned, dropped his pack and tried to raise his rifle.

A shot rang out. But not from Dade. The bullet struck Dade's rifle, flinging it out of his grasp, into the water.

Petter took his eyes off Dade just long enough to identify the shooter. Jesse stood at the base of the Douglas fir.

"No, Jesse, don't shoot."

"He killed Haven," Jesse shouted. He raised the rifle again.

"Let the Law take care of it. Listen. The helicopter." He jabbed his chin upward. "They're coming for us right now."

Jesse hesitated, taking his eyes off Dade.

"Jesse, you don't—"

A body slammed into his side. For a second, they both swayed. But Dade's weight carried them over the side.

The cold took his breath. Bubbles churned around, and currents sucked at him. Dade had a hold of him, dragging him under the water. Punches rained down from the big man. Water rushed into Petter's mouth. Rocks gouged at his legs.

One punch. He only needed one good punch.

The current swiveled their bodies. Now it sucked Dade downward. Petter kicked off the man's body, rose to the surface and gasped for breath. When Dade's head rose again, Petter was ready. The punch he delivered broke Dade's grip.

The river swept Petter over a rock, around another, shunting him toward the south side of the river. A jumble of boulders broke the river into two halves. Petter put his feet out in front of him to fend them off. Kicking off one of the boulders, he managed to grab the butt end of a partially submerged tree and pull himself out of the current. He crawled onto the pebbly bank, shivering and gasping for breath.

He watched the river. Where had Dade gone? There. On the north side. The icy river and the fight must have weakened him, too. The man was barely able to keep his head above water.

Petter huddled on the shore, shivering uncontrollably. His enemy's body washed on beyond his view. Maybe the Law wouldn't get a chance to deal with Dade Colton.

♩ ♪♪♫♪

Haven would not allow herself to rest. The current had pushed her to the north bank and deposited her almost gently onto a narrow beach. She struggled to her feet. Shivering and dripping, she looked up and down the river. Dade would be across the river by now, maybe searching for her. But what if he returned to the south side of the river? He could be anywhere. But she had to get back to Petter, to take care of him. Even Dade and his gun would not intimidate her. She climbed up the bank to higher ground and found cover in the forest, heading west. Shaking from cold and hunger, she willed her feet to keep on moving. *Please, God. Please, God.*

When she reached the fallen Douglas fir again and crossed to the south bank, she uttered a cry of horror. Petter was gone. She could clearly see how the grass had been flattened and the ground torn up by his struggle with Dade. She sank to her knees and covered her face with her frozen hands.

"God, where is he? Did Dade come back and do something to him?"

She searched the ground for clues as she crawled on her hands and knees. Blood peppered the ground. Blood and boot prints, headed in the direction of the downed tree. Tears clouded her vision and her chest heaved in silent sobs. "Petter, where are you?"

Movement along the bank made her jerk. A man's shape. Dade. He was back. Moving fast. Calling.

She hadn't the strength to jump in the river again. Heart thudding in her ears, she forced herself onto her feet again. She limped, shaky and gasping in the opposite direction. Her legs felt like lead and the man was gaining on her.

"No!" she screamed. He was nearly upon her. "No!" His breaths sounded like Dade. He put his hand on her shoulder and tried to stop her. She whirled around and beat blindly at him with her fists, trying to fend him off. He took her wrists and held them, bending over and calling her name over and over until she recognized him.

His clothes were as wet as hers and his beloved face was

bruised and swollen from his fight with Dade. When she stopped fighting him, Petter pulled her into his arms and held her, stroked her hair, soothed her with his gentle voice.

♩ ♪♪♫♪

The helicopter carrying Guy had to travel another half mile east and away from the river before a suitable set-down spot was found. Once landed, Guy jumped out and tore into the woods, running in the direction of the river. The Clear View police officer had a hard time keeping up. When they reached the water, they made their way upstream, looking for any signs of Petter or Dade. They found the backpack one hundred yards farther up the river, snagged by a downed tree branch. Boot prints were spotted moving from the river and up into the forest. They'd seen the two men go into the water, but where was Haven?

Guy ran to higher ground, moving west, scanning the river. Up ahead he spotted the fallen tree. That had to be the place he'd seen Petter and … Dade? He shouted Haven's name over and over. She had to be near. Unless. He tried not to think about her in the water. But maybe she had gotten away from Dade. Maybe that's why Petter and the other man were fighting. He called Haven's name again. A man answered. He followed the sound and started running, straining to see better. A hundred yards upriver, a man and woman half reclined on the grassy area between the woods and the river. Guy hurried to get a better look. Halfway there, relief and joy spread over his face. Haven. Safe.

Petter sat, holding her. Guy strained to run the last few yards, and when he reached the pair, he dropped to his knees and pulled

Haven into his arms. He buried his face in her pale, damp hair.

His heart was full, and there were so many things he could have expressed, but he said what comes first in a father's heart. "I love you, little girl."

"I love you, too, Dad," she sobbed.

Chapter Twenty

"For the Lord watches over the way of the righteous,
but the way of the wicked will perish."
Psalm 1:6

Jesse had waited until he was sure Dade's head would not pop up from the bottom of the falls. After that, he had to know what happened to Haven. But after spying Petter and Haven and her father reunite, then being surrounded by law enforcement, he returned to the falls and climbed down to the bottom. He found no evidence. No clothing, no boots. No body. He followed the river east for several hundred yards and searched. Then he found it. One large, distinct boot print near the water's edge. It could have been Petter's or some other big man, perhaps one of the search team. He just didn't know. He obliterated the print, then hiked back over the ridge before the police spotted him.

♩ ♪♪♫♪

Guy couldn't stop whispering his thanks to God for sparing Haven. She and Petter were admitted to the Clear View Medical Center. They had both suffered cuts, bruises, and abrasions. Haven was exhausted, cold and dehydrated. But Petter had suffered a mild concussion from the blow to his head and needed to rest quietly.

Guy stood before the news cameras. Detective Butler gave most of the statements and answered the lion's share of the questions. After the reporters and camera crews were satisfied, he went back inside the hospital and stationed himself beside Haven's bedside.

As she slept, he studied her face. When he drew his chair nearer, she opened her eyes. He cradled her hand in his.

When she tried to sit up, he gently pushed her back into her pillow.

"Dad, where's Petter? Is he okay?"

"He's being taken care of. The nurse said he's doing fine. You'll probably both be able to go home tomorrow morning."

Haven drew a drowsy breath and closed her eyes. "You should have seen him, Dad. My calm, gentle doctor," she murmured. "He grabbed Dade and took him down. Amazing." Her body relaxed. "I … had … no … idea." Then she drifted off.

Guy leaned over and kissed her, then settled himself for a night's sleep in the hospital chair.

♩ ♪♪♫♪

Petter took a week off to stay at the retreat so Haven could tend him. He'd decided that it was a better place than his apartment to hole up for a while. The media had created a sensation over their story. He and Haven had temporarily become celebrities and it became necessary to station a Cascade Springs patrol car at the entrance to the retreat. Fan mail began to arrive, mainly for Petter and mainly from female admirers.

"It's a funny thing about people," Haven declared as she joined him on the sofa in the great room. She handed him a cup of tea and sat down, cuddling close. "They see you on the TV and then they think they're part of your world."

He shook his head. "I'm glad I'm not famous. I'd hate to have to live like this all the time."

"Do you think this will all die down before the wedding? I don't want a hoard of cameramen and strangers following us when we're on our honeymoon."

"I think we'll be okay." He grinned and pulled her in for a quick kiss, wishing he could give her a longer kiss. "I'll shave my beard and wear dark sunglasses. And you can put on a wig and some frumpy dress."

"What? How come *I* have to wear the frumpy clothes?" Haven tilted her dainty face and her eyebrows arched with mock outrage.

"Okay," he sighed dramatically. "I'll wear the dress. But they're going to know something's up when they see my hairy legs."

Haven laughed and his heart soared. He loved her laugh. She reached up to rumple his hair. "I didn't know I was marrying such a funny man."

"Was I being funny?" He gave her a goofy grin.

Haven stood up and went over to the piano. She peered over the stand at him. "I'm going to ignore you now." Her glorious eyes sparkled. "But I expect you to come up with a better solution for our not attracting attention." She began to play softly.

He picked up his book and pretended to read. But he couldn't concentrate. It wasn't just that his head still hurt a little or that the woman he loved to distraction was seated ten feet away. He was remembering Jesse's words the morning they were getting ready to be discharged from the small hospital in Clear View. He could see Jesse now, sitting in the hospital room, his body tense and his face grim as he told his story. They were hard words to hear and he wondered how much of it he should tell Haven. She would have to know sometime. He didn't like to think what Dade might have done to her. She'd tell him when she was ready.

He'd made Jesse promise to say nothing to Haven. And, in the meantime, he would watch her and determine when she was ready to hear about Dade's disappearance.

♩ ♪♪♫♪

"I made sure we'll have the private corner on the deck at Giannini's." Petter started the Honda and they pulled out of the retreat's parking area.

"Oo, you mean that fancy restaurant that overlooks the bay?" What was Petter planning?

"Uh huh." A small smile played around the corners of his mouth.

"You're being awfully meticulous about tonight's dinner. What's with the new haircut and the suit? And you even got me a corsage." She bent her head and sniffed the fragrance of the delicate flowers. "I feel like I'm going to my high school prom."

"Hmm," was all she could get out of Petter the whole trip to the restaurant.

They were ushered through Giannini's main dining hall and taken outside to their secluded table. The sun was just dipping over the sound and the waves lapped gently against the pier and the little boats, docked in the harbor. Soft, romantic music caressed, and a flickering candle made the tableware and crystal glimmer. An envelope with her name on it and a single long-stemmed rose lay across her place setting. Petter seated her. His hands were moist and he flushed as he took his seat.

What could be making him so nervous? He'd already asked her to marry him and she'd said yes. She took the envelope and pulled the letter out.

My Beloved Haven,

A few months ago, I came home to my quiet apartment after a long night in the ER. It was about 3 in the morning. I should have been happy. Everyone I treated that day got better. No one died. I'd done all the right things. But in spite of this, I felt so empty and so alone. There was such an ache in my heart that I even prayed that night. I said, 'God, if you're really out there, if you do care, please send me someone who can help me. Not some know-it-all, religious, holier-than-thou, Bible-toting preacher. Just someone who cares.

When nothing happened, I realized that God didn't care. I forgot about praying and just concentrated on my work.

But one day, as I was jogging around the hospital, I passed a young woman. She looked up at me and I've never seen anyone smile like that. I tried to find out who she was, but she disappeared. But then Pal arranged for me to meet this other girl. I didn't want to go. We went to her little house in the woods and when she opened the door all I saw was that same wonderful smile. She invited us in and listened for what seemed hours while I talked about myself. She hardly said anything, but the few things she did say were fascinating. And that's when I began to wonder if God really did hear my prayer.

As the weeks, passed this sweet girl continued to listen. She heard all about my God-anger and had to listen to all of my mean comments about her faith. She kept telling me that 'bad things happen, but God never turns His face away from those who seek Him.' And just like God, she kept caring.

I don't think she has any idea how much I adore her. But if she'll have me, I'll spend the rest of my life loving her and protecting her.

My Darling, will you marry me?

Your Petter

Haven raised her head, tears spilling down her cheeks. She'd been so engrossed in the letter that she hadn't seen Petter get up and come and kneel next to her seat. He held a small box in his hands.

"I already said I would," she whispered, not trusting her voice. "Did you think I'd changed my mind?"

"No, but I didn't get the chance to do a decent, elegant proposal. And you needed to know how thankful I am for all you've done for me."

"All *I've* done?" She tilted her head, amazed at his humility. "You've saved my life twice. I'll never be able to repay you for that."

Petter had nothing to say. Instead, he offered the small box again. She opened it and gasped at the size of the diamond.

"You shouldn't have—"

"Shhh." He slipped the ring on her finger then continued to hold her hand.

She looked at him in wonder for a long minute, remembering God's urgent prompting months ago. "You must go up and help the doctor." But he had helped her as much as she had helped him.

Growing up, Dad had always told her, "When the right man comes along, he should be gentle and generous, and unselfish. He should listen to you, and take your cares as seriously as he does his own. Hold off until you find a man like that."

Petter held her hand. "Do you like it?"

"I like it. But I love you way more." She wrapped her arms around his neck and held him like she'd never let go.

Epilogue

"The angel of the Lord encamps around those who fear Him,
and He delivers them."
Psalm 34:7

Petter, dressed in his black tuxedo, waited, hardly breathing at the end of the rows of chairs next to Pastor Bernard and Pal. Haven had prayed that the cool fall weather would not bring rain, and it hadn't, allowing her to have the garden wedding she'd said she always dreamed about.

The beat of his heart drowned out the soft music played by a string quartet. Was it possible for a man to feel this much happiness and not shout or dance a jig or make a fool out of himself?

The quartet began to play Pachelbel's Canon. Haven's aunt Joy came down the steps and paraded across the grassy aisle, looking like she was trying very hard not to cry.

Pal leaned in close. "Now, take a deep breath, Little Brother."

Haven held her father's arm and began to descend the lodge steps. The guests stood and turned to face her. But she did not seem to see them. Her eyes rested steadily on Petter, and he struggled to catch his breath.

The last cloud, driven by a gentle breeze, finally drifted east and the sun's rays reached down and kissed Haven and her white dress, enveloping her in a dazzling beam of light. All three men in front of the altar gasped at the sight. But the effect only lasted seconds. Petter squinted and tried to see his bride. When Haven emerged from the beam she was smiling at him with such joy that, in spite of the music the audience broke out in spontaneous applause.

When his bride reached the end of the aisle, Guy whispered, "I love you, girl."

"I love you, too, Dad."

He kissed Haven, then took her hand and placed it in Petter's

♩ ♪♪♫♪

They'd moved the reception indoors due to a light rain. It was almost dusk before Haven had a chance to slip out of her screamingly-painful high heels, hidden behind the white tablecloth at the head table.

Glasses clinked, and Petter pulled her in for another kiss, amid cheers and applause. "Well, Mrs. Eriksen, now that we've cut our cake, and done our dance, do you think we could say our goodbyes?"

Joy leaned close and put her hand on Haven's arm. "You guys should go. The guests aren't going to leave until you do."

"Let's go, Haven." Petter stood and took the microphone. "Ladies and Gentlemen, it's been a long day and joyful day. Thank you all for coming to celebrate our wedding. And now, I'm sure you're anxious to throw birdseed all over us, and that's just fine with me. Mrs. Eriksen and I bid you adieu."

Dad grabbed a couple of packets of seeds from the bowl by the door and hurried in front of Haven with a goofy grin on his face. "I've been waiting twenty-three years to do this."

Haven held Petter's arm as they descended the steps amid a shower of birdseed and the laughter and well wishes of their guests, and hopped into Petter's Honda.

Guy followed them to the car and leaned his head into the passenger window. He gave Haven one last kiss on the cheek. "God bless you both." He stepped back and the car pulled forward slowly.

They drove down the gravel road toward the highway. At the intersection, Petter jumped out and ran to the back of the car. He snipped off the noisy cans and colorful streamers attached to the back bumper, then threw the whole lot into the trunk and hurried back into the driver's seat. Instead of turning toward town, he headed east. After a quarter of a mile, Petter pulled into a little-used gated service road back into the east end of Misty Mountain. He got out and unlocked the gate, pulled through, and locked it again. Minutes later they drove up alongside her cabin.

"I think our secret's safe," he whispered. He was about to open the car door when she stopped him.

"There's just one thing I need to tell you before we get out." How could she tell him?

Petter took a quick startled breath and he searched her face. He looked almost frightened. "You don't need to tell me."

"No, let me explain." She tried to keep her voice steady. *Lord, he doesn't need to hear everything, does he? I don't even know what all happened.*

"After he took me away from Fairhaven, he drugged me. When I came to, it was dark and I was in that cabin outside Remley. I pretended to be asleep so Dade would leave me alone. Later that morning I woke up again. Dade was standing above me, staring. I thought, 'I'm dead.' Inside my head, I screamed, "Jesus, help me!" Immediately there was someone else in the room, standing right behind Dade. The biggest, most powerful looking soldier I've ever seen. He held a huge sword and he was so gigantic that his head went right through the ceiling. But I could still see his face. The soldier didn't speak, but I knew he was there to protect me from Dade."

She paused to give Petter time to digest the facts of her supernatural encounter. "That's when my fear melted away. And I knew I would be okay. Because even during this awful time God had not abandoned me. Maybe Dade would hurt me or even kill me, but I'd still be okay. And I told the Lord that whatever He allowed to happen to me was okay because I trusted Him."

Petter covered her hand with his. His chest rose and fell in an erratic way.

She held his gaze. "Thank you for being the answer to the hope I've held in my heart for so long."

Petter released her hand. He got out of the car without a word and went around to her door. Opening it and holding out his hand, he smiled tenderly. "Welcome home, Mrs. Eriksen."

---

[i] Isaiah 43:2

Acknowledgements

Every author leans heavily on friends, writing associates, and editors to help them envision, write, and polish their manuscript. This manuscript is no different.

Thank you, Nancy Reinke, my dear friend, for listening to my first chapters and encouraging me to complete the story. I deeply appreciate the loving ears of my critique partner, Kim Stewart, who patiently listened to my pity-parties over the phone during the editing process, and prayed me into a more Christ-like attitude.

Thank you, my sweet Bruce Wallace. I am ever grateful that I married you. You are my soul mate, and I love you.

Marji Clubine, you are a wonderful editor and friend. I thank God that He led me to you and Write Integrity Press. Thank you for your hours of hard work on behalf of Haven' Hope. Thanks also to Brittany Clubine and Angela Maddox for their excellent edits.

About the Author

Dena Netherton was born and raised in the San Francisco Bay Area. She studied music and theater in the Midwest and in Colorado and taught music for thirty-five years.

In the 1970s, when Dena was just a teenager, her family took a road trip through the Pacific Northwest, ending with a stay in Anacortes, Washington, and a ferry ride through the San Juan Islands. She was captivated by the beauty of Washington's west coast and vowed she'd one day move to the area.

Forty years later God answered her prayer, and she and her husband relocated to the Seattle area.

Book One of Dena's suspense-filled series, Haven's Flight, released in April of 2017.

Dena's prayer as a Christian author is that her stories inspire and encourage your faith. Her goal is to write stories compelling enough to keep you 'up all night.'

Find Dena on her website: denanetherton.me.

From the Author

Dear Reader,

A suspenseful and romantic tale like *Haven's Hope* needs just the right setting, and even though I've lived on the east coast, the Midwest, the Colorado Rockies, and the California west coast, none of these locations could compete with the Cascade Mountains. Where else, in one hour's westward drive can one view skiers on snow-covered Mt. Baker, tour dirt roads where ferns grow thick under the cool darkness of moss-covered cedars, zoom past cows grazing in green pastures bordering the state highway, navigate through bustling city traffic to finally park and walk along one of the piers that overlook anchored boats bobbing in the gentle waves of the Sound, with the San Juan Islands as a backdrop?

Of course, when I originally envisioned *Haven's Hope*, I had only vacationed a handful of times in the area. My imagination and some thorough Internet research fueled the story. A few months after I finished writing *Haven's Hope*, and before I started editing the manuscript, I flew out to Bellingham (Cascade Spring's real town) to make sure I had written a believable tale. I found, to my surprise, that I'd written a story true to the actual layout of the town, the businesses, churches, the hospital, and the surrounding countryside.

For me, the funniest part of visiting a town where I've set my story is that I go inside a store, or drive down a particular street and think, "This is where Haven shopped," or "This is where Dade followed Haven." And I have to remind myself that my fictional characters are just that: fictional.

I hope you can relate to one or more of the characters in *Haven's Hope*. And I pray that some of the comfort and support Haven received from her friends is something your friends have been willing to give you, too.

Sincerely,

Dena

The Hunted: Book One

How can you flee from an unseen enemy?

Haven Ellingsen enrolled in Life Ventures Therapy Camp in the Cascade Mountains to help her heal from horrible memories of her mother's violent death at the hands of an armed robber. But now, a greater fear dogs her steps. The rustle of leaves or the snap of a twig could be nothing. Or it might signal the sinister presence of the stalker who won't stop following her. It seems like a cruel trick from God to throw Haven into another dangerous situation only a year after her mom's murder.

He hides near her tent and listens to the girl talk with the counselor. Mostly she talks about her father. She's unhappy, and he can't stand to listen and do nothing about it. He needs to rescue her. He needs to make sure she doesn't ever go back to that man. His own father was the cause of his mother's death. And Ruth's. He can't let that happen again. Not with this girl. When the time is right, he'll take her away to his hidden cabin where she'll be safe. And he will feel peace for the first time in years.

Can one month of survival training equip a girl to face all that the rugged wilderness and a madman can dish out?

Recent Releases from Write Integrity Press

Annalee Chambers: Poised, wealthy, socially elite.

Convict.

True, Annalee's crime amounted to very little, but not in terms of community service hours. Her probation officer encouraged her with a promise of an easy job in an air-conditioned downtown environment. She didn't expect her role to be little better than a janitor at an after-school daycare in the worst area of town. Through laughter and a few tears, Annalee finds out that some lessons are learned the hard way, and some seep into the soul unnoticed.

Carlton Whelen hides behind the nickname of CJ so people won't treat him like the wealthy son of the Whelen Foundation director. Working at the foundation's after-school program delights him and annoys his business-oriented father. When a gorgeous prima donna is assigned to his team, he not only cringes at her mistakes but also has to avoid the attraction that builds from the first time he sees her.

No one said the road to recovery would be easy, but Balaam Carter is also desperate to protect the woman and the little boy he left behind from a state full of drug lords who believe they have evidence that will tumble their lucrative cartels. Balaam's continued sobriety, his natural ability for finding his way out of trouble, and his prayers to God above for the strength to never let his loved ones down again are all that he has to protect Lyric and his son, and still, he doesn't know if he's up for the task.

Thank you
for reading our books!

Look for other books
published by

Write Integrity Press
www.WriteIntegrity.com

www.ingramcontent.com/pod-product-compliance
Lightning Source LLC
Chambersburg PA
CBHW070536260626
47161CB00002B/407